The S
of Versailles

An Affair of the Poisons
Book One

Cathie Dunn

Ocelot Press

About the Author

Cathie Dunn writes historical fiction, mystery and romance.

She loves historical research, often getting lost in the depths of the many history books on her shelves. She also enjoys exploring historic sites and beautiful countryside.

After having spent many years in Scotland, Cathie now lives in the south of France with her husband, a rescue dog and two cats. She is a member of the Alliance of Independent Authors and the Historical Novel Society.

Find her at **www.cathiedunn.com**, and on **Facebook**, **Twitter** and **Instagram**.

Books by Cathie Dunn:

An Affair of the Poisons (historical fiction) series:
The Shadows of Versailles – Book One
The Alchemist's Daughter – Book Two (due out in 2021)

Standalone:
Love Lost in Time – an award-winning dual-timeline mystery
Dark Deceit – a romantic murder mystery
Silent Deception – a Gothic romance novella

The Highland Chronicles (historical romance) series:
Highland Arms
A Highland Captive

The Shadows of Versailles

A Tale of Seduction, Loss and Revenge

"Dunn's masterful portrayal of the glittering world of the Sun King's court and the contrasting dark, human stew of 17th Century Paris, will delight any reader familiar with the Affair of the Poisons - and equally thrill those new to the period."

~ Kate Braithwaite, author of *Charlatan*

List of Characters

Main Fictional Characters:

The La Fontaine family:
Blanchefleur 'Fleur' de La Fontaine
Sophie de La Fontaine: Fleur's mother
Émilien de La Fontaine: Fleur's father (deceased)
Marin de La Fontaine: Fleur's uncle, writer and poet

Saint Denis, Paris:
Jacques de Montagnac: spy for La Reynie; investigator in the Affair of the Poisons
Claudette Arnauld: owner of a brothel; supporting young women in need
Angeline 'Ninou' Bourré: a young woman working at Claudette's brothel
Jeanne Bourré: Ninou's five-year-old daughter
Guillaume Tellier: twelve-year-old street urchin

Versailles:
Philippe de Mortain: ambitious young courtier from impoverished noble family
Henrietta de Brun: Philippe's fiancée

The convent of the Carmelites:
Sister Agathe: the Mother Superior
Sister Benedicte: midwife

Main Real Characters:

Versailles:
King Louis XIV: the Sun King, absolute monarch of France
Marguerite, Marquise de La Sablière: widow; host to literary circles of Paris
Marianne, Duchess de Bouillon: once close to King Louis XIV; a favourite

Françoise 'Athénaïs', Marquise de Montespan: longterm mistress of King Louis XIV

Marie, Marquise de Sévigné: writer of letters to her daughter about court and courtiers

The Police of Paris:
Gabriel Nicolas de La Reynie: Lieutenant General; chief of the new police force

François Desgrez: Captain of the Watch; investigator in the *Affair of the Poisons*

Characters closely linked to the Affair of the Poisons:
Marie-Madeleine, Marquise de Brinvilliers: condemned for poisoning her father and brothers; the first execution in what was to become the *Affair of the Poisons*

Abbé Guibourg: priest of the parish of Saint Marcel; conducted black masses

Catherine Monvoisin: midwife, poisoner, participant in black masses; known as 'La Voisin'

Adam Lesage: occultist; associate of La Voisin

Magdeleine de La Grange: arrested for forgery; suspected of murder; the first to hint at persons of court involved in the *Affair of the Poisons*

Prologue

They had gathered to watch her die.

The baying crowd fell silent the moment the tumbril carrying her entered Place de Grève. The sudden calm sent shivers down her spine. In their eyes, she noticed admiration, suspicion, disgust, horror, even lust. The worst, for her, was pity.

The thin white gown of the condemned exposed her bloated body. She could cope with the stares, but the compassion shown by many women – thronging the way from the Conciergerie to Notre Dame, where she had repented in public, and onwards to Place de Grève – was too much to bear. With gritted teeth, she swallowed back the tears.

No one would see her, Marie-Madeleine, Marquise de Brinvilliers, cry.

She raised her head high, no longer glancing at those around her, but gazing over their heads. Her hands tied with a rope that cut through the skin of her wrists, she clung to the wooden frame as the cart jostled across the uneven ground. A path, barely wider than the tumbril, opened in front of them.

Then Marie spotted him: her executioner. He wore a black hood concealing his identity. Of course, she knew who he was. All of Paris did. In prison, she'd arranged payment to ensure his sword found its aim without fault. At least, she would not die by the axe, like a commoner.

A dry laugh escaped her, and she moistened her sore lips with her tongue. Oh, the irony. Her body was still screaming in pain from the water torture that had finally made her confess. In the crowded cell, they had tied her backwards over a rack, forced her mouth open with prongs, stuffed a long piece of

5

fabric down her throat – and poured jug after jug of water into her until she could take no more. In the end, it did not matter whether she told the whole truth – which she had not.

Standing upright now cost all her willpower, when all she wanted to do was curl into a ball to ease the continuing cramps in her still extended stomach.

As her gaze roamed the narrow windows of the houses around Place de Grève, she was sure people she knew were hiding behind those half-drawn curtains. Too cowardly to show their faces, but too curious to stay away. Unlike the nosy courtiers who'd stared at her when she emerged from the Conciergerie! Her arrest and ensuing trial had become the gossip of the court. Even the king was said to have commented on it!

The marquise smirked. Oh, but she knew of ladies of her own standing – and even higher in royal circles – seeking potions and cures from well-known midwives and alchemists. She'd seen them enter certain establishments in search of a solution: to snatch or keep a highborn lover, to rid themselves of the competition or – as in her case – inconvenient family members. Or to advance into the higher echelons of King Louis XIV's magnificent court at the newly built palace of Versailles, his latest folly.

Oh, the scandal if I'd revealed everything...

But she would die knowing that their pride and greed, like hers, would eventually lead to their downfall. Men and women would suffer her fate.

No, she would always prefer the slow effect of poison. It left no visible marks. Had it not been for Sainte Croix's foolish notes...

Alas, 'twas no use dwelling on the past.

The smell of smoke from the pyre burning in the centre of the square hung thick in the air. It made her shudder. She was grateful that she did not have to suffer the fate of being burnt alive. Let them do to her dead body what they wanted!

The cart stopped at the bottom of the scaffold. The marquise sighed. Soon, it would be over. She did not want to think about the men in her life, with their demands, abuse, and deceit. They were not worthy of her last memories.

An overweight gaoler with grimy hands untied her from the wooden frame and helped her clumsily from the tumbril. The crowd moved in. All she saw around her was anger. The agitated fury of the masses. She'd witnessed it before, having watched executions over the years.

Marie gave a wan smile, then climbed up the steps to where Abbé Pirot waited. He had been a godsend in the dark weeks of her incarceration. The priest took her hands in his, and as she went down on her knees, he intoned the *Salve Regina*. Soon, voices from beyond the scaffold joined in.

"Salve, Regina, mater misericordiæ. Vita, dulcedo et spes nostra, salve.

Ad te clamamus, exsules filii Hevæ.

Ad te suspiramus, gementes et flentes in hac lacrimarum valle.

Eia ergo, Advocata nostra, illos tuos misericordes oculos ad nos converte.

Et Jesum, benedictum fructum ventris tui, nobis post hoc exilium ostende.

O clemens, o pia, o dulcis Virgo Maria! Amen."

Then a hush fell over Place de Grève, and she locked eyes with Abbé Pirot. It was time.

"Bless me, Father, for I have sinned…"

He made the sign of the cross on her forehead. "Repent, daughter, and prepare to meet the Lord. He will recognise those who have faith." He slowly released her hands and stepped back.

Discarding her cap, Marie revealed her cropped fair hair. She held herself as upright as the pain in her middle allowed, and ignoring the discomfort of her knees on the hard surface.

The executioner stood in front of her, a double-handed sword in hand. She caught the tiny nod he gave her and breathed a sigh of relief.

The Marquise de Brinvilliers closed her eyes.

I am but the first…

her spine. "Come!"

As she trailed Mother through the richly decorated rooms, she was under no illusion. Sophie had brought her here to find her a husband. The richer the better, and ideally above a marquis. Fleur rolled her eyes, giggling when a handsome young man she was passing laughed out loud. Had he seen her gesture? She smiled.

"Blanchefleur!" Sophie's polite façade couldn't hide her cold eyes.

Fleur sent him an apologetic glance, then rushed after her mother, who was crossing yet another vast room where groups of lords and ladies were chatting.

"Here." Sophie handed her a crystal glass that she'd picked off a footman's tray. "But do drink slowly. It's not *limonade*." She took a few sips before she cried out, "Ah, Valerie! How wonderful to see you."

Fleur's heart sank. Sophie's best – her only – friend, Valerie, Countess de Montmarché, waved them over. Fleur's good humour vanished. They would stay by the side of the Montmarchés for much of the night, she was certain.

"Ah, there's Blanchefleur. Finally, you're ready to join us." Valerie giggled. Mother smiled politely. "What do you think?" The countess waved a gloved hand around. "It does not quite compare to life with the nuns, does it?"

"No," Fleur said. She let her gaze roam the room. Large oil paintings, most of which depicted mythical scenes, covered most of the walls,. She'd learnt all about Greek and Latin mythology, and found it easy to recognise the old gods in their splendour. But it also gave her a sense of being hemmed in, the larger-than-life characters looking down on her, leering…

A hand slid into the folds of her gown and pinched her bottom. She jumped, almost throwing the contents of her glass at Mother. The hand disappeared as swiftly as it had arrived.

"Now if that isn't little Blanchefleur." The Count de Montmarché sidled up beside her, much too close for her liking. Their elbows were touching. He looked her up and down, then his eyes settled on her bosom, before a discreet cough by his wife brought him out of his reverie. "Welcome to our world, dear," he said.

"Thank you, my lord."

Sophie was beaming. She'd clearly not noticed his wandering hand or gaze. "Oh, Albert. Isn't it such a special moment?"

He nodded, his triple chins glistening with sweat beneath a thick layer of powder. "It is, madame. Your daughter will have no dearth of admirers." Montmarché sent Fleur a meaningful glance, and she considered herself fortunate that he was not a widower.

"I do hope so. With her being educated by nuns, to a high standard, I must say, I'm hopeful of a marquis."

"A count no less, madame, if not higher. Her beauty will enthral them."

Fleur shuddered at the wistful tone in his voice. The hairs on her neck stood on end.

Sophie giggled behind her fan. "Do you think so?"

"We have no doubt," Valerie said.

Whilst they were discussing her fate, Fleur sidled away under the guise of admiring the artworks. A few small steps gave her room to breathe. She took a sip of her wine, cool in her throat, and studied the painting closest to her. Amidst a dark, threatening sky, the sirens lounging on sharp rocks were luring poor sailors to their early grave. Bodies of drowning men littered the churned-up waves. Hands reached out for salvation that never came.

"Quite a dramatic scene, do you not agree?" A deep voice reached her.

Fleur turned to see a man of about twenty-five years. His dark hair fell in long curls around his head, deep blue eyes glistening in the light of the candles. Her mind skipped a beat.

"Umm… Yes, I do."

"Proof that beauty can sink even the strongest men." He grinned, then gave a deep bow. "Philippe de Mortain, at your service, mademoiselle."

14

Blushing, Fleur gazed at the painting. But now she found the exposed breasts of the sirens, and the seductive looks they sent out to the drowning sailors, disconcerting. Aware of her own revealing décolleté, she couldn't help but blush.

He sent her a lopsided smile, endearing. "May I have your name, pretty girl? I haven't seen you before."

Fleur swallowed. "I'm Fleur de—"

"Is everything in order, dearest?" Sophie's voice cut in as she appeared at Fleur's side, her eyes fixed on the young man.

Annoyed, Fleur glared at her mother. "Yes, thank you. I'm merely making polite conversations."

"So I see." Sophie looked at her sharply, then turned her attention to him. "And you are?"

Chapter Two

Over the rim of her fan, Fleur watched Sophie talking to Philippe de Mortain. Suddenly, Mother seemed impressed.

"Really?" Mother beamed. "Please correct me if I'm wrong – but from what you have revealed your grandmother was linked to the last Duke d'Orléans, His Majesty's late uncle?"

He nodded. "Indeed, my lady. She was a cousin to the duke's wife. I am named after the current holder of the title, His Majesty's brother."

"Oh, how exciting." Sophie breathed. "So you are distantly related to our dear king through his aunt-by-marriage?"

Fleur searched for the vial of smelling salts she carried in her pouch. Mother hyperventilated, and it was quite likely that she would need calming soon. And this was only her first *soirée…*

"But it is nothing, Madame. Here," he waved at a passing footman. "Let me get you a glass of wine." He scooped up two glasses from the tray and handed one to Sophie, who took it off him, still smiling.

Fleur shook her head when he held out the other glass to her. "I'm still on my first, monsieur, thank you."

"Oh, but it will have become warm by now, mademoiselle. It won't taste of anything. White wine has to be consumed chilled." With a wink, he took her glass off her and pressed the new one into her hand.

The coolness in her palm felt good, and she realised how hot it had become in the room. She took a tentative sip. The cold liquid made her feel better, so she took another. "You

16

were right. It is much nicer now; more refreshing."

"See! I told you." He grinned. "Perhaps you would allow me a dance tonight? I've already spotted several of my competitors watching you, but I wanted to ensure I was the first."

"Of course Blanchefleur will dance with you." Sophie had found her voice again. "But not more than once." She was gazing across the room, and Fleur had a sinking feeling in her stomach. Philippe de Mortain had just reminded her mother that there were other eligible young men here, a minor fact she seemed to have forgotten earlier when the name of Orléans had cropped up.

"Are you interested in tragedy, or would you prefer the musical piece tonight, mademoiselle?"

With Sophie's attention diverted by the arrival of another lady, he'd taken a small step closer to Fleur. She breathed in his perfume. Notes of patchouli and citrus hit her, and she dared not to think of the expense. Was he rich? Not that it mattered much to her, but as regards Mother…

"Oh, I don't know. Mother hasn't yet shared her plans for the evening with me."

"It has to be the music. The grove where the small chamber orchestra plays is wonderfully secluded, and the trees and shrubs provide much-needed shade. It has a fountain in its centre, though, from what I've heard, the design of it will also change in the coming years. But for now, it is the perfect spot for listening and…conversing."

"It sounds idyllic. I love parklands, and Mother said the gardens here are breathtaking." Surely, a grove would be preferable to the Orangerie where Iphigénie was due to be performed later. And she was too excited to watch a tragedy, anyway.

He nodded, leaning a little closer to her ear. "They are, and they're constantly being extended. You should see the great lake! I would take you there if your mother allowed, but it may all be too much for one night. Perhaps later in the week?"

Fleur blushed. Was it this easy to find an agreeable

husband? Her heart soared. And there she'd feared having to suffer the company of old or ugly suitors for months…

With his good looks and charm, a proposition would not go amiss, though his ardent attention still mystified her. Philippe was charming, with the sweetest smile and his eyes full of mischief, yet he seemed a little too keen for someone who'd only just met her. Fleur took a small step back and bumped into the fleshy back of Albert de Montmarché.

Startled, she said, "I'm very sorry, my lord."

He took her by the arm to help her regain her balance. "Do not worry, little Blanchefleur. I'm glad you did not injure yourself."

His thumb brushed up and down her upper arm. It made her skin crawl, and there was no polite way to get him to let go. "I did not, my lord, thank you." She edged away from him, but caught in a tight space between the count and Philippe de Mortain, she suddenly felt sick.

Sophie finally turned back to her. "Blanchefleur, don't be so clumsy." To the count and countess, she made her excuses. "Will you excuse us? I've just seen someone I'd like Fleur to meet." Sophie smiled at the Montmarchés, who politely inclined their heads.

"We shall see you later on in the evening," the countess said, pressing Sophie's hand.

With an apologetic shrug and a sideways glance, Fleur passed Philippe de Mortain.

"Until later, sweet Flower." He bowed with a flourish that made her giggle.

Her mother grabbed her elbow and pulled her into the next room, where she led her into a quiet corner.

"That young man may have loose family links to the royal house, but his clothes are not of the latest fashion."

Fleur blinked. "What?"

"You can be so obtuse, child! Or have you no sense because you always keep your nose in books, day and night, like your Father did?" Sophie sighed. "What I mean is that Monsieur de Mortain might not be as rich as he would lead us to believe. As for his pedigree, I will ask around. But in the meantime, I it's best to secure more dances and get the attention of the young men of the higher nobility. At least, we know where we stand with them."

"Higher titles are no guarantee of money, Mother," Fleur quipped. "From what Charlotte said, half the nobles of France are in great debt." She opened her fan and cooled her hot cheeks. The air in these rooms was stifling.

"Shh! Don't!" Sophie's eyes widened, and she looked around, as if to reassure herself that no one was listening. "You will only get us into trouble. One lesson to learn, now you're out of the convent – don't gossip with the staff! And never listen to their chatter. It's demeaning."

"And informative," Fleur argued, then stilled when her mother sent her a sharp glance.

"Oh, you are so like the de La Fontaines. No sense of business or station. If we're not careful, you'll end up like your Uncle Marin."

Fleur smiled. "But doesn't he write poetry? I thought he was popular."

Sophie snorted, much to Fleur's surprise. Hers was an unusual reaction. "He might be a welcome guest in many houses, but his writing doesn't earn him a fortune. Last I heard," she lowered her voice, "was that he lives at the home of a lady patron. I'm still amazed how he gets away with it."

"Will I meet him?"

"Who?" Sophie's gaze roamed the large room.

"Uncle Marin."

"Most certainly not. The last time I saw him – thank God – was at your father's funeral."

This puzzled Fleur. "But why? He's our family."

Her mother turned back to her, pointing with her index finger. "He is *your* family, Blanchefleur. If I'd had my wish, I'd have married a count or a duke."

Not an impoverished marquis…

Fleur had heard the story many times, how poor Mother had to settle for Émilien de La Fontaine because her father deemed him the most suitable. Fleur's grandfather had gambled away most of her inheritance, something Sophie had never forgiven him. But it wasn't Fleur's fault that her own father had no talent for business, but instead had been lost in his books or travelled to the New World, taking copious notes of flora and fauna found far away.

A sense of sadness washed through her. She'd not seen him often during her childhood, but when she had, she loved the tales of adventure he made up just for her.

"Blanchefleur? Fleur!"

She blinked. Mother stared at her. "You were far away, child. Look, I know for a fact that the gentleman over there lost his wife a few months ago, and I noticed he's been admiring you. He is a count, from near Bordeaux."

"Bordeaux? But that's on the far side of the country?"

Her mother's mouth formed a thin line, which she hid from view with her fan. "You'll end up where your husband is. That's how it goes."

"But I don't want to live in Bordeaux. I want to stay at home." Panic rose in her chest, and Sophie gently tapped her arm.

"Whoever marries you will take you to his estate, child. But fret not, it won't happen for months yet. And you'll get our home – when I'm dead."

Sophie snapped her fan close and waved it towards them, showing her approval for a man to approach them. A thin gentleman in ridiculously colourful attire. He wore a short-sleeved doublet of rich green over puffed sleeves tied at upper arm and elbow with red ribbon. An embroidered long shirt hung fashionably down to his thighs, and his skinny calves clad in white stockings and pointy shoes with a bow matching the ribbons on his arm.

Worst of all was his wig, long dark curls trailing over his shoulders. It made his face look horselike. He clearly tried to emulate the king, but failed.

Fleur sighed. Then, to please her mother, she put on a wide smile.

***

apothecary."

Jacques straightened. Ninou's honest nature of one who'd fallen on hard times through no fault of her own was enough for him to know she told the truth.

"Has the doctor seen her?"

"That old quack? No. I go straight to Monsieur Moreau on rue Saint Denis."

He nodded. "That's probably wise. What does Jeanne have need of?"

"Nothing you could help with, thank you." Ninou stepped back and preempted his offer. "I don't accept charity."

Jacques grinned. "You're too honest for this business, Ninou. Let me think of a line of work that would suit you better."

Ninou nodded with an expression that told him she'd heard this phrase too often, and he vowed to make real enquiries. There had to be something else she was skilled at.

A noise behind them made him turn around to see two men, no older than thirty, approach the brothel at a steady pace. Their clothing marked them as comfortably off, and their weaving gait revealed they'd partaken of alcohol, but fortunately did not seem too drunk.

With a wide smile, Ninou sauntered towards them, her narrow hips swaying. Another woman who'd been lurking in the doorframe joined her. Business was resumed.

Jacques went inside, nodding to Pierre, the burly giant who sat on a chair at the bottom of the steps, and entered the front room where Madame Claudette perched on a settee lined with red velvet. Normally, he'd consider the interior with its cheap drapes and curtains distasteful. Crude paintings depicting couples involved in many intimate activities lined the walls. It was most definitely feminine, intended to entice men into sin.

But he'd come to know the owner well over recent years. Her heart was in the right place. In her sheltered establishment, she'd saved many a lost girl from a worse fate on the streets over the past decade.

"Oh Jacques, what brings you here?" Claudette stood and

embraced him with a kiss on each cheek. The scent of citrus engulfed him. Not for her the lavender pouches so fashionable with the ladies at court. She beamed, though in the dim light the lines beneath her eyes stood out darkly on her heavily powdered face. The wig of flaming red hair, decorated with peacock feathers, did not help make her face look natural. But then, that was the intention. Only a few people, including him, had ever seen her without the *accoutrements* of a bawd.

"I couldn't sleep, and I thought sharing a glass of your wonderful wine would help."

"For you, always."

She slid her arm through his just as Ninou entered with one of the men Jacques had seen outside, followed by the second girl with the other. Claudette welcomed them with a coquettish smile. "Good evening, kind sirs. Our humble abode is at your disposal. Please make yourselves comfortable over a glass of something...fortifying." She opened her fan and hid behind it, giggling. It was to appeal to the male egos of their customers, leaving the impression they were dealing with a creature of lower intelligence. Jacques knew it was far from the truth.

"Pierre," she trilled, "please see that the gentlemen have everything they need."

At her signal, Pierre joined them. "Of course, Madame Claudette."

Jacques exchanged a swift glance with Ninou, who gave him a light, reassuring nod, then allowed Claudette to drag him through a side door into her parlour.

Chapter Four

"And don't forget, Blanchefleur, you still owe the Count de Maquaire a dance. You treated the count abominably last night."

Fleur rolled her eyes, then reached out to steady herself as the carriage jolted across the paved streets. "I will not dance with him, Mother, ever! Twice, he tried to grab my bosom when we walked from the ballroom to the refreshments. And on the way to the terrace, he fondled my bottom."

Sophie sighed, her mouth forming a thin line. "Your future husband will do an awful lot more than that, child. Get used to it."

"He's old enough to be my grandfather, and I don't appreciate the way he leers at me – or at any female who displays a bit of flesh…"

"Which you're sadly lacking." Mother's gaze went to Fleur's *décolleté*.

Tonight's gown was more daring than the ones she'd been wearing since her arrival at court a fortnight ago. It left little to the imagination. Fleur detested the way Sophie had made her dress. She felt like a whore. Over the past week, her gowns had grown more revealing, low cut at the front, the puffed sleeves pulled down to her elbows, the stomacher even tighter to push up her small breasts. The smell of the powder on her face made her gag, and the rouge on her cheeks made her skin itch, but she was not allowed to scratch it. Today, her mother had also added a beauty mark just beneath her right eye. Apparently, men found them irresistible. Fleur thought it looked cheap. Three weeks at Versailles, and without a firm offer, she was flogged off to the highest bidder, like cattle on the market.

"What did you say?" Sophie eyed her sharply.

Fleur startled. Had she spoken out loud? "Me? I didn't say anything, Mother."

"I'm certain you said something about cattle."

She snorted. "Surely not. Why would I think of animals?"

Sophie leaned back, though her gaze never left Fleur. "Why indeed? So you will grant the Count de Maquaire the first dance. Then we have," she consulted a tiny book where she'd scribbled down names of potential suitors, "the Count de Roumère and the Marquis de Brêve. And yes, I haven't forgotten *Monsieur* Philippe de Mortain. Although in terms of wealth he's well behind the others, so a far less admirable prospect."

"But I like him." Fleur had noticed Mother's emphasis on Philippe's lack of a title.

"You are not the only one. And he has not proposed marriage to you, has he?" Sophie's hard tone chilled Fleur to the core. "Two nights ago, I heard rumours that he's been courting other young ladies when he doesn't lure you out of my sight. One such is a plump thing called Henrietta de Brun, daughter of a rich merchant. I did not want you to grow concerned; that's the reason I had not told you yet."

Fleur smiled. She'd heard this as well. "The court is always full of rumours, Mother. Even I know that. It's what courtiers live for."

"We shall see." Sophie pulled the curtain aside and looked out. "Ah, we're here. Now, be a dutiful daughter and catch a wealthy husband!"

Hiding behind her fan, Fleur yawned. Three hours had passed, and she longed to cast off her tight shoes and this ridiculous gown.

How could time go so slowly? Of all the evenings she'd spent here, tonight was the dreariest. Her mother had paraded her like a new filly, and Fleur had almost expected one of the lords to check her teeth. Thankfully, this had not happened. But they had been so tiresome, their conversations – if they got their words out – dull!

Most men she'd danced with tonight had barely raised their eyes above her half-exposed breasts, never mind met her gaze. She fumed. They had not even pretended to be interested in her words. Why, the old Count de Maquaire had positively drooled down her *décolleté*! She shuddered.

Fleur had sneaked out of doors when Sophie's friend, Valérie de Montmarché, distracted her. Fleur enjoyed the cooling breeze that came up the gardens from the Grand Canal. She watched as people were milling about on the terraced lawns, envying them their freedom to do so, but after her mother's anger on discovering her sitting with Philippe in the semi-darkness on her first night, Fleur had not dared to venture out again.

"A *louis d'or* for your thoughts, Mademoiselle Fleur…"

Recognising Philippe's voice, Fleur turned around, keeping her face hidden behind her fan. Had her thoughts conjured him up? He'd not asked for his dance yet.

Aware of where she was, she was determined to not let him charm her into following him into the gardens again. After their first encounter, he'd tried repeatedly to convince her to join him again, but she'd not given in. Torn between her growing attachment to him and irritation at his continuing insistence that they abscond from the crowds, she said coolly, "Ah, Philippe! I've not seen you all evening."

He stepped back and pulled a face, holding his cheek dramatically – as if he'd received a slap. "Oh, my beautiful Fleur! Why the harsh voice? Have you missed me?"

"Shh, don't!" She looked around, but nobody was close enough to overhear his words. Picking up her skirts from the dusty tiles, she moved to an even quieter spot at the top of the steps.

To her dismay, she found Philippe had not followed her. Leaning against the stone railing and looking out over the illuminated gardens, she caught her breath. Had she chased him away for good this time? She hoped not, but she'd been quite rude. Her heart pounded in her ears. All she needed to know was whether the rumours about him and Henrietta de Brun were true.

And his intentions towards me…

"Ah, Fleur. There you are." Philippe approached her, carrying two glasses of chilled wine. Relieved, she gave him a wan smile. "I think you need this. The heat in the ballroom is most unhealthy." He handed her a glass, then took a sip of his.

Fleur relished the taste of the wine, the cold liquid in her throat as she swallowed it.

"Forgive me, Philippe. Mother has become unbearable in her quest to find an agreeable husband for me."

"So I've noticed." He grinned. "The men she makes you dance with every night are mostly deplorable old goats."

She laughed, remembering her own thoughts about cattle at the market. "Old goats – I like that."

"I fear for you, little Flower." He drew nearer, his mouth close to her ear. "I can't bear the thought of their grimy, fleshy hands on your delicate skin."

His breath, hot in her ear, sent a shiver down her spine; a tingling sensation coursed through her body.

"The idea is inconceivable. But I may have no choice…" Her voice quivered, and she looked at him. If he was serious about her, now would be the time to reveal his intentions.

Philippe's gaze remained intense. He stood beside her, not backing away. "Perhaps we can see what we can do about that."

She swallowed hard. "What do you mean?"

He straightened and glanced around. "Shall we walk a little?"

Fleur blinked.

"Do not worry, we don't have to go far. I would simply prefer some…privacy…to speak with you properly."

"What about? Henrietta de Brun, perhaps?" The name had escaped her lips before she could stop herself, and she bit back the tears that threatened to well up.

He stared at her, then took a step back. "The de Brun girl? Why?"

Heat rose in Fleur's cheeks. She opened her fan. The air helped steady her racing thoughts. "Well, you must have heard the rumours about…"

Philippe placed his weight on his right leg and crossed his arms in front of his chest. "About what, Fleur?"

"Well, about you and Henrietta."

"What about it?" He snorted. "That's nonsense."

She breathed a sigh of relief and reached out to touch his hand. "So it's not true…that you're engaged?"

"Why would I be?"

"Please forgive my insolence, Philippe. I merely wanted to know the truth."

He eyed her in a way she found disconcerting. "The truth, Fleur? All these people…" he waved his hand in the air, "they thrive on spreading gossip and lies."

He sounded bitter.

Fleur wanted to soothe him.

"Then let us walk, yes." She looked around. "But where to?"

Philippe smiled, then took her offered hand. "That way. There's a lovely grove behind those trees."

"It's not too far, is it? I must still be able to hear Mother if she calls me."

He shook his head. "It's close enough. Barely a few minutes. Come."

Darkness surrounded them as they walked through the rows of shrubs planted several years earlier. Away from the lit paths, a sense of unease hit Fleur, but she shrugged it off. Philippe would declare for her, and then she would no longer have to live with Mother. Instead, she would be Madame de Mortain. The thought appealed to her.

The scent of summer flowers hung in the air. Here, in between the greenery, the air seemed cooler. Fleur took several deep breaths, relishing the freshness.

"It's a lovely spot, is it not?" Philippe asked. He led her to a bed of flowers and soft grass, pulling her down with him. "It's all dry, so it won't show on your gown."

Fleur checked the ground with her hand. He was right. She lowered herself into the tantalising scent. "It's beautiful. So calming."

Philippe reclined, propped up on his elbows. "I discovered this spot last summer, by coincidence." He lay back, his hands under his head. "If you lie flat, you can see the night sky. All the stars…"

Fleur looked up, but her neck soon grew stiff, so she carefully lowered herself on the grass. It was dry, so her gown should not carry any stains. She leaned back a little, holding herself in a sitting position, cursing the stomacher that made it so difficult for her to wriggle.

The view made it worthwhile. He'd been right. The night sky was beautiful, twinkling with thousands of stars. Never had she seen them so clearly; never had they appeared so close.

He took her hand and kissed her knuckles one at a time. "Isn't it beautiful?"

Unsure whether he referred to the stars or the sensations he sent through her skin, she nodded. "Uh huh." A delicious shiver ran down her spine.

"Oh…you're enjoying this?" He asked, trailing kisses up her bare arm.

"Mmmh." The delight she felt at his touch was nothing she'd ever experienced. She closed her eyes. Was this what marriage was like? Mother's guidance had been different.

Philippe edged closer to her. The scent of his perfume, rich and musky, enveloped her. His fingers were exploring the outlines of her face, before trailing down her throat, lower down towards—

"No!" Her eyes flew open as her hand clapped on his before it reached her half-exposed breasts. The stomacher pushed them up, something she was still uncomfortable with.

And she did not want him to touch her there. Was that not reserved for the wedding night? But one glance at his face made her feel guilty. Had she hurt his feelings?

With a loud sigh, he turned away from her and sat staring into the trees.

"I…I am sorry, Philippe. I didn't mean to—"

"It's fine, Fleur. We shared a beautiful moment… Now it's gone." His mouth formed a thin line.

Chapter Five

Jacques read the note La Reynie had sent him. After memorising the words, he ripped it up, cast the pieces into a clay bowl, and burnt it. The ash he discarded in the empty grate.

Three more infants had gone missing, two taken away by nuns and one by the midwife, all without the mothers' consent. He whistled. So now the holy sisters were involved?

From what he'd seen so far, it was not a surprise. Rumour had it that several priests in Paris conducted black masses.

He snorted in disgust.

But the children had not disappeared from the nearby convent of the Filles-Dieu – the Daughters of God – where former prostitutes had found their faith, and a safe escape. No, this particular convent lay outside of town.

Where noble ladies go to hide their pregnancies…

Again, no names were revealed, nor the details of the mothers. How on earth was he meant to find out what went on?

He would seek out the nuns first. Later, he'd speak to Claudette again. Of course, she would not reveal her associates – midwives who were conducting abortions of unwanted children of desperate women – but he was certain she would not hide murderers of children born alive and healthy.

At least, he hoped not.

Jacques grabbed his coat from a hook in the wall of his narrow corridor and left his lodgings, locking the door behind him and securing the key safely into the inner pocket of his coat. He walked for half a mile until he reached a small stable where he hired a gelding for the rest of the day. Shortly after, he rode through the gate of Saint Denis and into the sprawling areas that had sprung up around the old centre. Already the largest city in Europe, Paris was expanding at a fast rate.

Once through the gate, he turned east, and soon, he left the buildings behind. Despite the heat, he relished the breeze. Perhaps a dwelling outside the old town walls would be his reward once he had saved enough. Growing up in the countryside of Languedoc, where he'd enjoyed sweeping views over rolling hillsides from the bedroom he'd shared with his older brother, he found life in Paris suffocating at times. But he became accustomed to the constant noise, the filthy streets and stale air. So on the rare occasions that he ventured outside of the gate, he made the most of his freedom. Taking deep breaths, he urged the horse into a trot towards the Carmelite nunnery five miles away.

Out here, the road was as bustling as in town. Traders, travellers, and nobles leaving for or returning from Versailles all vied for a space. Soon, he left the buildings behind. On either side of him, fields and orchards now lined the way. Jacques blinked in the bright sunlight, and a yearning he had not felt in months took hold inside of him. His life could have been different. His mother had intended for him to join the Church.

Jacques grinned. Bless her. She'd meant well, but it was not the life he'd sought.

Up ahead, he saw the high walls of the convent. He slowed to a walk. The fresh air had distracted him.

When he arrived by the sturdy door, he dismounted, tied the horse to a ring in the wall, and knocked. Within moments, a small grille inset into the solid oak wood opened.

"Yes?" The wrinkled face of an elderly nun appeared. She stared at him down her long nose as if he were a beetle.

"I would like a word with your Mother Superior, sister."

She tutted. "And on what grounds, sir?"

Jacques had decided to be blunt. "The abduction of

infants."

"The wha—?" Her hand flew to her mouth, and her gaze turned even more suspicious. "There are no infants here, sir. We are a religious order if you haven't noticed."

When she tried to close the grille, he reached his hand through it and held it open. "I know what you are, sister. Yet my sources are accurate. Your Mother Superior?" He raised an eyebrow. "Or would you prefer I spread word in Paris that your order is complicit in the removal of children for black masses?"

The nun went pale. "By all the saints." She crossed herself with a trembling hand. "Black…" she croaked.

She has no idea.

"Yes. What is it to be?"

A key rattled in the door. He withdrew his hand from the grille. She stepped back as he entered. Behind him, the door clanged shut, and the nun locked it again.

"Wait here. I shall inform the Mother Superior." With a shake of her head, she trundled along the cloister and out of his sight.

Jacques looked around. Exposed to the elements, the walls were bare, but the small courtyard in the centre was blooming with roses and herbs. He saw rosemary and lavender, but also nightshade and other herbs he did not recognise.

What did nuns need nightshade for? He stepped into the yard to take a closer look when a voice echoed around the walls.

"You wish to speak to me?"

He turned to find himself face to face with the Mother Superior. Tall and thin, with cold grey eyes, her mouth drawn into a thin line, she was a far cry from the kindly nuns he'd met in the past.

"Yes. Thank you for agreeing to speak to me. Is there anywhere more private for us to talk?"

"I won't enter a room with a man, so the garden will suffice." She walked to a bench at the far end, between pots of flowers, the type of which he had not seen before. Small, bright petals shared a warm scent. To his pleasure, bees were busy carrying pollen.

The joys of nature.

His gaze met hers. It jolted him back into reality. "I'm Sister Agathe, and what you are accusing us of is preposterous." She sat down but did not offer a space to him.

"Is it?" Jacques was pleased he had the advantage of height, something she seemed to realise when he inclined his head to look down at her.

She interlinked her fingers in her lap so strongly, the knuckles were white. "Of course it is."

With slow steps, he paced along the narrow path between the plants. The cloister walk was empty. No one was around to overhear them.

He faced her again. "Why do my sources point at your house?"

She shrugged her shoulders. "That I don't know. Who are you anyway to raise such…spurious accusations?"

"Forgive me, Mother Superior." He gave a slight bow. "I'm Jacques de Montagnac. I work on behalf of the Lieutenant General. You may have heard of Monsieur de La Reynie, *non*?"

"Who has not," she said, her tone acerbic.

"Indeed. So you rest assured that our sources are reliable. What happened to those infants?"

"There are no infants here, monsieur."

"That's what the sister who admitted me said already, and it may as well be correct – that there are no children here *right now*. But you can't deny that women often stay here until their confinement, or you give away their children for adoption. Others…" He stopped in front of her.

The Mother Superior jumped up, her haughty gaze on him. "How dare you accuse us of assisting in this vile trade?"

Jacques lifted his hands in defence. "I merely state what I was told. So, what happens to the newborn babes?"

"There are no—"

He silenced her with a glare.

Sighing, she sat down again. "This stays between us." She

looked around, but the cloisters were deserted. "Occasionally, we offer shelter to girls who need to disappear from society for a few months. They are usually daughters of courtiers or rich merchants."

"Seduced by the shining lights at court, no doubt."

"Probably." She pulled a face in disgust. "But we always give the infants up for adoption. The notion of us supplying children to be murdered in black masses is ludicrous."

He nodded, although her reassurance lacked conviction, he thought. "Who is the midwife you use?"

She sighed. "Sister Benedicte looks after the expecting mothers. She was a midwife before she joined our order after the death of her husband."

"I see." Jacques nodded. The nuns kept everything in-house. "And how do the adoptions work? Do the young women not have a say in what happens?"

"Of course not!" Sister Agathe hissed. "They give birth before they return home to recuperate. It's usually the parents of these fallen girls who advise us of their intentions."

"Ah." A convenient way to rid yourself of an unwanted child, and to avoid rumours. The thought chilled him to the bone, and he suppressed a shudder. How lacking of emotion this business was. "And the babes?" he asked again.

"Often, the poor children are stillborn." Her left eye twitched, and she averted her gaze.

Was she lying? Her words sounded false to Jacques' ears. "How often does this tragedy occur?"

She glared at him. "We do not keep records. We offer a service to families of good standing who do not wish to publicise their…misfortune. Hence, no written records exist."

Jacques shifted his weight to his left leg and folded his arms. "But you must have an idea, surely. Is it two out of ten? Five out of ten? Or, perhaps, eight?"

"As I told you, I have no knowledge of this. Sister Benedicte deals with this sort of thing. We do have a small cemetery in our grounds for the infants who are baptised before they die. Only a priest can do this. For the lost souls, there is a small patch behind our walls, beside a field. You understand – if they haven't received the holy sacrament, they are eternally condemned to hell."

"And of course that's the fault of the poor children!" Anger rose inside Jacques, and he took a deep breath. He walked a few steps to calm himself.

"I did not make the rules, monsieur. 'Twas ever thus."A resigned look crossed her features.

"Yes. It must be pleasant to live with such an absolution of responsibility. So I ask you again. How many die? And how many do you give away for adoption? And where do those end up?"

She rose abruptly and stepped closer, her cheeks reddening. She pointed a bony index finger at his chest. "As I told you, monsieur, I do not know."

"In that case, I will need to speak with Sister Benedicte."

"That is not possible."

Jacques' patience was wearing thin. He placed his hands on his hips. "And why not?"

"Because Sister Benedicte is not here."

He blinked. "Where is she?"

"In town."

"Alone?" He raised an eyebrow. The good sister appeared very independent, for a Carmelite nun.

The Mother Superior looked past him, unable to meet his gaze. "Yes."

"What is her business in Paris? Where does she go?"

She lifted her chin in defiance and glared at him. "The nuns don't have to tell me everything. Often, Sister Benedicte has tough decisions to make, so I won't put any further pressure on her." She huffed. "Now, you better leave."

With a flourish of his hat, he gave her a bow and a thin smile. "I shall return."

Chapter Six

Late September, 1675
Paris

"Are you certain that the nun is involved in something sinister, Jacques?" La Reynie, his mouth pursed, leaned back in his high-backed chair and regarded him.

"Yes, I'm sure, sir. Sister Benedicte has so far evaded to answer my questions, but…"

"You don't want to have her arrested yet?"

"No. It's too soon."

"But you've been watching the nunnery now for over a fortnight, and nothing happened since that priest arrived the previous Sunday."

He nodded. "Abbé Guibourg, yes. Ostensibly to give mass, but you were right – he has something to do with the disappearances. He stayed for much longer than the service lasted. I heard their bells."

"Ah. You think he works hand in glove with that Sister Benedicte?"

"I do. Tomorrow is Sunday. I'll keep watch again."

"You do that. But don't forget your leatherwork. The people of your *quartier* must not suspect anything."

"Don't fret, sir." Jacques grinned. "My shop opens every day at eight o'clock. There is a bell on the door, so if I fall asleep in my workroom, I wake when a new customer comes in."

La Reynie laughed, something Jacques saw rarely. The Lieutenant General had the hardest post in Paris. Any failure would lead directly to the king's displeasure. A high risk.

But even a small error on his own part could see Jacques floating face-down in the Seine. He sobered. It was their line

49

of work.

"Stay onto the priest and the nun, Jacques. We've had no new reports of abducted infants, so perhaps you have rattled them with your presence."

"Or perhaps they've found another way. Prostitutes often sell their newborn children to priests, a habit my source cannot stop. But she has mentioned this particular priest in Saint Denis, before. That's why I recognised him; as unsavoury a character as you can find."

"But obviously intelligent enough to obscure his trail."

"He'll make a mistake one day, sir. We need patience."

"I need results, Jacques." La Reynie sighed. "But I believe our plan will work. A dark cloud hangs over Paris, and we have to chase it away."

Jacques nodded. "We will get them, sir."

"We shall." La Reynie stood. "Report to me when you can."

Two days later

Jacques was in his usual spot, on the edge of a small copse of trees a few hundred yards from the entrance to the Carmelite nunnery. As it was Sunday, he had arrived before dawn, rather than in the middle of the night.

As expected, Abbé Guibourg had entered the cloister before prime. Now the bells were ringing the end of the service, and Jacques awaited the priest's reappearance.

As last Sunday, the man took his time in leaving, and Jacques silently cursed him.

It had drizzled all morning, but now the rain was turning into a steady downpour. He looked up, then retreated deeper beneath the cover of the trees, but it was futile. His wide-brimmed hat drawn deep over his face, he shifted from one leg to the other, but he was still getting drenched. When the door finally opened, Jacques breathed a sigh of relief.

Abbé Guibourg emerged, turning to speak to someone. His hands were flailing, his round face contorted with anger.

Guibourg's raised voice reached Jacques before the priest lowered it again, glancing around. Did the man suspect he was being followed?

Jacques slid behind the oak tree he'd been leaning against. After counting to ten, he took off his hat and dared another look.

Guibourg was pacing up and down beside his horse, with the odd glance to the door. Moments later, Sister Benedicte emerged carrying a bundle that Guibourg swiftly placed into a saddlebag. At silent nod, the nun turned and shut the door behind her.

Jacques stopped himself from whistling as a shudder ran down his spine. Did the wrapped bundle contain an infant?

Would the priest risk discovery, carrying a dead child in broad daylight?

Guibourg mounted and nudged his horse into a leisurely walk.

He clearly was in no hurry, not wishing to attract attention, Jacques thought. Given the rain, no one would have wondered about a faster pace.

Should I apprehend him?

Jacques untied his horse from the hiding place inside the copse. Once the Abbé was out of sight, he urged his hired mount into a canter. Not long after, he watched as Guibourg passed the outlying settlements and entered through the gate of Saint Denis.

Jacques followed Guibourg more slowly as he weaved his way around people, horses and carts. The priest stopped outside the church of Saint Marcel. He unbuckled the saddle bag which he tucked under his arm and threw the reins of the horse to a waiting boy who took it away.

Guibourg entered Saint Marcel through the side door.

It was still too early for Sunday mass, so if Jacques were to follow him inside, he might risk discovery. Still, he had to try.

Looking around, Jacques spotted a familiar face. Guillaume was sitting on a rag in the shelter of the doorway of Saint Marcel. Jacques waved him over. The lad's initial reluctance to leave his dry spot soon changed at the sight of a copper coin Jacques held up.

"Morning, sir." The boy's voice was hoarse, as if he had a cold. His skin was pale, and his wet blond hair hung limply over his shoulder. He was thin – too thin for a boy of twelve.

The injustice of the children living on the streets hit Jacques once more, but he brushed his concerns aside. He could try to save a few, but not all of them. Using their help when he needed it ensured that they earned enough to feed themselves and their family for a few days.

"You're out early, Guillaume."

"Couldn't sleep."

"Ah." Likely, his mother kept him awake. Yet another whore vying for men's attentions – and full purses. "I'm sorry to hear that. Could you do me a favour?"

"Of course, sir." A reluctant smile broke on Guillaume's face. A favour for Jacques meant coin. And coin meant food.

"Can you hold on to this horse for me for a little while? I need to…umm…say a prayer…for a friend."

Guillaume grinned, revealing several missing teeth. "I'll gladly do that, sir, but can I wait over there?" He pointed at a large weeping willow behind the chancel. "We can shelter from the rain."

Jacques nodded, then gave the boy's shoulder a squeeze. "You do that, Guillaume. I won't be long."

As he entered Saint Marcel through the main door, he glanced around. Only a few elderly women, their heads bent forward, sat on benches. No one looked around.

Jacques took off his hat as he slid behind a pillar. Of Guibourg, there was no sign. He waited as he looked around the church. Oil paintings depicting biblical scenes decorated the walls, and candles in two large candelabra, hung from the wooden roof by thick ropes, cast a warm light over the nave. It was his favourite in all of Paris, but with Guibourg as sacristan, Jacques felt Saint Marcel was desecrated, its holiness tainted. Not that Jacques was religious…

He heard the rattling of metal and looked towards the side where steps led down into the small crypt. The priest

Chapter Seven

Château de Versailles

Fleur strode up to the couple, her heart pounding as Philippe stilled mid-movement.

He stared at her. "Fleur!" Rolling off the girl, he fiddled with his breeches.

She scrambled to her knees and pulled her gown up to cover her breasts. "What's going on?" she whined.

It fuelled Fleur's anger – at Philippe, and at herself. How could she have been so stupid?

"Indeed," she growled. "That would be my question too. Perhaps Monsieur de Mortain can enlighten us."

"I…" Philippe swallowed hard, then he stood. "Fleur, I…"

"You what?" The girl asked, blinking. She held out a hand, and he pulled her up, barely glancing at her. She adjusted her gown, but the layers of her skirts lay limply around her hips, and without her stomacher, the front of her dress was in disarray. Her curls were squashed. She was in no fit state to return to the palace.

"What are you doing, Philippe?"

"I…" His mouth twitched in a nervous smile. "You're back, Fleur. I haven't seen you for weeks."

"You know this person?" The girl asked, pouting. "What does she want from you?"

Fleur shifted her weight from one foot to the other and crossed her arms in front of her, tapping her closed fan against her upper arm. "What I want from him is an answer. And I don't want to repeat myself."

"Well, Fleur, I…" Ruffling his hair, Philippe gave her a rueful smile. "I didn't know when you'd return."

"You could've written to me. You know where my home

59

is." Her voice wobbled, and Fleur hated herself for this sign of weakness. She would let two pitiful people intimidate her. "So, what is this?" With her fan, she pointed at the girl.

"What do you mean, mademoiselle?" The girl stood upright, with an arrogance Fleur found astonishing. "I'm Henrietta de Brun, daughter of a count. And Philippe here is my betrothed." She grabbed his hand, clasping it firmly in hers.

Fleur swallowed back the bile that rose inside her. "Ha! Really? Since when?" She stared at Philippe. But instead of meeting her gaze, he studied his shoes.

"Our parents announced our engagement last week, here in Versailles. You must have missed it." A thin smile played on the brunette's lips. "So we may wish to ask what *you* are doing here, interrupting a romantic evening *à deux*!"

Don't faint! Breathe.

Calmer now, Fleur blinked. "But what if he was already engaged? That would render any other engagements nil and void, would it not?" She kept her voice light, not wanting to show them how miserable she felt inside.

"Philippe?" Looking alarmed, the girl nudged him. "Is this true?"

"Etta—"

"What?" Her face like thunder, Henrietta stood with her hands on her hips then took a step closer until they were almost nose to nose.

It would be comical if it were not so serious, Fleur thought.

Then Philippe looked at Fleur with eyes that begged for forgiveness. "Fleur, I…I'm sorry. This match was agreed between our parents a long time ago."

An icy chill gripped her heart. "When?"

"Three months ago, but Father only announced it last Friday."

Reality hit Fleur like a fist. "So you knew of…this," she pointed at Henrietta, "when you promised marriage to me?"

"I'm sorry, Fleur. I…I didn't think. You were new and beguiling."

won't cost me too much money – though they'll want to be paid well to hush up a potential scandal. And I shall simply announce to our friends at court that you returned to our estate to recuperate from a sudden illness."

"They? Who?" Fleur's heart was pounding. The sense of dread deepened.

"The Carmelite convent outside Paris. It is secure. You won't be able to escape – because I know you'd try. And rest assured, they've been very obliging to acquaintances of mine. Nuns will do anything for gold coin. And once your… trouble…is over, we can see if some lord or other would be happy to take damaged goods. But heed my words, Blanchefleur – beggars can't be choosers!"

***

Early October, 1675
Paris

It took Jacques a week until the opportunity arose to explore the crypt of Saint Marcel.

He waited until Guibourg had left to hold Prime at the convent. To his relief, the priest had unlocked the church. People could enter for prayer all day.

He slipped inside where the gloom swallowed him. At this early hour, well before sunrise, no one was about. Only a handful of candles were illuminating the arches. Shadows stalked the aisles. He lit the candle he brought and soon, his eyes adjusted.

Creeping down the narrow steps into the darkness of the crypt, Jacques pulled a large pin, part of his set of tools he used regularly, from his coat pocket. He inserted the pin into the large lock and wriggled until it sprang open. He grinned. Every time he picked a lock, he told himself he'd missed his calling.

He tucked away the pin and, as quiet as possible, pulled the strong chain off.

Best not risk getting locked in.

Then he opened the metal grille, slipped through, and closed it again, putting the chain on the floor.

He entered the vaulted room and looked around. The hairs at the nape of his neck stood on end as he walked between several old sarcophagi in the flickering light. These people were long dead, and he did not believe in ghosts. What he was looking for was very much in the present.

He searched the crypt, peeking into every corner and across the floor. The walls were solid, with no niches or shelves. It was in vain. He'd found no trace of any bundles containing dead children, nor their bones, nor any other body parts.

Jacques swore as frustration soared through him. Time was of the essence. Guibourg must not find him poking his nose into the stone coffins. He stared at the first one when a thought crossed his mind. Could something other than their rightful bodies be *inside* them?

As he passed each sarcophagus for the second time, he checked the lids. All were solidly in place...except one at the far side of the crypt. That lid, a little thinner than the others, lay slightly skewed.

His pulse quickened. From the carved name and date, faded in time but still legible, it predated all others. The resting place of a fifth-century bishop would be perfect for the *abbé*'s nefarious actions. No one would ever dream of checking.

He gave a corner a sharp push, and the lid slid back with a crunching sound. The light of his candle revealed only an ancient shroud, thin and torn in places, with the outlines of a skull and bones beneath, but no bodies of infants or their swaddling clothes. Jacques was about to push the lid aside further, to peek into the bottom half of the sarcophagus, when he heard a door shut.

Had Guibourg returned already?

"Damn," he whispered. If he moved the stone back, anyone in the nave would hear it. He leaned into the space as much as he could, holding his breath to avoid the musty smell. Close to the foot end of the coffin, he spotted something, but even as he stretched, he knew he could not reach it without shifting the lid.

The sound of footsteps alerted him, and he blew out his candle. Behind the row of sarcophagi, he felt his way back towards the entrance, he realised that whoever was there had halted. A light went up in the stairwell, and Jacques crouched behind a coffin.

If it was Guibourg, he'd know something was amiss when he saw the chain on the floor inside the grille door. Jacques put the candle into his pocket, suppressing a hiss as the hot wax dripped over his hands. He held his breath when he heard the person sauntering through the crypt; the light showed the way. After it had passed his hiding place, he peeked around the coffin. It was as he thought.

Guibourg, carrying a lantern, was heading straight for the back of the crypt.

I'm right – he's hidden something there.

But now was not the time to find out what it was. Guibourg placed the lantern on the floor, then pushed the lid of the last sarcophagus.

Jacques had no intention of getting locked in. Whilst Guibourg rummaged inside the coffin with the half-open lid, Jacques slid out and took the steps two at a time into the nave. Darting from pillar to pillar, he finally reached the side door.

To his relief, it was unlocked, and, as footsteps echoed up the stairwell, he pushed his way outside and ran into an adjacent lane, then turned off, down a narrow path behind the houses. He only stopped running when he was certain he was not being followed, taking deep gulps of air to catch his breath. Moments later, he walked into the direction of the Châtelet, plotting another secretive visit into the crypt.

But the following Sunday, Jacques found Saint Marcel locked, and when he returned two weeks later, both church and the crypt were unlocked and the old sarcophagus contained nothing but the bones of the dead fifth-century bishop.

Guibourg had got the better of him. For now…

PART TWO

A Time of Sorrow

Chapter Eight

Early June, 1676
The Convent of the Carmelites, Paris

"You've missed a corner, over there!" The harsh voice grated on Fleur's nerves, but knowing what awaited her if she disobeyed Sister Benedicte's order, she nodded.

"I'm sorry, sister. I did not realise." Dipping the horsehair brush into the bowl of now-muddy water that stung her raw hands, Fleur grimaced. Then she began to scrub the floor where the old nun had indicated. Sweat ran down her forehead, and she wiped it away with the back of her hand. Certain she'd cleaned that part of the church earlier, she still kept quiet, else the sisters would whip her again.

This close to giving birth, she could not risk punishment for what the nuns considered her 'wicked ways'. She'd counted down the days, weeks and months of her stay by etching lines into the wall behind her bed. Another fortnight, perhaps, and she'd have her baby.

Resigned, her attention returned to the stone floor.

Later that afternoon, as she sat on a bench in the sparse visiting chamber of the convent, she thought back to the last time Sophie had visited. Snow had covered the grass in the cloisters. It must have been over three months ago. So when the Mother Superior had announced that Sophie would come to see her today, Fleur had been more concerned than relieved.

Sophie had left her at the convent a fortnight after Fleur's revelation the previous autumn, when they were certain Fleur was expecting a child, and had given the nuns permission to treat her daughter as they saw fit. Fleur had to earn her keep.

She never dined with the nuns, but received pottage or stale bread and old cheese to eat in her cold cell.

None of that could have been good for the baby, yet it still thrived in her belly. Often, she lay awake at night, a hand on her extended stomach, feeling the babe move. The experience amazed her, and she came to love the little person who grew inside her. How could she not? It was not the child's fault that the father was a seducer.

The nuns forbade her to speak to the other handful of women she'd seen over recent months. Sister Benedicte always kept them apart from each other. The new mothers disappeared shortly after having given birth. Clearly, Fleur was not the only one who'd met her fate the same way.

Confined to her cell except for prayer and chores, she escaped the nuns' clutches once or twice, exploring stairwells and corridors, until one day when the Mother Superior had found her in a room devoid of furniture apart from a birthing chair and a plain table. Was this where she would give birth? Punishment had been severe. Fleur shuddered at the thought of the scars on her back.

The last time she'd come, Mother had told Fleur, with great satisfaction, that Philippe had wed Henrietta in a lavish ceremony. Fleur had bitten back her pain, hiding behind a polite façade, until she'd returned to her sparse chamber, where she'd burst into floods of tears. Then the baby had kicked, and she realised that she no longer yearned for Philippe. The mirror had cracked. Now, she saw through his deception, but the unfairness of the situation made the anger inside her rise every day. He was leading the life of luxury, no small thanks to stupid Henrietta, whilst Fleur was cooped up in a convent, with nuns who enjoyed using the rod on defenceless girls.

Once her child was born, she would find a way to support them both. She could sew or become a companion. It was impossible to return home. The revelation would lead to scandal.

In recent months, Fleur had written to acquaintances she'd made at Versailles, but it was likely the Mother Superior held back any letters for her, as Fleur had received none since her arrival.

The door opened, and Sophie entered, devoutly crossing herself, before she took a seat on Fleur's bench. She sent her a cool glance that took in her face and belly.

"How are you?"

Fleur smiled coldly. "Why do you ask, Mother? It's not like you to care."

Sophie pursed her lips. "You've become rude, Blanchefleur. It doesn't suit you."

"Does it not?" Fleur snorted. "I suppose I have much time to think, stuck in this pigsty." She waved her hand in the air.

"And rightly so," Sophie snapped. "You needed to reflect on your sin."

"My sin? As if I'm the only one who…" Fleur returned Mother's glare. "Rumours of your behaviour have reached me here, and they're not complementary."

Sophie blanched, but quickly recovered her composure. "What I do is between me and the Good Lord. At least, I was married when I carried you."

"And now you're not, and still take a lover, from what I heard."

"Oh, don't be nasty. Soon, this," Sophie pointed at Fleur's belly, "will be history. Then you will come to realise what life is really about."

Fleur frowned. "What do you mean? Of course, I will. I shall provide for my child, as most mothers do."

Sophie laughed out loud, the sound echoing across the bare stone walls. It sounded false. "By doing what?"

"Well, I can sew, or I can become a companion to a lady. I've written to—"

"I know." A gleam in Sophie's eyes sent a shiver down Fleur's spine, and a coldness gripped her heart. "I burned all those pathetic letters."

Fleur stared at her. "You did what? You had no right, Mother!"

"I have every right, Blanchefleur. We must never reveal your little…misadventure…to anyone."

"What? Once I leave this hellhole, my child and I will—"

"There won't be a child for you to keep. Be realistic! Do you really think I will allow you to venture into Paris with a bastard? Everyone would laugh at us. Why, at the moment, all our friends think you're recuperating from a sickness in our country home."

"I'm sure they're aware of what's really happening."

"Whether or not they do is of no significance. You will leave here once the…thing…is born, a married woman." Sophie sent her a triumphant look. "It's all arranged."

Fleur's mind whirled. What had Mother done? Tears stung her eyes, but she bit them back. She would not cry in front of her. "And what happens to my child in your master plan?"

"It will be given up for adoption, I suppose, or whatever the nuns want to do with it. If it survives the birth, that is… You're thin, apart from your enormous belly. The child might not survive."

Black spots appeared in front of Fleur's eyes, and she dug her fingernails into the flesh of her hand to dissolve the threatening blackness. "Of course he or she will live. My babe is thriving."

Sophie snorted. "To be honest, I don't care either way. Once it's over, you'll wed. The child won't play any further role in your life."

Fleur swallowed hard. "And what if I refuse?"

"Trust me – after giving birth you'll hardly be in the condition to object. Abbé Guibourg will perform your marriage ceremony to an acquaintance of mine, who will then take you far away from Paris."

"I see." Her mind numb, she asked, "And who is this friend of yours?"

Sophie's smile was as cold as the stone walls that surrounded them. "Why, he's a rich merchant you have never met, from Brittany. He likes his women young…and pliable."

"How old is he?"

"It doesn't really matter, but if you must know, he is close to three score years. You will submit unto him, as a good wife should. And don't think you can play tricks on him – he

refused to consider them 'holy'; in fact, he considered their behaviour less than Christian.

He held the note over the flame of a candle and dropped the burning parchment into the cold ashes of the small fireplace opposite his workbench.

"A visit to the nuns it is." He stretched, then put on his boots. He could not remember taking them off, but he must have done.

His double life was wreaking havoc on his mind. He must keep his wits about him. That meant he needed a proper sleep at night.

"There aren't enough hours in the day," he said, and rose. Raking his hand through his hair, he walked over to the chair on which he'd abandoned his cloak and hat in the night.

Jacques blew out the candles and left, locking the door behind him. If anyone came looking for him, they'd have to return later.

With a sigh, he walked towards the stables again. A fresh griddle cake from a street vendor he knew helped restore his spirits, and when he eventually rode through the gate of Saint Denis, he was finally fully awake.

Chapter Nine

Early June, 1676
The Convent of the Carmelites, Paris

The walls of the convent towered in front of him when Jacques stopped outside the entrance. From the upper levels, two small, rectangular windows overlooked this side. It resembled a fortress more than a religious house. From the corner of his eye, he thought he spotted a shadow moving behind a window. Had the nuns seen him approach?

He tied the hired horse to a solid iron ring set into the stone and knocked on the door. Several moments passed before a young nun opened the grille.

"Yes?"

"Good day. I wish to speak to Sister Benedicte."

"The sister does not receive visitors at this moment, monsieur."

Had they seen him approach? The negative response had been too swift.

"I can wait."

The nun inhaled sharply. "No, you can't. I mean, she will not…" She looked around before whispering, "She won't speak to you."

Jacques grinned. "So she was watching my arrival? Ah."

"I never said that." Her eyes widened, and the sudden sharp tone in her voice showed her fear.

"I'm sure you didn't, sister. I could always speak to the Mother Superior instead."

Again, the nun shook her head. "Please leave, sir."

"No." He leaned against the stone frame. "I'm in no hurry."

"You can't stay there!"

"Why ever not?" He extended his arm in a sweeping gesture. "It's a beautiful day. The sun is shining. Out here, the air is fresh. No, 'tis as I said, I can wait."

"As you wish!" The nun shut the grille, leaving him standing in front of the closed door.

As he expected, moments later she returned and unlocked it.

"Please enter." She stood aside as he walked into the entrance room. "But wait here! The Mother Superior will see you shortly." She disappeared down a narrow corridor.

Jacques glanced around, but all was silent – except for a swishing sound coming from the cloisters. Intrigued, he stepped through the adjoining door. In a corner to his right, a woman, heavily pregnant, was sweeping the floor.

Should she be doing this in her advanced condition? But then, he remembered the many women in his *quartier* who undertook much harder chores than merely cleaning the floor, right up to the day they gave birth. A new respect had grown in him as he'd watched them. It was something that rarely occurred to men, especially those of a certain station. Perhaps women were indeed stronger than men, not physically, but in their minds? A thought that would no doubt outrage the learned professors.

But what he wanted to know whether this woman was one of those who came here to have their child, only to never see it again? Looking around, he saw no sign of any nuns. He coughed into his fist to alert her to his presence and approached her in swift strides.

She pivoted towards him. Her youth surprised him. She could barely be seventeen, if that.

"Good day, mademoiselle."

"Oh, monsieur." Her hand flew to her mouth.

The girl was too thin for one so heavy with child. A simple linen gown hung like a sack off her frame, stretching over the rounded belly. Her blonde hair was tied back in a tight braid, and the pretty face appeared tired. Only then did he realise that her eyes were red-rimmed, her eyelids puffed. She'd been crying.

"Please help me."

His heart tugged at his conscience, and he clenched and unclenched his fists. "What can I do for you, mademoiselle?"

Her gaze flew across the cloisters before it settled on him with a beseeching look. "You must help me escape. Today."

"Are you held here against your will?" Anger rose within him when she nodded. "You can accompany me to Paris if you wish."

"Oh, thank you, monsieur."

"Where would you want to go to?"

At that, she paused. Did she not have any family?

"I…I need to get away from here. I…" Her eyes widened as she stared behind him. Footsteps echoed around the stone walls. "No!" the girl screamed.

He spun around and looked straight into the barrel of a pistol Sister Benedicte aimed at him.

"Out!" the nun ordered, her cold eyes staring at him.

"No, let me go!" Two nuns who had appeared as if from out of nowhere dragged the girl away. "My child!"

He was about to follow her, to wrestle her from the sisters when the cold metal was pressed against the back of his head. "Don't think I won't pull the trigger. You've made a nuisance of yourself here for the last time, Montagnac. Now leave!"

"Not without this woman."

"She's of feeble mind and due to give birth any moment. See, her clothing is staining. 'Tis time. I have to attend to her."

He cursed himself for not being armed, as they hauled the girl away. A trail of liquid was running down her skirt.

Hell! She's giving birth.

He had to help her, but first, he had to escape the clutches of Sister Benedicte. He turned swiftly, but found himself staring not only down one, but two barrels. A second nun, her wrinkled face distorted, her mouth pressed into a thin line, had appeared, and together they nudged him back to the entrance and slammed the door shut behind him.

Outside, he swore as he untied his horse. Then he urged it into a gallop on the road back to Paris, but once he lost sight of the nunnery, he veered into the copse of trees he'd been hiding in before and led the gelding through it.

He realised he had come across their secret. They were trading the newborn babes of young women caught in compromising situations. But Jacques would not leave this girl to her fate. Yet with her family's explicit approval, there was little the police could do.

But how long would it take until her babe was born? She'd looked gaunt, her cheeks sunken, the green eyes – too large for her small face – full of sorrow. Given her desperation, she was likely put there by relatives to give birth, and then what would happen? Whisked off to the countryside, to be hidden from view, her infant abandoned, given up for adoption, or worse – killed in a black mass?

"Of course." Why had he not thought of him before? He would look out for Abbé Guibourg. Then he spotted a nun leaving the convent on a donkey. She rode in the direction of the gate of Saint Denis.

And on to the church of Saint Marcel?

Torn between staying in hiding or following the nun, he sighed. As she was about to disappear, he mounted his horse and, keeping as close to the trees as possible, followed her.

A short while later, she entered the city and soon stopped outside Saint Marcel.

Biting his lip, Jacques nodded slowly. It was as he'd expected. He dismounted and led the horse into a side lane from where he could see if the priest would emerge. He cursed himself for not bringing his pistol, but entering a convent had not instilled in him the sense that he needed to be armed. He always wore his dagger on his belt, but that would do little against two weapons loaded with gunpowder.

He did not have to wait long. Guibourg rode ahead on his gelding, with the nun following. Now that he was closer, Jacques recognised her as the one who'd stood beside the midwife, pointing a pistol at him.

Now, all he needed was proof.

At a safe distance, he followed them back to the convent and hid in the trees again. An hour had passed at least, if not more. He wondered how far the birth had advanced. Leaning against a tree, he kept his eyes on the gate, occasionally scanning the countryside for any unusual movements. On the main road, he watched as riders and carriages vied for space as they approached the gate. Traders and merchants with their carts mingled with messengers rushing past them on fast horses. Paris was the biggest city in Europe, but sometimes Jacques yearned for the peace and calm of his native land in the south. But then he remembered how bored he'd been, growing up surrounded by vineyards and forests. Thinking of the poor babes that were murdered for the folly of the rich made him glad he was here.

Such as the one being born right now.

Of course, there was the risk it could be a stillbirth. The girl had looked small, and so young. What had befallen her?

A carriage approached the gate, and he straightened. A woman emerged, her face covered in a black veil. A footman pulled a small trunk from the roof and carried it to the door where he knocked sharply.

Was this the girl's mother, coming to take her home? It was too soon after her confinement. Surely, the girl would not be ready to travel yet.

To his surprise, a portly man, shorter than the woman, stepped off the carriage and looked around as if to make sure he was not observed. The father?

Jacques did not like the look on the fleshy face. The man lifted his hat and patted his forehead and temple with a handkerchief. His wig was elaborate, his clothes of excellent quality.

He is rich.

Was this man the girl's father, or perhaps buying the infant? Jacques' breath hitched.

The door opened, and the woman strode in, followed by the well-dressed man and the footman who took the trunk inside. Moments later, the footman reappeared. The driver secured the carriage and stepped off, and together they disappeared behind it, likely waiting beside the horses, out of Jacques' sight.

"She's asleep." Sophie huffed. "And still bleeding, by the looks of it."

"I can't wed her with all that...stuff dripping down her legs." The man's voice was whiney. "Look at her!"

"Don't worry about that," Mother said. "It will soon stop. She shall be clean."

"I hope so. How long until her...er, you know what I mean...narrows again?"

Fleur suppressed a shudder, now knowing full well what he meant. She was tempted to open an eye to catch a glimpse at her intended, but decided against it. If her mother knew she was awake, she might insist she got up.

"A few weeks." Sophie's voice sounded detached. "Take her to the country, come back to Paris for some entertainment, and then go back to her later. She'll be perfect for your...preferences."

"She's so slender, true." His tone turned dreamy. "I shall pay for another night's stay at the inn and return tomorrow. We must find Abbé Guibourg and tell him about the delay."

Fleur felt like gagging. To her relief, the door closed, and the voices receded. She counted to fifty before she dared to blink. The room was empty.

What was that man going to do with her? A shudder ran down her spine. Mother had sold her to the highest bidder, it seemed, and not cared at all about Fleur's happiness.

Thinking back, she realised she'd never really known Sophie. Mother had never paid much attention to her. The little time Fleur had spent with Father had been precious. He'd introduced her to reading; the library at their country home was full of books, including those of his brother, Marin, a celebrated poet and writer.

But it was clear to Fleur that Mother had always regarded Father as weak. Memories of their arguments returned. Mother had demanded to attend court, when all Father wanted to do was travel the world and fill journals with details of strange animals.

His death in a riding accident eight years earlier had come as a shock. The next day, Sophie had sent Fleur to a convent to be schooled. She'd not even allowed her to say goodbye to Father at his funeral.

Fleur felt the tender flesh between her legs. With relief, she realised the pain had stopped. Hopefully, Sophie and the strange man had left. It gave her time to search for her babe. Surely, the boy would scream for her?

She removed the rags and wiped away the last drops of blood. Spotting a clean linen cloth on the floor that the sister had overlooked, she inserted it gently. She hissed at the discomfort, but it would have to do. It was the only way she could be certain no more blood would escape.

Fleur stopped by the door and listened, but only silence surrounded her. Slowly, she prised it open and looked around. She found herself at the end of a narrow aisle that led to a larger one. She opened two other doors which led into similar rooms like the one she'd been in, but they were empty. Daylight greeted her at the end of the corridor, and she blinked. Only then did she realise that the room she'd given birth in had no windows. How strange! Was fresh air bad for babes?

She tiptoed along the corridor on this upper floor, where she knew the nuns' cells were. This section overlooked the cloisters. Finally, she turned a corner and spotted two small windows towards the outside. She hid in an alcove between them, catching her breath, listening for footsteps, but all remained silent. Where could they have taken her son?

It was clear now that most nuns did not understand what went on. *Was the Mother Superior aware of this?* If they gave away infants to families, the woman would have to know. Otherwise, her status would be at risk. Fleur had no doubt that the old crone would happily hand over innocent babes to waiting hands, to get back at the sinners who'd delivered them.

A wailing sound reaching her from outside the wall raised her from her thoughts. She looked out of a window and realised she was above the main entrance. Leaning forward, she saw Sister Benedicte and Abbé Guibourg emerge. The priest always unnerved her. Even when he said mass, there was something about him that made Fleur's skin crawl. To her horror, he held a bundle in his arms, which he stuffed into a saddlebag.

Fleur whimpered. Was that her boy? And was he really dead? If so, why did they not bury him behind the convent walls, as she'd seen other unfortunate babes disposed of? Instead, her child was wrapped up like a parcel and carried away by the sinister priest. Fleur was certain it was her son. A moment later, Guibourg mounted, waved at Sister Benedicte and rode away.

With tears in her eyes, Fleur fumbled with the lock of the window to call out to him when a hand covered her mouth and another wrapped around her waist.

Chapter Ten

The Convent of the Carmelites, Paris

"Please stay calm." A low voice whispered in her ear. "I'm going to help you."

The stranger from this morning? It seemed like a lifetime ago.

She nodded, and he removed his hand from her mouth. "My babe…" she whispered as she turned around.

It was the young man who the nuns had threatened with their pistols.

"Come with me, quickly."

She glanced up and down the corridor. "Where to?"

He grinned. "Out of here."

"But," Fleur pointed at the window, "he has my son."

His expression changed instantly as he turned serious. "I thought so. Come!"

He took her hand, and she followed him, her mind whirling. "Who are you?"

"My name is Jacques. I'll explain everything later. First, we need to get back to where I got in. You're not safe until we reach my horse."

Should she trust him, or was he leading her into another trap? The way he stalked ahead, sword in one hand now and her hand in the other, was calm and assured.

What have I got to lose? A lecherous husband? An uncaring mother?

Still. "Where are we going?"

He sent her a swift glance. "To Paris. I'm afraid we don't have time to collect any of your belongings. Sister Benedicte will probably be on her way to your birthing room now that she sent Abbé Guibourg on his way."

Fleur breathed in sharply. "You know the man?"

He nodded, his face grim. "I do. Not far to go." Clearly, Jacques was no friend of the priest.

They hurried down a narrow aisle and into what looked like a storeroom. Piles of clean, folded linens lay heaped high on a table. Two shelves held bottles of various substances. She shuddered when her gaze fell on one particular bottle prominently displayed: arsenic.

"What is this? Arsenic?" She pointed at it. "What do nuns need poison for?"

The stranger regarded her for a long moment. "I wonder." He closed the door behind them and pulled a low cupboard in front of it, blocking the way. After a glance out of the narrow, open window, he looked around the room. "Ah. Take an armful of these." He pointed at the fabrics.

Puzzled, she picked up a large pile of them and followed him to the window. "We're not jumping, are we?"

"We are, and we'll be fine."

"But we'll break our legs!"

He smiled. She liked the way the left side of his mouth quirked. "We won't." He threw the linens outside, before he beckoned her closer. "See that? It will stop your fall."

"A cart?" Alarmed, she stared at him. "Are you serious?"

"A cart filled with straw," he clarified. "It's the only way, I'm afraid. The straw will temper your fall. One of the sisters stays near the entrance hall. She'd ring a bell to warn the others. Believe me; I don't want to be facing the open barrel of Sister Benedicte's pistol again."

Fleur swallowed hard. "Nor do I. How did you get in?"

He snorted. "By standing on my horse and climbing up. There are plenty of gaps in the stone. But I wouldn't recommend it for going down, especially not with your bare feet. We have little time."

She stared at the fidgeting beast tied to a stake in the wall beside the cart. It looked…unsafe.

He took the bundle from her and threw it down. Then he collected another pile and threw it on top. Satisfied, he leaned back. "This should do. I'll go first, but you must follow me immediately." He pressed her upper arm. "Trust me."

A sob escaped her. Philippe had said this, and look where she'd ended up! But the look in Jacques' eyes showed genuine concern for her. Fleur nodded. What choice did she have?

He swung his legs over the ledge. With a last glance at her, he slid outside and jumped.

Fleur rushed forward to watch him landing neatly on top of the pile of linens in the cart. He waved at her.

"Your turn now," he called out.

Her heart beat a steady drum in her ear. The drop was not too steep, but it was enough to hurt yourself. She'd given birth recently. Her body was still weak. Would the jump harm her?

Behind her, a bell sounded from inside the convent, and shouting ensued. Had Sister Benedicte discovered she'd gone? How soon until they found her?

As voices drew nearer, panic rose within her. She took a stool and stepped on it. Cautiously, she sat on the ledge and squeezed her legs outside. Unable to sit upright, she nudged forward. Her shift rode up her legs, and she pulled it down, fully aware she wore nothing beneath it.

Better lose your dignity than be abused all your life.

Her hands trembled, but she forced her body to calm. By the time voices outside the storeroom grew louder, she'd decided. "Sweet Mother, help me!" With a prayer in her head, she pushed herself off.

She closed her eyes, relishing the air on her skin before she landed, the impact softer than expected. Still, it winded her. Her body rolled, but firm hands caught her deftly.

"I have you."

Fleur opened her eyes and realised she was lying on top of the linens. But Jacques had already jumped off the cart and reached out his hand to help her descend.

As she moved, blood trickled down her thighs. She grabbed a handful of the linens – she'd have need of them – and disappeared behind the cart, out of his sight. "A moment, please, monsieur."

"Of course, mademoiselle." As if he'd guessed…

She ripped a sheet into small strips. Then she pulled out the bloodied rag, discarding it beneath the cart, and replaced it with a clean one. Finally, she dabbed the blood from her skin. Her face on fire, she emerged, clutching the bundle of clean fabric pieces.

But he merely smiled at her. "Come. You'll ride sideways in front of me."

A dreadful thought occurred to her. "But what if I…if the blood…"

"Don't worry about that. We must get you to safety first. A friend will look after you." He took two large sheets and draped them over the saddle.

"And my son? That priest took him away."

Would she never hold her boy? Her breath hitched.

He met her gaze calmly. "I know where to find Abbé Guibourg and will search for your child once I've dropped you off."

Nodding, she let him hoist her onto the horse. He mounted and wrapped the sheets around her. She felt like a swaddled babe.

Safe. Unlike my son. Tears stung her eyes, but she quickly blinked them away as her saviour guided the horse towards a line of trees nearby.

Close to him now, she tilted her head, studying his profile. His skin was darker, which was unusual for people in Paris who preferred a paler complexion. His home must be in the far south, perhaps the Languedoc. Beneath his hat, wavy blond hair fell over his shoulders. He glanced at her with warm brown eyes.

Fleur wanted to trust him, but the past year had left its mark. "Who are you?"

"I'm Jacques de Montagnac, and I…" He hesitated before he seemed to make up his mind. He smiled. "I'm also with the police. And you, mademoiselle?"

The police? Perhaps he would really find her son! "My name is Fleur de La Fontaine. Blanchefleur, really, but only my mother calls me that."

"Ah." He looked as if something had occurred to him. "Earlier today, a tall woman arrived at the convent, together with a short, rotund man. Are they your parents?"

Fleur shuddered. "Yes, that was my mother. But the man with her was meant to become my…husband."

He raised his eyebrows. "You were going to get married – straight after giving birth? What kind of mother is she?"

She'd wondered about that herself, but it sounded so much worse when another person spoke her own thoughts out loud. "To be honest, I have no inkling. She never bothered with me. Father did, but he travelled a lot. And he died years ago."

"I'm sorry. Yours doesn't sound like a contented childhood."

A smile escaped her. "Oh, whilst Father lived, it was wonderful. He preferred to stay in our country home, looking after the estate, when he was not abroad. I grew up reading and walking and listening to him explain the sciences and other works. His brother, my uncle, sometimes joined us."

"It sounds idyllic."

"It was – until his accident. His horse threw him. Father broke his neck."

Jacques eyed her. "Was he riding out alone when it happened?"

Fleur nodded. "Yes, and I understand where your thoughts are taking you. I've often wondered myself if Mother had a hand in it."

"But you don't have any proof?"

"No. I wish I'd paid more attention, but she sent me to a convent in the north, and I never had a chance to speak to anyone about it."

"I'm sorry," he said again. "It must have been a distressing time for you."

"It was."

"And now you're supposed to wed that old goat that arrived with your mother?"

She laughed. "Yes. The idea is ridiculous."

"Though, sadly, not rare. Many young girls have to marry older men."

Fleur gritted her teeth. "I can imagine."

For a while, they rode on in silence. Fleur barely took in the many people who frequented the road. Her body weak, she was grateful for Jacques' firm hold, else she would slide off the horse.

"There we are." He pointed up as they rode through an archway. "The gate of Saint Denis. We're nearly there."

They turned away from the big streets, from one narrow lane into another. The *quartier* was not one she was familiar with, and a sense of unease gripped her. He'd not told her anything about himself, yet she'd spoken at length about her childhood. "Where are we going?"

"To a good friend of mine. You might find the accommodation…unusual, but let me reassure you that Madame Claudette has helped more young women in need than anyone else in this city."

"She must be a very kind lady."

He smirked. "Yes, she is. Claudette has a good heart, but she's also a shrewd businesswoman. If I could give you one word of advice," he guided the horse around a stray dog crossing the street. "If she ever asks if you wanted to work for her, please say no."

"Why is that?" Fleur asked as she stared at the buildings rising on either side. This was not the pretty Paris she remembered. The men and women passing them by wore tattered clothes, often badly mended. Children ran around without shoes, their feet filthy. This *quartier* was much poorer than her own; more grimy.

They came to a halt in front of a narrow, tall house. Jacques dismounted. Fleur immediately missed the heat of his body behind hers. She'd not realised how tired she was.

The red door stood open. Two young women leaned against the wall outside the entrance, staring at them. Their plain gowns revealed more flesh than Fleur had seen in Versailles. Who were they?

Jacques held out his hands and helped her off the horse. Aware of the bloodstained shift, she wrapped the linen sheets tight around her.

"It's fine. Don't worry," he said. "My friend, Madame Claudette Arnauld, manages this establishment."

The two women approached, looking her up and down. The younger one glanced at Jacques. "What happened?" she asked, her voice soft.

"I found this young lady in the convent, Ninou. She needs our help. She's just given birth."

"Sweet Lord!" The girl called Ninou walked up to her and embraced her. Fleur briefly closed her eyes. She did not remember the last time a female had handled her so gently. "Come in, ma chère. You're safe here."

Fleur stared at the doorway, where a woman in her forties appeared, watching them.

Realisation hit her, and her heart sank. "A brothel?" Without warning, her body shook, and Ninou tightened her grip. Fleur blinked frantically, struggling to breathe. "You've taken me to a brothel?"

Darkness claimed her.

***

"Can you help her?" Jacques stood in the open door, feeling useless.

He'd carried the girl up two flights of stairs and placed her in a narrow bunk bed in a small chamber beneath the roof. Only a small window on the low wall below the slanted ceiling let in the daylight. Here, they were safe from any prying eyes.

Claudette glanced at him across the room. "Of course. How long ago did she give birth?"

He shrugged his shoulders. "I don't know. Guibourg left with the infant when I found her. It can barely be more than an hour."

"Goodness! It's too soon for her to be up and about." She rinsed the cloth in the bowl of water Ninou had brought from the kitchen and dabbed Fleur's face.

How young the girl looked, Jacques thought. How vulnerable! "Is there anything else I can do here?"

Claudette shook her head. "No. She's losing blood, so I will attend to her. We'll wash and dress her in a fresh shift. I might have to visit the apothecary, if she suffered any injuries. Will you pay for him?"

"Monsieur Moreau? Of course." Jacques nodded. He could barely afford to mend the soles of his worn boots, but always found coin for girls in need. La Reynie kept his spies on low wages.

"I'll come back later. In the meantime, I'll go to Saint Marcel, to see what the good abbé has done with the child. A boy, I believe."

"I pray he's alive, but…" Claudette's words echoed his own doubtful thoughts.

"Please do." Without another word, he turned and went downstairs. At the entrance, he stopped beside Ninou. "Keep an eye on the girl, please. She's too young, and all alone. Oh, and her mother might send men looking for her. Don't mention her arrival to anyone."

"Her mother?" Ninou's eyes widened.

"Yes. She was going to marry her off to an old *débauché* today. I'm certain she does not take kindly to Fleur's escape."

"Parents can be a Godsend – or a curse."

From the look on Ninou's face, hers belonged to the latter group. He sighed. "How is Jeanne?"

"Safe and well." The young whore smiled. "And looked after by my elderly landlady."

He had no doubt. Ninou had told him before that the owner of her small lodging was keen to help her. *You find people who support you in the strangest places.*

Smiling, he took his leave. She may not have Fleur's family status and upbringing, but the two girls had much in common. He hoped they'd become friends.

He took the horse back to the stables, then turned in the direction of the church of Saint Marcel. Grey skies were looming above, threatening more rain, and the wind whipped at his hat. He lowered his head to brace himself.

The side door to the church was unlocked, and he slid in and closed it quietly behind him. Inside, a strong smell of incense lingered in the air.

A useful way to hide dead bodies.

Jacques removed his hat and ruffled his hair that had stuck to his skull. To his surprise, the church was empty. No praying widows today. There was no sign of Guibourg.

Weaving his way across the church, he halted behind a pillar from where he could observe the steps to the crypt. He berated himself for not having been able to find any traces of newborn children here. Guibourg was guilty, Jacques was sure. No sound emerged, so he moved to the steps that led downstairs. Below, the grille door was locked, the crypt beyond in darkness.

So where had the priest taken the boy?

A sound from the front of the church made Jacques look up. Standing by the alter stood Abbé Guibourg, a triumphant smile on his face, but the eyes that met his were as cold as the sarcophagi in the crypt.

He's been expecting me. A shiver ran down his spine.

"Monsieur de Montagnac, have you come to pray? Or for your confession?" Guibourg ambled towards him, his narrow frame upright, hands folded behind his back.

Hands that had the blood of innocents on them!

Jacques shrugged, trying to keep his confusion under control. How did Guibourg know his name? Had someone revealed his identity? "I've said a brief prayer, yes, but somehow I don't think I have to confess to as much as you do…"

Guibourg pursed his thin lips. "Ah, and what would that be? That I am remiss in looking after the poor widows of Saint Denis?"

"I could not say, abbé. Although I don't think you're too concerned about what the Lord thinks of your types of… masses." Jacques kept his breathing steady and did not let the old priest out of his sight.

"You are wasting my time with baseless insinuations." The old man waved a bony hand in the air, then looked Jacques up and down. "I want you to leave my church and never set foot in here again."

"You can't throw me out of a church."

"Yes, I can." Grinning, Guibourg looked pleased with himself. "For today, let me merely give you a warning. Next time, I won't be so obliging. There are ways us priests can handle…thieves."

By crippling them, or worse, no doubt.

A moment later, Jacques heard the now familiar click of a pistol and the feeling of cold metal pressed against the back of his head.

"To the door over there!"

He did not recognise the deep male voice. An associate of Guibourg's? Of course, the network might contain dozens of men and women across Paris. The idea chilled his bones. So far, he'd thought Guibourg and Sister Benedicte acted on their own. How careless of him not to consider other members of their circle! He sauntered towards the side door. "I will leave. But don't think I won't be coming back, Guibourg. Next time, I won't be alone."

"I wouldn't be so certain, Montagnac. I will make sure the Lieutenant General will receive my complaint."

"Why don't you kill me? No one would ever find out."

A dry laugh came from Guibourg. "Do you consider me that stupid, Montagnac? If you don't report back to La Reynie, his *policiers* will tear my beautiful church apart."

Jacques snorted. "We might do that anyway." He reached the door and stopped.

A hand clasped his shoulder and dug into it. "It's time you accepted the inevitable, Montagnac. Without proof, you'll always leave empty-handed. I am a respected priest in an impoverished parish. I have nothing to hide. Therefore I'm certain my warning will be heeded."

As Jacques opened the door, he half-turned, but the man holding the pistol moved into the shadows, out of his line of vision. Was it someone he knew? "I wish you good fortune in your endeavour." Smiling at the priest, he bowed and flourished his hat. The movement allowed Jacques a brief glance over Guibourg's shoulder at the shape of a tall, broad man whose face remained hidden.

Jacques hurried away, his mind in turmoil. Was the stranger a member of La Reynie's police force? If so, how many others, perhaps up to the highest ranks, were involved in this sordid affair? He'd recognised the voice from somewhere.

He had to get a message to La Reynie urgently, but that henchman – or others working with him – would be there to intercept any such messages.

Jacques needed a different strategy. First, he'd have to discover the name. Only once he was certain would he tell La Reynie. The Lieutenant General might consider it fitting to have the man observed, rather than move swiftly against him.

With new plans swirling in his head, Jacques was heading to Claudette's when he spotted Guillaume, a threadbare blanket thrown around small shoulders.

"*Bonjour*, Jacques."

"Guillaume. Where are you going?" A thought struck him. "Not to Saint Marcel, are you?"

The lad nodded. "Yes, there's going to be a funeral later of some woman popular in the *quartier*, old Madame Bouvier." A shy grin spread across his face. "Mourners are generous as funerals remind them of their own mortality."

Jacques laughed out loud. "And so they should be, sinners, the lot of them. Could you also do me a favour? Over the next few days?"

"Of course." Guillaume beamed at him. Food would be secure for a while.

"Thank you. I'd like you to keep an eye on someone, a man." He fished out a couple of *ecus* and passed them to the boy.

"What kind of man?" The coin disappeared into Guillaume's pockets.

"Tall, about my height, but much broader around shoulder and middle. He has a hooked nose, dark hair, and a stubble. That's all I can tell you. He's in the church now."

"Ah yes. I've seen him before."

Jacques raised an eyebrow. "You have? Who is he?"

Guillaume shook his head. "I have no idea, but he's

102

around sometimes, especially after dark. Though, to be honest, he doesn't strike me as devout."

"Me neither. Can you follow him one day or two?"

"Sure. No problem."

"Thank you. Please leave word for me at Madame Claudette's if you spot anything of interest." Jacques looked over his shoulder, to ensure no one was shadowing him, but there was no sign of Guibourg's associate.

"I'll do that, Jacques." Guillaume circled him, then hobbled along towards the church.

"Good luck with the mourners!"

A wave showed him the boy had heard. Soon after, he was gone.

Guillaume – like many children – faked his injuries. But the lad was already learning skills that might come in handy once he was a few years older.

Pleased, he strode on towards Claudette's. He had to reassure himself young Fleur fared better before he would return to the workshop. Several orders lay half-fulfilled on the workbench, and it would take him well into the night to complete them.

Chapter Eleven

Early July, 1676
Châtelet, Paris

"We have her!" La Reynie's fist thumped his paper-covered desk, and a broad grin spread across his face. "She is now locked up in the Conciergerie."

"Her? Who?" Jacques was puzzled for a moment,

"Desgrez finally caught her in the Low Countries." La Reynie's eyes glinted.

"Ah, you mean the Marquise de Brinvilliers? The poisoner?"

The Lieutenant General nodded. "Desgrez arrived with her this morning and deposited her in a cell in the Conciergerie. The trial will be held in the coming days."

"Are you certain you'll want to hear all she might tell?" Jacques cocked his head. Would she reveal her sources? He had his doubts.

He had his thoughts confirmed when La Reynie calmed, leaning over the desk. "So far, she denies everything, Desgrez said. Of course, her fleeing to England had nothing to do with us wanting to question her." His tone was dry, but the corner of his mouth twitched. "And he has quite a tale to tell. He tricked her into revealing herself in the convent where she was hiding."

"Did he?" Jacques grinned. Desgrez was one to bend the rules when needed – as he did. "I'm impressed. She led him on a merry dance, that woman."

La Reynie sat behind his desk and leaned forward. "She tried to outwit him several times, but ultimately, they all make mistakes. Her hope of forgiveness was her downfall. How naïve of one who so meticulously planned to murder not only her father, but her two brothers, with no one suspecting her." He smiled, clearly pleased with himself.

"What will happen to her now?"

"The trial will prove her guilt. Fortunately, thanks to her late lover's sense of mistrust, we have the written admission of all their deeds in great detail. The letters Sainte-Croix left behind are damning. Yet, despite all that, she gives nothing away. But we have means…"

Torture.

Jacques nodded. It was the last attempt at gaining answers. Over the years, he'd sometimes witnessed torture by water or by the rack, though he preferred not to. The pain broke people's spirit, and often it mattered little if the defendant was guilty or not. Even innocent men and women would admit to anything when their bones broke or their stomach extended to an unnatural size.

"The threat of such ways might make her confess."

"You don't know La Brinvilliers, Jacques." La Reynie slowly shook his head. "The woman is cold, unfeeling. She will not admit to anything until we break her." He sighed. "You mark my words."

"She will be executed after her trial?"

"Without a shadow of a doubt. As a member of the gentry, she will likely die by the sword, not by axe or even burnt alive. Witch that she is, burning is what she deserves for all the pain her poor relatives faced." La Reynie nodded. It was a triumph for the Lieutenant General to have caught the marquise – finally. "And that execution is why I called you in today."

"Yes?"

"I want you to observe the crowds. Find people who look concerned – scared, even."

"I shall. Will other men from the police attend?"

"Of course. Our men will be in different places between the Conciergerie and Place de Grève. Desgrez and I will watch her too, from a discreet distance. I wouldn't want to be seen gloating."

"Not at all, no." Jacques paused. "Any others?" He had to

find out.

Would Guibourg's helper be there? Guillaume had followed him on the day Guibourg caught Jacques, but lost him. Days later, Jaques had a result: the attacker's address. According to the boy, the rogue went to the Châtelet almost every day, but surprisingly, his paths had not crossed Jacques' again.

La Reynie was looking at him. He shook himself out of his reverie.

"Why do you ask? My men are all over Paris." The Lieutenant General stroked his chin absent-mindedly.

"They are, sir." How best to approach it without giving too much away?

"Spit it out, Jacques. Something worries you. Tell me!"

Jacques sighed and met La Reynie's gaze. "There may be a traitor in the police; a man who secretly works with the darker elements of Saint Denis."

"Elements like…?"

"Abbé Guibourg." Jacques lowered his voice. He glanced over his shoulder, but the door was firmly shut.

La Reynie understood and leaned forward. "Who it is?"

"I can give you a rough description and tell you where he lives." He wrote down the street and added the man's features as he remembered them. "He was with Guibourg when the priest threw me out. Guibourg addressed me by my name."

"Hmm. A fortnight ago?"

Jacques nodded.

La Reynie tapped on the paper, then pursed his hands, almost as if in prayer. "I have a suspicion, but will need to verify the address first."

"Thank you. He might expect us."

"I understand. I shall send one of my most trusted men – who looks nothing like the description you gave – to follow him for a few days." The Lieutenant General cocked his head. "What took you so long to tell me?"

"I wanted to find out who he was before telling you. I'm certain I've come across him before, but so far my memory has deserted me. One of my sources has been shadowing him."

"I hope your…source…is careful. That henchman doesn't sound like he has any problem getting rid of people. Is that how Guibourg might have found out your name?"

Jacques nodded. "It's the only conclusion I've arrived at. The abbé's associate must have seen me come in here."

"That's not good. You could end up floating in the Seine, face-down." La Reynie looked grim.

The thought had also occurred to Jacques. Since the encounter at Saint Marcel, he'd kept away from narrow or deserted lanes at night and secured the door to his lodgings with an additional lock to ensure he noticed any potential intruders.

"We will identify him. Leave it with me, Jacques."

"Thank you, sir." He rose but stopped when La Reynie lifted a hand.

"How fares our abbé these days? No new sightings with strange bundles?"

Jacques shook his head. "No. I've not been back at the church, but there has not been anything unusual during his Sunday visits to the Carmelites. I think Fleur's escape – and my presence in Saint Marcel – have halted their actions, though I'm sure, given time, they'll continue. I shall focus my observations around Guibourg, rather than the convent."

"Should we arrest him?"

"Not yet. Let's wait until they feel safe enough to get back to their terrible acts, then we can pounce."

"I agree," La Reynie said. "And the young woman you saved, Fleur…?"

"Fleur de La Fontaine? Her healing continues, but she is still mourning the loss of her son. Guibourg spirited the infant away, and I found no trace of him. We fear he is dead." Guilt still racked him, but he kept his expression neutral. It would not do well, showing how much the boy's fate affected him.

"It's incredibly sad for her, although I doubt her mother would have allowed her to keep the child. Given time, the girl might get over it."

Jacques was not so certain, but he decided not to voice his doubts. "I'm on my way to Madame Claudette's now to learn how Fleur fares. I'll be in contact once I have news about Guibourg."

"Good. In the meantime, if you want to join the interrogations of La Brinvilliers, ask Desgrez."

"I'm not sure it's a good thing for me to be there. I prefer to hear about the revelations from a distance." Jacques suppressed a shudder. Unlike some men, he saw no pleasure in the torture of women. It baffled him how admission of culpability gained through violence was so widely accepted. But he would not voice his doubts to anyone.

La Reynie nodded. "So be it. Until next time."

Jacques left the Châtelet by the back door to avoid being seen. Outside, it was already dark. The wind whipped at his coat as he walked through the passageway that connected the yard of the Châtelet to rue Saint Denis. The autumn storms had arrived several days previously, with strong gusts and heavy rain. Jacques grunted, holding on to his hat as he strode towards the river, the wind howling in his ears.

Something made the hairs on the back of his neck rise.

Reaching for his sword, he swung around, but behind him, the road was deserted. Was his mind playing tricks on him? Jacques sighed and turned back when something hard hit his head, and he collapsed, half-conscious. Someone knelt on his back, pinning him down, and pressed his face into the muddy cobbles. He tried to wriggle free, but the attacker was putting all his weight onto him.

"Stick to your leathers, Montagnac, and stop poking your nose into affairs not of your own!" The voice was hoarse; not clear enough for Jacques to recognise it.

Could it be the man he suspected to be hand in glove with Guibourg? Had he watched him arrive at the Châtelet tonight? Again, Jacques twisted, but the grip was too strong. A heavy-set man. It was likely.

With his mouth pressed into the mud, he was unable to respond.

"Don't make us harm you! After all, it would be a pity if something happened to Claudette or her girls, wouldn't it?"

Jacques froze. Whoever the man was, he knew too much about him.

"Ah, you understand now. If not for your own sake, but for theirs – stay away from us! Am I making myself clear?"

"Humph…"

"Good. Now go home!"

Something heavy hit Jacques' head.

**

Fleur sat in Madame Claudette's private sitting room, a gown spread out across the table in front of her. She was mending a sleeve of a dress belonging to Annette. A client had been too vigorous in his fumbling and almost ripped it off. Fleur focused on the stitches in the dim light of a gas lamp.

She'd been here for over two weeks and had looked for a way to thank Claudette for the care that had been so freely given. Without it, Fleur would have bled to death in the aftermath of the birth. Any initial trepidation had vanished when the girls told her about how Claudette had helped many young women in distress. But not all ended up employed in the brothel.

Several had found posts in households across Paris and beyond.

Claudette had offered Fleur the chance to work in the business for her keep, but she'd politely declined. After the way Philippe had let her down, and the danger she'd faced after she'd given birth, Fleur did not want to be near any man ever again. Claudette had smiled, accepting her decision. Fleur had suggested she helped with household chores, and they'd quickly discovered that she had a talent for sewing. Claudette had not mentioned any other form of payment again, but Fleur had to find new lodgings soon.

Ninou had told Fleur that Claudette had faced a similar situation to hers. Thrown into the streets, with no protection,

Claudette's had been a fight for survival and respect.

Today, Claudette's establishment had gained a reputation for fairness to the girls who worked for her, and the safety she provided for them, with the help of her assistant, Pierre. The former soldier, his kind nature hidden in a broad, powerful body, ensured there was no trouble. Fleur called him The Bear. She smiled.

Pierre had dragged the man who had mishandled Annette – whose dress Fleur was mending – from the building.

A twinge in her belly made Fleur straighten up, and she secured the needle in the fabric. Stretching carefully, she took a deep breath. The pain was subsiding slowly, but the occasional pang brought back the painful memories.

Truth be told, her son was never far from her mind, but despite Jacques' best attempts at tracing him, they were no further forward.

Deep inside, though, Fleur accepted that the boy was dead, and her heart would always remain broken. Anger coursed through her body, something that happened more and more often, yet she would never speak to anyone about it.

Philippe had to pay. If only there was a way of hurting him…

I will avenge you, my sweet boy.

At a commotion from outside the room, she turned towards the door which burst open, revealing Claudette followed by Pierre The Bear carrying Jacques towards the settee in the corner. Fleur rose and threw needles and threads into the basket, quickly folded the gown and placed it on top. She stared at Jacques. Her heart pounded at the sight of his pale, dirt-streaked face. On his temple, blood mingled with mud.

"What happened?"

"We don't know," Claudette said, closing the door behind her. "He was dragging himself along the lane near the Châtelet when Annette saw him and alerted us. Quick, fetch a bowl of water and some clean cloths from the kitchen."

Blinking back tears that threatened to flow, Fleur rushed from the room to collect the items.

When she returned, they had already removed Jacques' coat, shirt and boots, and laid him flat on the bed. He was mumbling incoherently.

"Here," she indicated for Claudette to take the linens she'd tucked under her arm. The bowl she placed at the woman's feet. Claudette sat on the edge, gently wiping the dirt from Jacques' face and hair. Soon, the water in the bowl had turned a reddish brown, and Fleur went back and forth twice more before the older woman was content that she'd removed all the filth.

Jacques' eyelids were fluttering, but he was finally calmer.

"Thank you, Pierre. I think he'll stay put now," Claudette said, and The Bear nodded and left for the front room, where he'd keep an eye on the comings and goings.

"Have a look here," Claudette waved Fleur closer, pointing to a deep gash still oozing blood on the side of Jacques' head. "We need to bind this before it turns. If you go to that cupboard over there, you'll find a bundle of linen strips. Pick a long one and the bottle of alcohol beside it."

Fleur opened the cupboard door and stared at the contents. On the lower shelf sat a pile of linens, all neatly folded, but above them stood rows of flasks, containing liquids of various colours, but not all labelled. She wondered briefly what Claudette needed all these for, but shrugged off her suspicions and picked a strip of fabric and a clear bottle. She held it up. "Do you mean this one?"

"Yes, bring it over."

Fleur closed the cupboard doors and went back to the bed. Jacques' eyes were now closed.

"Is he...?"

"He's breathing, Fleur, so he'll be well again soon." She held out a small square of linen. "Pour some liquid on this, please. Carefully!"

Fleur removed the cork stopper and tipped it lightly onto the cloth in Claudette's hand.

"Thank you." Claudette dabbed Jacques' wound with it, and he hissed.

His eyes flew open, and he tried to remove her hand.

"What are you doing?"

"Hold his arm down, Fleur!" To Jacques, she said, her voice soothing, "Try to rest. This will help you heal."

Fleur sat on the edge of the bed, firmly taking Jacques' wrists. He writhed as Claudette dabbed the wound again – and passed out.

"You can let go of him. He won't feel the pain now," said Claudette. She discarded the dirty cloth, took a clean strip and placed it on the wound. "Please hold this."

Fleur crouched at the top end of the settee and pressed the cloth into the wound as Claudette wound the long stretch of linen around his head. Fleur held his head up, so the older woman was able to complete her task. Moments later, Claudette tucked the end into the tight bandage and rose. "That's all we can do for him."

Fleur regarded his face, the calm expression belying the nasty wound they'd treated. "I wonder what happened."

"Someone attacked him, that much is obvious."

"Was he alone?"

Claudette nodded. "Yes, I suppose. It appears someone in the *quartier* discovered he's working for La Reynie."

"Hmm, could Abbé Guibourg be behind this?" Fleur lit another gas lamp and put it on a small table beside the bed. Jacques' breathing was deep, his chest rising and falling steadily.

Claudette put a cover over him. "Who else? He'd been watching that priest for weeks. All of us need to be more careful now." Her expression was serious as their eyes met. "Stay with him, please. I must look after our customers."

"Of course. I'll clear away the discarded clothes, then I'll sit with him."

Claudette smiled. "Thank you. If you need help, call me."

"I should be fine. I'll bring over The Bear's shirt, so I can sew the loose button back on. I can easily do that over here, rather than be at the table."

"You don't have to, Fleur. There's time tomorrow for this."

"I know, but I'd like to keep busy. Don't worry, I won't let

Jacques out of my sight."

Claudette walked to the door. With her hand on the handle, she turned. "Why do you call Pierre, The Bear?"

Heat shot into Fleur's cheeks. She'd revealed her secret name for their protector. "Because he's huge, broad, kind, but ferocious in the defence of us girls."

"Ah," Claudette said, smiling. "I'm sure The Bear would be delighted to know how highly you regard him."

Fleur gasped. "Oh, please don't tell him! I'd rather it stayed between you and me."

"Fret not, Fleur. It will. Until later." Claudette entered the public sitting room and closed the door behind her, shutting out the noise of talking and laughing men and women.

In the calm of the small chamber, Fleur picked up the shirt, and a needle and thread. She placed a chair beside the bed and settled on it, crossing one leg over the other.

Jacques stirred for a moment, but settled again. Fleur held her breath until she was certain he was asleep again. She took advantage and studied the man who'd saved her from Mother's clutches.

His feet were hanging over the edge of the narrow bed, and it was barely wide enough to hold his broad frame. Her gaze wandered over his closed eyes, down the straight nose to the wide mouth. He was handsome, she had to admit.

Handsome and kind.

She jerked away from the thought and focused on The Bear's shirt. Never again would she trust a man like she'd trusted Philippe. Not even one who'd come to her rescue. She would remain alone for the rest of her life, and that was just as well. With Claudette's help, she would find an honest occupation and be independent.

She would move on, perhaps even leave Paris, and Jacques would become a memory.

With vigour, she stuck the needle into the fabric and began to reattach the button.

Never again!

Chapter Twelve

The wailing infant lay naked on a large stone slab, tiny fists punching the air. But no mother came to soothe her, no wet-nurse to feed her. The surface around the babe was stained dark red. On looking closer, Jacques realised it was dried blood.

A man wearing a black gown with a hood that hid his face pressed a knife into Jacques' hand and led him to stand beside the stone. Realisation hit Jacques – it was an altar.

The babe looked up with wide blue eyes, her cheeks puffed from crying. Tiny fingers stretched towards him. A small creature looking for comfort.

The cloaked man gripped Jacques' wrist and forced it down so the tip of the knife pointed at the infant's heart. Jacques closed his eyes, but the blue gaze, full of trust, haunted him.

Then the man pushed down the hand that held the knife, and it plunged through soft bone and sinew. Blood spurted from the wound, droplets covering Jacques' arms and face.

The wailing stopped, and the light faded from the blue eyes…

"No! No, I won't—"

"Jacques! Jacques, wake!" The voice was soft, feminine, calming. Someone dabbed his forehead with a damp cloth.

He pushed it away. "I don't want to do it. No!"

"You're dreaming, Jacques. Nothing has happened." The voice grew firmer. "Open your eyes, and you'll see."

"You're safe, Jacques," intoned a second female voice. "You're with friends."

Light banished the darkness as he blinked. "What? Where am I?" He moved, and a sharp pain shot through him.

"What's going on?"

"It's nothing serious, but you must wake."

Claudette? What was he doing in her house? With an effort, he opened his eyes and stared at Claudette and Fleur hovering over him.

Jacques tried to rise, but Fleur gently pushed him down. Exhausted as he felt, he did not mind.

"Ah, you're coming back to us." Fleur smiled. "You had a nightmare, from the sound of it. You screamed."

The memory returned fleetingly, and he shuddered. Had he dreamt of the fate of Fleur's son? It would upset her too much if he mentioned it, so he'd keep the details to himself.

"I...I can't remember," he said instead. His gaze met Claudette's, and she nodded. Years of close friendship had made them understand each other without words.

"Never mind your dream, I'm glad you've returned to us. Do you know what happened to you?"

He frowned, trying to think back. Where had he been before the darkness had swallowed him?

Guibourg. La Reynie. The Châtelet.

The passageway.

He sat up too fast for them to stop him. "I was attacked." The searing pain shooting into his head made him grind his teeth together. He propped himself up on one elbow and touched his temple. A bandage covered what felt like a large bump.

"Yes, you were," Claudette said grimly. "Guibourg must have become concerned."

Fleur went to rinse the damp cloth in a bowl on the table, then sat on the edge of the bed again. He was about to protest when she raised the cloth to his forehead, but she silenced him with a sharp glance. "You had a fever, which appears to have broken. But we need to make certain you continue to get better. Now, please lie back again, so I can take care of you." Her tone reminded him of his mother, admonishing him when he was a child. He grinned.

"Yes, *maman*!" He did as he was bid, and she dabbed his face.

She tutted and looked at him from beneath long eyelashes. He'd already regarded her as a beguiling creature, sweet and caring, but he realised that she had a determined side. It pleased Jacques that she worried about his health, though he kept any such thoughts to himself. Her family was above his in standing. He would help her find her way, then their paths must diverge.

Claudette watched them both, a smile on her lips. He'd seen it often whenever she tried to find him a wife who was suitable. Did she really think he was a match for Fleur? He would speak to Claudette in private to rid her of the idea.

"I didn't see who hit me, but it was definitely a man, about my height." Try as he might, he could not see beyond the swift moment when he'd turned around. "He kneeled on my back as I lay face-down on the ground. That's all I remember."

"Annette told me as much. She was the first who saw you stagger into our street, covered in blood and dirt."

"Did your acquaintance by chance discover who it was?"

"No. Someone saw a broad figure emerge from the passageway moments before you came out. A tall bearded man wearing black breeches and a long black coat. They didn't pay any attention, though. That's why we don't have a better description."

Jacques cast his mind back at the men he'd seen in La Reynie's service. The description sounded familiar, but he still could not think of a name. He looked at Claudette. "Do you think your friend—"

"Acquaintance."

"Your acquaintance could watch the entrance to the Châtelet, to see if they could spot that man again? I don't think I'd have any results if I were lurking around there."

Claudette laughed. "No, you wouldn't. He would not dare show his face as long as he knew you're there. Yes, I shall ask her to look out for that rogue."

"Her?" Somehow, Jacques had assumed Claudette's associate was a man.

She grinned. "Why, yes. You men are so gullible, thinking

women can't possibly be excellent spies."

Fleur giggled, sharing a conspiratorial glance with Claudette.

Embarrassed, he picked an imaginary fleck of dust from the pristine cover to distract himself. Then he stared at his clean hands as a thought occurred to him. He touched his hair above the wound. It felt fresh. Staring from one woman to the other, the heat in his cheeks grew deeper. "Did you wash me?"

Claudette raised an eyebrow. "Of course. Did you think I'd allow you to stay in my sitting room stinking of horse dung?"

***

"What are you planning to do?" Jacques looked at her as he ripped a chunk of bread off and placed a cut piece of cheese on it.

Fleur watched him take a big bite. It was good to see he'd recovered his appetite. He'd soon regain the few pounds lost over the last three days. To her relief, the gash on his head also healed well. Claudette's cupboard of potions and ointments held salves that aided the process. The array had amazed Fleur, though she only handled those items she needed.

"I'm going to write to my uncle. I've spoken with Claudette who thinks it's a good idea. He has contacts to the noblest families, so I hope that I'll find service with one of them."

"Service? But you shouldn't…"

She held up a hand. "I know, but what choice do I have? I don't want to join Ninou, Annette, and the others. It's not for me." She glanced at the hands in her lap, interlinking her fingers until his hand covered hers.

"I didn't expect you to choose that path, Fleur. But I'd rather see you lead the life you deserve. You should be at court."

She burst out laughing, not caring that ladies of her station did not do that. "No, Jacques. You saw what that place did to me. Never again do I wish to be at the whim of a courtier – or any man."

He flinched, withdrawing his hand, but there was nothing else she could say. She had to guard her heart, and her life, carefully, even against kind friends like Jacques. It was impossible to give him more than she was prepared to give.

"But if you go into service, you might end up there anyway, be that as an *accompagnante*, or a maid if I have to."

The thought had occurred to her as well. "I'd hoped that I'd do better under protection."

He nodded. "That may be the case, but much depends on the family. Who is your uncle?"

"Have you heard of Marin de La Fontaine?"

"The writer?" He stared at her.

"Yes." She smiled, pleased he knew Uncle Marin. "He is father's cousin, and Father always spoke highly of him."

"When did you last see your uncle?"

"Hmm, when I was about eight, I think. I listened as he and Father discussed some poem or other. I didn't understand any of it, but I found it fascinating. Mother hated it." She grinned. "Of course, there is a risk that Mother has told him of my escape, but I'm sure he would never reveal my location to her. They did not like each other."

A frown appeared on his forehead, and by now she knew that something troubled him. "You do not think Uncle Marin would help me?"

"Oh, he might. But do you know where he lives?"

She shook her head. "Not yet. One of Claudette's friends is making enquiries. Someone mentioned he has been attending the literary salon of a rich patroness. We're going to get in touch with her."

Jacques did not seem convinced. He finished chewing his last bite, regarding her. Then he leaned back. "And what if he doesn't remember you?"

Fleur blinked. "You mean if he doesn't want to help me?" She shrugged. "I don't know. I suppose I will offer my skills as a seamstress. Claudette has been very content so far."

"I can see you do very well, but that's no life for you. You belong in salons, at recitals and plays, not sitting in dimly lit rooms mending shirts."

"Well, I have not much of a choice, do I?" She stood and paced the room, aware of him watching her. "I cannot risk my mother finding me. If she does, she'll take me to wed that monster. I'd rather die."

He took a sharp breath. "It won't have to come to that, Fleur. We'll make sure you're safe."

She gave him a sad smile, her heart heavy. "You're kind, Jacques; you, Claudette, and everyone here. I can never express just how grateful I am to you all. But I can't rely on your kindness forever. I must make my own way."

"It's good to see you looking forward, not back."

Fleur knew what he meant. "I'll never forget my time at the convent, nor the horrors they inflicted on me and my babe, God bless his soul." She crossed herself. "And one day I will find out what happened to him, and the culprits will pay for it." She clenched her fist so hard, her nails dug into her skin. Tears pricked behind her eyes, and Jacques knelt beside her, took her hands in his, stroking them softly.

"I'm having nightmares about abducted infants, scenes of the cruellest kind. Details I do not wish to share with you."

She let the tears roll freely. "I have long suspected what the abbé is doing. The way he carried the bundle – my boy – away, he cared not if he lived or died." Her voice broke, and she rested her head against Jacques' shoulder, sobbing, letting all the pain wash from her.

His arms encircled her gently, and his strength gave her hope, courage even. After a while, the tears dried up, and she pulled back, wiping the moisture from her face. He stayed close but gave her enough space to compose herself.

"Better?" He smiled.

Fleur nodded. "Yes, thank you. I don't know what I'd do without you…and Claudette."

He sat back in the chair he'd vacated. "That's what we're there for, to help girls like you get your lives back in order."

'Girls like you.' Fallen girls.

She took a deep breath. "Until I hear from Claudette's

acquaintance, I should get on with my work. And you should be out there, spying on people!" Her voice sounded too bright in her ears. Fleur was certain he'd noticed, but she had to get a grip on herself.

The look he sent her proved her right. "We'll find out what happened to your son, Fleur. I swear."

"Don't make promises you might not keep, Jacques."

His face was solemn, his gaze intense. "I have every intention to uncover the truth, however long it may take me."

They fell silent for a moment, and Fleur was unsure how to continue.

'Girls like you.'

She could not trust any man ever again. Not even Jacques.

He sighed. "After your escape, I've never seen Abbé Guibourg carry another bundle from the convent. He only goes there on Sunday mornings now, for mass. Nor have I seen any more ladies enter."

"They are covering their tracks," she said. "And with the attack on you, they're hoping that you'll investigate elsewhere."

"I might. Just for a few days."

"Oh, doing what?"

"The trial of the Marquise de Brinvilliers begins tomorrow. I want to attend the court, to see if any of our suspects make an appearance."

"The poisoner? Has she confessed?" Fleur had read about the woman who'd dispatched her father and brothers through slowly poisoning them – and who'd got away with it for years. Part of her wished she had the marquise's courage. What would she give to exact her revenge!

Disturbed by her own thoughts, she brushed them away.

"Not yet, but La Reynie hinted at more convincing methods to make her talk." His mouth formed a thin line, and Fleur blinked.

"Torture?"

He nodded. "Yes, by water."

Fleur could not imagine how it would feel to have pitcher after pitcher of water poured into you. "It sounds painful."

"It is. The stomach extends so much that your entire body feels in agony."

She shuddered. "I hope she confesses before it comes to that."

"I'm not so sure." He picked a small chunk of cheese he'd cut earlier off the board. "She is a stubborn lady, not giving any answers to the magistrate's questions. He was quite put out, I heard this morning."

"Can I come with you?" A sudden surge of curiosity made her want to see the woman. "I promise I won't make a nuisance of myself."

Jacques grinned. "You, a nuisance? Well, if you insist…"

"You…!" She slapped his wrist in play, laughing. "I'm talking about watching the trial."

"Oh, and there was me thinking you insisted on being a nuisance." The glint in his brown eyes held warmth, and something else she could not fathom.

I must not think further of it.

"Of course you can come with me. I'll pick you up tomorrow morning. The court gathers at eight of the clock."

Fleur clapped her hand in excitement. It would be her first outing beyond this street. Then a thought struck her. "Will I need to conceal my face?"

He shook his head. "No, I don't think so. Your mother would hardly grace the trial of a wanted woman. Though a cap to cover your hair might be useful."

"Yes, a good idea. I shall ask Claudette if I may borrow her black gown and shawl. That way, nobody would suspect I'm a sinner." She was only half-jesting.

"You'll never be a sinner to me, Fleur." Jacques stood abruptly, then put on his coat. He busied himself with the buttons, and she watched him, puzzled. Then he took his hat. "Thank you for sharing your food with me. I shall collect you in the morning. Be bright and early."

Fleur rose and placed a hand on his wrist. "Thank you. I shall."

As the door fell shut behind him, her mind was whirling. Absent-mindedly, she gathered up the plates and knives, and wrapped up the cheese and the half-eaten loaf of bread.

She must not get attached to Jacques. As much as he did to help her, he was still a man.

Like Philippe de Mortain. Like the old deviant Mother wanted her to wed. Like all men!

Grinding her teeth, Fleur suppressed the anger that always surged through her at the memory of Philippe. The sooner she knew where Uncle Marin's lodgings were, the sooner she'd be gone from here – and from Jacques.

Chapter Thirteen

July 16th, 1676
Paris

Tomorrow, the Marquise de Brinvilliers would die by beheading, her remains burnt, and the ashes thrown into the Seine. Paris expected a riveting spectacle of the kind people had not seen in a long time.

As the crowds on the viewing platform jostled for a final peek at the doomed woman, Fleur was glad for the firm clasp of Jacques' hand in hers. When he'd mentioned that he was going to attend the hearing, she'd decided to join him. Claudette had shuddered and declined, mumbling something about 'justice being served'.

But now Fleur was here, watching the once proud marquise slumped on her stool, her heart cried out to the woman. Her mind drifted away from the judge's monotonous voice.

The marquise, broken under the water torture, was a shadow of her former self. Nodding quietly, she sat bent forward, cradling her stomach. The fabric of her grimy chemise stretched tight over thin shoulders. Blonde hair stuffed beneath a frayed cap, her face gaunt, the poisoner merely stared ahead, unmoved by the pronouncement – or by the ensuing chaos.

As if she has accepted her fate...

At that moment, the condemned woman looked up, and her gaze met Fleur's. A faint smile appeared on the marquise's lips, and a strong sense of understanding surged through Fleur. Her mouth went dry.

"Don't feel sorry for La Brinvilliers." Jacques's voice was close to her ear, so she could hear him over the clamour. "She is a pitiless murderer."

Had he read her mind?

Fleur blinked back a stray tear. "Nobody deserves to be treated like that."

"Some do." Her gaze met his, and she stood still.

Then she understood. If it were Sister Benedicte in place of the condemned woman, Fleur would have felt no shred of sympathy. The nun had the blood of children on her hands, just like La Brinvilliers was guilty of murdering her father and brothers. The lady had shown no remorse.

She nodded. "I see. You're right, of course."

To cries from the crowd, the prisoner was half-carried, half-dragged through the door that led to the cells. Fleur noticed that it was mostly the men who shouted abuse. In stark contrast, many women crossed themselves, their mouths forming silent prayers. She pointed it out to Jacques. "Why do they pray?"

"Apparently, La Brinvilliers has discovered her faith in recent weeks." He rolled his eyes. "Rumours have spread that she's a saint."

"A saint?"

He grinned. "She's a convicted criminal, but some people don't let that stop them from twisting the truth. Something about redemption, and all that."

Fleur regarded him. "But it could be true."

Jacques leaned closer as people brushed past them to leave. "She has shown no regret, has she? So how can her soul be redeemed?"

"Hmm." Fleur looked away, not wanting him to read her mind. The idea appealed to her. Even a condemned murderer had the right to reflect on their sins. It did not mean they'd have to reveal their contemplations to the public, who'd likely ridicule them anyway.

To her relief, the courtroom soon held but a few men and women, no doubt lingering to savour the morbid atmosphere.

"Let's go." Jacques pulled her gently towards the door.

"What happens next?"

"Abbé Pirot will stay with her and take her confession.

Then, tomorrow morning, they will take her to Place de Grève for her execution, like the judge said." His querying glance reminded her she'd stopped listening to the magistrate's words.

"Ah." Fleur followed him down the stairs. After the bustle of the courtroom, she wanted to be alone now. There was much to think about. Much to prepare. But it was important that Jacques did not suspect her thoughts.

Outside, the heat hit her like a wall, and she fumbled for her fan.

"Shall I take you home?"

"Yes, please. I'd like to rest awhile."

"The trial was tough, I agree. We've not had one like this in a long time. Come." He linked her arm in his.

They fell silent as he guided her through the packed streets. He was right. But to Fleur, the haughtiness of the judge matched that of the marquise, at least before they had put her under torture.

Finally, they arrived outside Claudette's, and Jacques stopped by the closed door.

"Would you like me to collect you in the morning? We could head to the Conciergerie, or to Notre Dame where she's expected to repent in public, or straight to Place de Grève. That is – if you want to see the execution at all. It makes for a grim spectacle."

She looked away. More and more, an invisible bond grew between her and the condemned woman. La Brinvilliers' eyes haunted her. But she must reveal nothing to Jacques.

"I'd like to go to Place de Grève. It will prepare me for the day I shall see the abductors of my son punished, whenever that may be."

"That makes sense. The cart carrying her will trundle through the streets, surrounded by an awful lot of angry people. We will get to Place de Grève in plenty of time to find a quiet spot."

"Good. Now please excuse me, Jacques. I need to lie down. Until tomorrow."

She sent him a shy smile, then rushed inside and straight

up the stairs to her chamber. Leaning against the door, she let out a long sigh.

Never must she share her feelings with anyone; least of all, a man.

Fleur knelt by the bed and prayed for the soul of La Brinvilliers.

July 17th, 1676
Place de Grève, Paris

Fleur stood inside a doorway, watching men and women rush past. A throng of people had gathered around the scaffold, another near the pyre. No one wanted to miss a moment of the execution of the year. The crowd was like an animal ready to pounce on its prey. She felt their energy, raw and angry. Then she spotted several women standing still, heads bowed in prayer. Some were on their knees, hands reaching towards Heaven. It surprised Fleur that they were not knocked over.

She had never watched an execution. The thought thrilled and scared her alike. Last night, she'd finally found peace after hours spent praying. When Claudette had knocked on her door asking if she wanted anything to eat, she'd sent her away. Today, Fleur was ready to take the marquise's hand and help her towards eternal life – if only inside her head.

As promised, Jacques had found a calmer spot where they sheltered from the worst of the pushing masses. Standing beside her, he craned his head as if looking for someone. Who did he expect? Guibourg? Or associates of La Brinvilliers?

She followed his speculative gaze to a group of women not far from them. One was clearly their leader. Clad in black, a veil obscuring her features, she held herself erect as much as her imposing figure allowed. She exuded authority. Her companions were of working background, their gowns and caps simple, even stained. Were they servants? But something in their exchange made Fleur doubt it. Deep in conversation, they stood cluttered around her, not behind her like maids. When one wailed, the woman in black abruptly gestured to her to keep her voice down.

Were they friends of the Marquise de Brinvilliers?

Fleur startled when Jacques raised his hand to wave at someone. A stocky man approached them. A peacock feature adorned his hat, perched on a wig of long, dark curls. The hawk-like features and sharp eyes sent shivers down her spine. His coat, surprisingly thick for the warm summer day, was of the highest quality. Of an upright stature, with his head held high, he emitted an undeniable sense of authority. A powerful man.

"Who is he?" Trepidation surged through her.

"The Lieutenant General. He was expecting us."

"Oh. From what you told me, I expected a giant. Though he still seems impressive."

Jacques grinned. "He is, in his own way."

La Reynie reached them. "Good morning, Jacques. Mademoiselle." He briefly inclined his head. His voice was firm and deep. "If you wish to be safe from the rabble, follow me." He pointed at a nearby building.

Jacques nodded. "Come, Fleur. This space is fine, but we might have a better place from where to watch everything."

Fleur frowned. "Is it unsafe to attend an execution?"

"Sometimes, violence can erupt, although I doubt it would do today. La Brinvilliers is not your usual murderer…"

"Ah," she said, silently agreeing with him when she remembered the praying women. She let him guide her towards the tall town house outside of which La Reynie awaited them.

"Mademoiselle de La Fontaine, it is a pleasure to meet you, despite the…unfortunate occasion." He gave a curt bow.

"Lieutenant General. I've heard much about your work across the city."

"The good and the bad, I presume." His mouth quivered.

Despite her earlier trepidation, Fleur liked him. La Reynie's reputation preceded him. He was known to be dogged in his investigations and ruthless in gaining confessions. "Indeed," she said, smiling.

"Where are we?" Jacques pointed at the building.

"The house belongs to an acquaintance of mine. We can see the whole square from the upper floor."

"Does your acquaintance not object to you bringing visitors here?" Fleur asked. Surely, it was polite to ask.

"Not at all, mademoiselle. The house is at our disposal, since the proprietor is currently in the Bastille on account of unpaid debts." La Reynie grinned.

Fleur's mouth dropped.

"We will have it all to ourselves," he announced and unlocked the front door.

Whilst she conversed with La Reynie, Jacques exchanged a few words with a man she did not recognise. His coat was worn, and he was unshaven. Before she stepped over the threshold, she noticed the man walk to the spot where they had stood but moments earlier.

Jacques followed her inside and turned a large key inside the lock. "Can't risk people taking advantage." He smirked.

"Who was that?" she asked.

"What? Who? Oh, outside? Desgrez. A colleague."

"Will he be spying on those women you were observing?"

Jacques looked at her for a long moment. "Yes. Come."

Fleur gazed in awe as she followed La Reynie and Jacques up the stairs to the first floor. Whoever the house belonged to must do well for themselves, as it put her own family's Paris home to shame.

Oil paintings and tapestries lined the high walls. When she crossed the threshold into a bright sitting room, a gasp escaped her. Large windows let the sunlight in, bathing the furniture in a golden glow. Two plush settees stood in the centre opposite each other. Small, square coffee tables sat either the side of each. She wanted to stroke the sumptuous, velvety cover, but folded her hands instead. The pale yellow of the fabric made the room shine even brighter. Wallpaper in light blue and green stripes lined the walls. A large ornate sideboard stood beside the settees, and a small desk at the far end. A small mirror hung above it, which struck Fleur as strange. When you sat at the desk, you would look at yourself all the time.

And you see everything – or everyone – behind you.

"One could say the owner is a little vain. He's a marquis, known for his high opinion of himself."

Fleur turned to see La Reynie scrutinising her. He'd read her thoughts well. "Ah, that explains much." Her earlier apprehension returned. Here was a man who easily wheedled information from people. She had to be on guard.

Jacques grinned, then opened a set of glass doors that led to a narrow balcony. "Here is your front row, mademoiselle." He gestured to her to step outside.

"Goodness!" She was not sure whether to be concerned or thrilled as she looked out over Place de Grève. A wooden pyre was erected in the corner opposite, but the scaffold was close to where she stood.

"The best view in Paris, mademoiselle," La Reynie said as he stood to her left. His voice held a hint of sarcasm.

Fleur had to agree. The best and the worst view alike was a more fitting description.

Jacques slid to the right of her. His hand briefly touched her waist. It comforted her. Then he leaned over the wrought-iron railing.

She followed his gaze across the masses of people gathered. "Why, there must be hundreds."

"At least four hundred, if you count all the children milling about."

"Children?" She frowned. "Why would anyone take children to an execution?"

A glance passed between Jacques and La Reynie. Eventually, the Lieutenant General spoke. "Many take their children as this is their only form of distraction. Others, to scare theirs into behaving, and to give them a sense of what happens if you choose the wrong path."

"And then there are the street urchins – the beggars and cutpurses." Jacques' tone held a hint of understanding.

"Thieves?" she asked.

"Yes, those too," La Reynie said. "But we'll catch them all, eventually."

Jacques' mouth twitched, and Fleur knew he disagreed with his superior. She quickly looked away into the square.

"There she comes!" Jacques pointed at a tumbril that entered the square.

The condemned woman frowned as the crowd grew more raucous. Where there had been sympathy, there was now disgust.

When the marquise stepped onto the scaffold, Fleur clasped the railing. A shiver ran down her spine when the priest intoned the *Salve Regina*. Soon, a chorus of mainly female voices joined in, quietly at first, then it grew louder.

Closing her eyes, Fleur recited the words. The nuns had taught her well. An eerie calm washed over her. Before her mind's eye, a light grew brighter until it turned into a burning inferno. She breathed deeply, relishing the heat.

With a sense of clarity, she realised what she had to do. *Vengeance is mine*.

"Amen," she finished with a whisper. A weight had dropped off her shoulders. Silence had fallen across the square. Fleur opened her eyes and stared at the scaffold.

Jacques touched her elbow. "You don't have to look."

"I want to." Fleur gritted her teeth. I must "I have to."

The sword came down swiftly, and the head of the Marquise de Brinvilliers dropped to the floor with a thud.

Fleur's hand went to her throat as the executioner lifted the head, showing it to the crowds. A roar rose from Place de Grève.

Swiftly, the body was placed on a stretcher, together with her head, and carried across to the pyre. Unable to reach the stake in the growing fire, they threw the remains onto the pile of wood.

Fleur's heart beat a steady drum in her ears. She swallowed back the nausea that threatened to overcome her. *I must watch.*

She repeated it over and over in her head as the flames lunged up towards the sky. *I must watch.*

In her mind's eye, Fleur imagined Sister Benedicte tied to the stake, her body writhing as the flames licked her skin. *I must watch.*

When her own face appeared in her vision, Fleur shook. *No, not me!*

A hand in the small of her back rattled her from her vision. "Fleur, Fleur? Are you well?"

"Y-yes." She sent him a dry smile.

Smoke mingled with the smell of burning flesh and drifted across the square

"We better go inside." La Reynie stepped inside.

Fleur's gaze drifted across Place de Grève. The memory of this day must remain etched in her mind.

Wait! She stared. Could it be?

"Mother!" she hissed.

Jacques leaned in close. "Your mother? Where?"

"Over there." She pointed at a tall whitewashed house near to where they were. A group of people, all dressed too colourful for such a sombre occasion, had gathered on a balcony.

There she was: Sophie, her arm linked with a dark-haired man young enough to be her son. She was laughing at something he said and placed a hand on his chest.

"What on earth is she doing?" Fleur muttered.

Jacques had seen her too. "Have you met the man she's with?"

Fleur shook her head. "I've never seen him before, but I recognise her friends, the Montmarchés."

"Ah. Best go inside before she spots us."

But it was too late. Their eyes met. The icy glint in Mother's glare was present as ever.

Sophie pointed a finger at her before she flew into a rage, her voice carrying even above the din of the crowd below. Already, her companions turned their way.

"Come, quick!" Jacques led Fleur inside. "We must leave before she can reach us."

"Who?" La Reynie asked as Jacques closed the balcony doors.

"My mother." Fleur looked from the Lieutenant General to Jacques. "I must return to court."

"To court? Why? She'll find you there."

Now it was clear what she had to do. "She won't, don't fret. But I need my uncle's help to return. Have you found out yet where he is?"

Jacques shook his head. "No, but I'm expecting word of his whereabouts any day."

"Who is your uncle?" La Reynie asked casually as they made their way down the stairs.

"Marin de La Fontaine, my late father's cousin."

"La Fontaine, the writer?"

She nodded.

La Reynie turned to her and grinned. "Why, everyone in literary circles knows he resides at the house of Madame de la Sablière, in rue Neuve-des-Petits-Champs."

"Truly? Oh, thank you." Fleur's heart beat so loud, she feared the men would hear it.

She ignored the dark look on Jacques' face. He would not understand.

Vengeance is mine…

"A black mass." Their eyes met, and she saw the shock in his. "Monsieur de Montagnac has been investigating the disappearance of newborn infants for over a year, but every time he discovers a new trail, a door shuts in his face. It sounds like there's a group of people involved, and they're keeping their secrets to themselves."

"Hmm, I have heard of such practices, but was uncertain if they were true or not."

"Oh, they are true, Uncle Marin. And that's why I need to return to court. I need to find out who's involved. The rumours are that several highborn ladies and lords are after black masses, as they believe the Devil will provide them with what they seek."

"But surely that's dangerous for you, Fleur." He stood and paced the room. "And what if you find out what you're looking for, what then?"

She straightened, blinking to dry her eyes. "I shall report them to Monsieur de La Reynie."

"You have met the Lieutenant General?" He sounded impressed.

"Yes. Jacques works for him."

"That is of some comfort. But even so," he looked at her evenly, "you might endanger your life."

"I have to take that risk, but first…I will need your help."

"What can I do?"

Fleur took a deep breath. "Do you know a lady who might require an *accompagnante*?"

"A companion? Let me think." He walked over to a cherrywood cabinet on which stood a tray with a carafe of dark red liquid and four small glasses. He filled two and handed her one. Then he sat on his chair again, cradling the glass in his hands. "It would have to be someone powerful enough to protect you, and you must be honest with her."

"But what if he or she – whoever they may be – is also involved in those practices?"

"It's the risk you have to take, Fleur. Perhaps hint at seeking revenge from that wastrel, Philippe, but omit mentioning your son."

"Yes, that would work."

"And you could only attend court disguised. Sophie might otherwise have someone abduct you."

The thought had not occurred to her. "Would she go that far?"

He nodded. "Just look how far she'd gone already – wanting to marry you off to an old pervert the same hour you gave birth! I never trusted her, and nor should you."

"What can I do, then?"

"Shall we ask Madame de la Sablière? She knows people at court better than I do."

"But does she need to know my story?"

Marin shook his head. "No. All we'll tell her is that you seek revenge and must stay safe from Sophie's grasp. Marguerite is curious, but she can keep a secret. Do you agree?"

"Yes, please."

Her uncle rang a bell and instructed the maid to ask the marquise to join them if she was free.

Minutes later, the lady entered, glancing from Marin to Fleur. "You wished to speak with me?"

Marin led her to the settee, and she sat down beside Fleur. "My niece needs our help, Marguerite. She requires to be in the household of a lady at court. She is seeking revenge of a young man who wronged her."

"Oh, I see." Madame frowned, looking Fleur up and down, taking in her plain clothes, then her gaze returned to Marin. "But we can't have the girl *work* in a household. That would not be suitable for a La Fontaine."

"I agree," Marin said. "It would be preferable if she were to become an *accompagnante*."

Fleur thought it best to stay silent as her uncle and madame exchanged glances.

"Yes, I suppose that could work." She turned sharp eyes on Fleur. "What do you do with your time, mademoiselle? Do you read? Can you discuss the sciences and philosophy?"

"I've had a limited education in a convent, madame, but now I'm away from my mother, I'll be happy to learn."

"As a child, young Fleur used to join me and her father as we discussed literature, but, alas, her mother had her raised by narrow-minded nuns. Sophie is a shallow female who never nurtured Fleur's intellect."

The marquise's eyes glinted. "So you would be happy to read as much as you can, perhaps over the next month, to build up basic knowledge of, say, recent literature – including your dear uncle's poems and articles – and scientific papers?"

Fleur's heart beat faster. Excited, she nodded. "Of course. I feel I've missed out on much over recent years, and as Mother kept me away from our library at home, I'd be delighted to catch up."

"Excellent. I have an idea, with your uncle's permission. If you agree, then I shall be willing to find you a lady who will take you to court with her, so you can seek your revenge." She clapped her hands. "I'm always partial to a touch of revenge. Too many men out there who take advantage of a young female – present company excepted, of course."

Marin inclined his head. "Thank you. I am honoured that you exclude me from that particular group."

"What would you like me do, madame?" Fleur asked. A shiver of anticipation ran down her spine.

"Move in with us here, Fleur."

"Truly?" Marin exclaimed. "That is very generous of you, Marguerite."

Fleur held her breath. "You are too kind, madame. But if I were to do as you suggest, I wish to earn my stay."

The marquise smiled. "Oh, in that case, please read as many books as you can. Join my soirées and take part in our discussions of the sciences, such as astronomy and the latest inventions. I hold weekly gatherings, and they would be the perfect occasion to introduce you to society. The next step follows on from there."

"You would be under Madame de la Sablière's protection, Fleur. Sophie could not touch you."

Madame nodded. "Indeed."

Fleur dared hardly breathe. Then she remembered Claudette – and Jacques. Could she really leave them behind so soon? Would they deem her ungrateful?

She was certain Claudette would be happy for her, but Jacques? The thought of not seeing him again made Fleur sad, but her plans for revenge came first. Perhaps her position would even help him with his investigations? She might live outside his *quartier*, but that did not mean they could not stay in contact. Or did it?

"Thank you so much, Madame la marquise. I'll gratefully accept."

The gates to Versailles had just opened…

***

Four days later

Jacques stood by the carriage that held all of Fleur's recent possessions: a small chest with threads and needles and a large bag that contained a few gowns and other types of clothing. It was sad to see a young woman having so few belongings, but given that she'd fled the convent with merely the soiled shift she wore, she'd done well for herself during her stay.

He watched as Claudette and Fleur hugged, both with tears in their eyes, and looked away. The driver of the carriage sent by Madame de la Sablière sat motionless, his eyes scanning the lane. Jacques smirked. He did not think the poor man had ever ventured into the less savoury *rues* of Saint Denis.

"Do tell us how you're faring, please." Claudette urged, and Fleur nodded. She extricated her hands from the older woman's grasp, then embraced Ninou and Annette, who'd also come out to bid Fleur goodbye.

"I'll never forget you, all of you," Fleur said as she took a step back. With the back of her hand, she wiped away her tears. "And I shall visit." She turned to him, and Jacques' heart sank.

She won't come back.

"Take care, little Fleur." He hated how his voice wobbled. Would he see her again, or would she soon forget about them as she pursued life where she belonged?

"Oh, Jacques!" She rushed towards him, then stopped short. "I will write to you, I promise."

Of course you will...

Out loud, he said, "I'm looking forward to hearing from you soon. Don't let your mother catch you." He could not hide his concerns for her, but it pleased him she looked happy. "And I will inform you if I find out more." He did not need to say what. She understood as she blinked back tears.

"Thank you for everything. I'll never be able to thank you enough."

"You already have." He let go of her hands and folded his behind his back. It would not at all be appropriate to embrace her, in broad daylight, and in front of the driver and various passers-by. Instead, he opened the carriage door, and she climbed inside. "Be safe!" It took all his willpower not to climb in beside her, but he had to let her go.

She doesn't belong here.

Closing the door firmly, he smiled at her through the window. "Don't forget us!" Then he nodded to the driver and stepped back as the man urged the two horses into a trot.

Claudette stood beside him and placed a hand on his shoulder. "She'll be fine, Jacques." To his questioning glance, she replied, "Fleur's a survivor."

"But she's exposed to dangers there, especially if she returns to court. If not her mother, then others who don't want her to poke her nose into their dark affairs."

Ninou and Annette joined them, and together they stared until the carriage turned a corner and disappeared from sight.

"You heard what she said, Jacques," Ninou said. "She'll keep us informed. That's what matters."

"And she won't forget you," Claudette added, a smile playing on her lips. "I know that for a fact."

"Don't be silly," Jacques shrugged her hand off. "She's above all of us in station, so there's no point in even thinking that way."

"Oh Jacques, don't be so hard on yourself. Let her find her way to court, then you can help her again. She'll still need you."

"To find out what happened to her babe, yes." His thoughts grew morose. Deep inside, he'd held hopes of Fleur allowing him to woo her, but her uncle's intervention had destroyed any such chance. "Nothing more."

Claudette sighed. "I think you need to take a walk, Jacques. Go to the park, or the river. And stop thinking about her and focus on your investigations."

He snorted. "I've hit a dead end, Claudette. You know that. The priest is lying low, and I can't find anyone who would inform on him."

"You will. I've no doubt," Ninou said. "And when you do, he'll face justice."

"Then Fleur will see right by you," Annette added.

He glared at all three. "It can take years to flush out all those involved. You know nothing."

Turning, he marched off towards the Seine. He needed space to think.

Silly women with their stupid ideas!

Late that evening, Jacques was getting ready to leave his shop, where he'd completed an order for an elaborate sword belt, and return to his lodgings when a knock on the door stopped him from extinguishing the last of candles by his workbench. The door to the street was locked, and the anteroom lay in darkness. Since the attack on him, he'd become wary, so he grabbed a hammer and walked towards the door, staying out of the light filtering from the back as much as possible.

"Who is it?"

"Me," came the abrupt reply. A voice demanding and haughty; one he'd always recognise. He unlocked the door and opened it to let La Reynie in.

"Good evening, sir. This is a surprise. Are you alone?" He glanced up and down the street, but all was still.

La Reynie walked towards his work room. "We must talk."

Jacques followed him inside, then closed the door, so

nobody could watch them from outside. He gestured for the Lieutenant General to take the only seat.

"No, thank you. This won't take long." La Reynie leaned against the workbench.

Jacques nodded. "You have news?"

"Yes. I believe I've identified the man who attacked you."

A sigh of relief escaped Jacques. "Who is he?" La Reynie's mouth formed a thin line, and Jacques became worried. "Can we not get to him?"

"I'm afraid we can't. You were right; it was one of our men…"

"Was?"

"He is dead; washed up with his skull caved in. His name was Boucher."

"Not someone I knew. They killed him?"

"Yes. I recognised him from your description, as I hinted during our conversation. His death confirms it."

"Was it Guibourg?" Jacques' mind whirled. Would the priest himself do the dirty deed, or had he handed it over to another henchman?

"Possibly, but we have no proof, Jacques."

"Can I see Boucher?"

"Of course. But you will have to come with me now. He'll be thrown into a shared grave tomorrow."

"I was ready to go home anyway, so let me fetch my coat and hat, and I'll be right there."

"It's him." Jacques regarded the dead man's face with mixed feelings. Part of him was glad Boucher was dead – he would never harm anyone again. But the man's death also frustrated him. How could he prove Guibourg's guilt with no witnesses? Looking over his shoulder, he checked whether anyone was within earshot, but only heard voices in the distance. Still, he kept his voice low. "Guibourg must have deemed him too great a risk."

"Yes, it would appear so. My theory is that the priest didn't know about Boucher's attack on you at the Châtelet, and he may have worried that you'd recognise the man, eventually. Boucher was part of a team that was checking on the brothels."

"The perfect place to abduct newborn children."

"Indeed."

"So we're back at the beginning, only now Guibourg and the nuns are aware of our interest and have stopped their... habits."

La Reynie nodded. "Walk with me, Jacques."

He followed him, keen to leave the stink of the room in the basement of the Hôtel-Dieu, and soon they stepped out from under its Gothic archway. Breathing in the fresh river air, he walked in silence beside La Reynie, passing by the toll house without paying their dues, until he stopped in the middle of the Pont de Double. Jacques smirked. It was worth being in the company of the head of the Paris police.

La Reynie leaned over the railing, staring into the swirling waters. Jacques leaned against it, looking around, but they were alone. It was past midnight, and only the unsavoury characters of Paris would lurk in the streets at this hour. He'd have to watch his back on his way home.

"I think we should halt our investigation, Jacques."

"You mean into Guibourg and the nuns?"

"Yes. We clearly worried them, so they won't do anything until they feel safe again."

Jacques understood. "So me backing off for a while will help us?"

"Yes, it shall."

"I see. It makes sense, of course, but we might then miss something crucial."

"That's a risk we have to take. For the time being, I'd rather you focus your attention on the cutpurses that pester the good people of Paris." La Reynie held up a hand as Jacques opened his mouth. "I know you're friendly with some children, but I'd rather see them in suitable homes, being fed and educated."

"But they have their own families, sir."

La Reynie sighed. "I'm aware of that. But often, those families cannot look after their children. It can't be that boys and girls go begging day and night, or worse, stealing from honest people going about their business."

Jacques gritted his teeth. "They steal to survive, sir."

"Listen, Jacques. I don't want them punished – unless the parents urge them to steal. Then, they're breaking the law."

"Which you know they do."

"Yes." La Reynie's repeated affirmation grated on Jacques, but he held his tongue. "They are taught how to rob innocent people, Jacques. When we dissolved the Court of the Miracles, we helped many of the orphans. They are now either in education or in service, learning a trade where they can make a living for themselves. Is that not what you want for them?"

He nodded. "Of course. But we cannot remove them from their families."

"Then they remain criminals. It's simple, really." La Reynie turned to face him. "Help us save those children. We can provide them with a better life. You know it, deep down." He tapped Jacques' heart.

"You're right. But it still feels wrong to separate them."

La Reynie threw his hands in the air. "Then they can look after their parents when they earn a wage. That way, both children and parents benefit."

Jacques sighed. He had nothing to say against that. Improving the lives of the many boys and girls on the streets – boys who'd turn from stealing to deeper criminal actions and girls who ended up in the many brothels dotted across the fast-growing city – it was what he wanted to do.

But he did not want to give up on Guibourg and the convent. Perhaps he could combine both tasks, but less obvious to the priest, so the man would consider himself safe.

"You're best placed to discover whether children are exploited or fighting for survival. Focus on them, and we'll see safety improved on the streets of Paris."

Jacques nodded. It would keep him busy and stop him thinking about Fleur. Then he realised he'd not thought about her all evening.

Chapter Fifteen

Late November, 1676
Paris

"Thank you, Charlotte, that will be all." Fleur dismissed the maid Marguerite de la Sablière had allocated to her on her arrival and stared at her reflection in the mirror.

Gone was the gaunt look. Even her body had filled out again courtesy of the wonderful meals Marguerite's cook prepared each evening, and her cheeks regained their natural colour. Tonight, Charlotte had added a touch of *rouge* to emphasise her high cheekbones and gathered her hair at the back of her head, leaving a few loose strands playfully cascading down her back.

Though nothing could banish the sadness from her eyes, Fleur kept her innermost thoughts hidden well from those around her. And whilst Uncle Marin and Marguerite had an inkling of her plan to seek revenge, they would never challenge her.

Marguerite was not always around – she travelled often, visiting friends. But when she was *at home*, the evenings at her salon always drew interesting groups of scientists, philosophers and alchemists, all enjoying a lively discussion. Uncle Marin's presence attracted many writers, as the literary circles of Paris sought his opinion on matters of poetry and to listen to his recitals.

Fleur's gaze fell on her gown. She now only wore black, as a reminder of the child she had lost. The reason for her revenge. Her thoughts wandered to Jacques. It had been nearly a month since she had last seen him. He'd visited her a few days after she moved into Marguerite's spacious home. She'd been pleased to hear about his new mission to reduce

146

the number of children working the streets, often involved in criminal activities. But when he told her of La Reynie's order to stop tracking Abbé Guibourg's movements, she could not understand it. The priest was guilty. Hurriedly, Jacques had reassured her he would continue to watch Guibourg, which consoled her a little.

Justice must be served.

Brushing aside her morose thoughts, she sighed and straightened her shoulders. Tonight's special guest was the Marquise de Sévigné, recently recovered from a mystery illness. The lady's letters about life at court –written to her daughter in Provence – were often leaked to Paris society. With a sprinkling of dry wit, the marquise described courtiers and their ruses in the most intricate detail. No one escaped her acerbic tongue, and Fleur had already gleaned great insights which might help her on her return to Versailles.

I must keep on the right side of Madame de Sévigné.

Fleur clipped the second of a pair of pearl earrings – a gift from Uncle Marin – in place when a knock on the door occurred, and his voice came through.

"Fleur, may I enter?"

"Of course. Come in." After a last glance at her appearance, she rose and turned as Uncle Marin entered. "I wanted to speak with you before our guests arrive."

Fleur frowned. "Is something amiss?"

"No, no." He shook his head vigorously and bid her to sit again, as he lowered himself onto a vacant chair by the door. "Not at all. I have good news for you."

"Oh?" Fleur dropped back into her chair, draping one arm over the back. "What is it?"

"Marguerite and I have discussed your wish to enter a lady's household, to gain access to court." He looked at her expectantly.

She nodded. "Thank you. And?"

He beamed like a child. "We have found the right lady. I wrote to her on your behalf, and she's going to attend tonight's soirée."

Fleur's heart stopped for an instant. "Not Madame de

Sévigné?"

"What? No, not her. Better."

She smiled. "You must tell me, Uncle Marin. I haven't really met anyone of importance."

"It's the Duchess de Bouillon, a great friend and patron of mine." He clapped his hands together, clearly pleased with his endeavours.

"I'm familiar with the name, but—"

"She and her sister are in the inner circles, close to the king!" His voice turned hushed.

"Ah." Now, Fleur understood. "And how can she help me? Would she be willing to?"

It was kind of Uncle Marin to find a position for her, but did the lady in question realise what Fleur was looking for?

"Oh yes, she is. Madame la duchesse likes her secrets, and a young girl looking for revenge is someone she'd happily help. She loves playing tricks on people."

As if her plot included mere tricks... But she did not wish Uncle Marin to become suspicious of her actual plan. "She knows Mother?"

"Not personally. But as Sophie doesn't move in the same circles, the duchess is quite certain there won't be any danger of your discovery. You will like her. She and her sisters are quite," he paused as if looking for the right word, "... intriguing."

Two hours later, Fleur found herself scrutinised by the redoubtable duchess seated diagonally from her at the dining table.

She nibbled at the venison, enjoying the earthy taste, whilst she listened to the lively discussion between two gentlemen about clock-making and time. Did time run according to the clocks? No, you would have to adjust them regularly. It was no surprise that, soon, the men's tone turned argumentative.

"Do you enjoy a good debate, Mademoiselle Fleur?" The Duchess de Bouillon's voice was deeper than Fleur had imagined. Yet her open face and friendly eyes kept her at ease.

148

Fleur liked the woman from the moment Marguerite had introduced them. Blunt and direct, she stood by her opinions as she exchanged views on one of Monsieur the King's Brother's *amants* with Madame de Sévigné, seated a couple of spaces to Fleur's left.

Fleur had gathered something new: that men could seek their pleasures with other men rather than women! The thought would have outraged her mother, but these ladies did not seem to put too much emphasis on it. *It was what it was*, Madame de Sévigné had concluded. And Fleur concurred.

"I enjoy a debate." She nodded. "I find the idea of challenging existing views invigorating."

"Good. That will serve you well." The eyes of the duchess flashed. Fleur suppressed a giggle. It would be rude to laugh. "We have much to talk about."

"Oh, about what?" Madame de Sévigné's voice piped up. She – and the quiet gentleman sitting between them – stared at Fleur.

"Dearest Marie, the child has been through much. We must not dwell on it here." The duchess swiftly changed topics, ensuring all attention was on her, much to Fleur's relief. She stifled back a smile at being called a 'child'. Marianne de Bouillon was barely a decade older than herself. "Have you heard of the latest letter that country bumpkin has sent home?"

Madame de Sévigné leaned forward. Her complexion was still pale, naturally so, but she seemed otherwise well-recovered. "No, please tell. What is she complaining about now?"

"Who is the country bumpkin?" Fleur asked, intrigued. Although she was learning so much during Marguerite's gatherings, it was impossible to keep abreast with it all.

Madame de Sévigné placed a bony hand on Fleur's wrist, as the man between them made himself even smaller. His gaze darted between the women.

"Oh, dearest, you probably have not met her yet." A glint entered the older lady's eyes, and Fleur saw a sparkle of humour. "We are talking about Elizabeth Charlotte, or

Liselotte, of the Palatinate, known at court as Madame Palatine. She is the second wife of Monsieur the King's Brother's."

"Ah, yes. I've heard of her."

"Good." The marquise patted Fleur's wrist, then withdrew her hand to pick up her crystal glass of red wine. "She is quite…common."

"Mostly, because she comes from a noble family with crude manners. Their castle in the provincial town of Heidelberg in the Palatinate is somewhat…rudimentary, compared with our own palaces. As is she…" The duchess looked wistful. "I've always wondered how she could ever hope to blend into our society when all she wants to do is stalk around the countryside shooting animals. What a tedious thing to do."

Madame de Sévigné laughed. "I find her highly entertaining, dear Marianne. She is a man at heart, born into a woman's body."

"What do you mean?" Fleur worried she'd come across as ignorant, but the ladies looked at her with a sense of understanding.

"What we mean is that she is most unusual, Mademoiselle Fleur. But the poor woman has to put up with Monsieur's… personal preferences, his favourites. Sometimes, I feel sorry for her."

"I would if she were a weak female, desperate for his attention," the duchess said. "But she is quite courageous for a lady born into such a grand heritage. I think she can look after herself. Although she needs to watch what she puts into her letters. The king has them copied."

Fleur's eyes widened. "The king would spy into her private correspondence?"

"Why, of course!" Madame de Sévigné said, bursting out laughing. "I am under no illusion that someone reads my own letters to dear Françoise before they are dispatched. That's why I'm careful," she added with a conspiratorial wink. "I use my sense of humour so no one could ever accuse me of slander."

"Although you float close to the edge at times, my friend," the duchess said. "Mademoiselle Fleur, have you read Madame de Sévigné's anecdotes?"

Fleur nodded. "Yes, Marguerite has introduced me to certain extracts."

The marquise laughed. "I hope you find them useful."

Smiling, Fleur met her gaze. "Oh, I do."

It had long gone past midnight when the circle of visitors eventually broke up, and everyone headed for their carriage.

Fleur had enjoyed listening to more of Madame de Sévigné's witty observations, a new poem written and recited by her uncle, and a geographic article for a scientific magazine one gentleman wanted to share prior to submission to the journal.

Her head was spinning with all the new impressions and views, but as she said goodbye to each guest, she was in her element. Here was a circle she felt comfortable in; people holding intelligent debates where nobody merely talked about clothes or appearances – the two things foremost on Mother's mind.

As she prepared to say goodbye to the Duchess de Bouillon, the lady pulled her to one side and leaned close to Fleur's ear. "Dearest, I have agreed with Marguerite and Marin that you shall join my household from next Friday. Are you content with that?"

Excitement coursing through her, Fleur nodded, even though she had no idea how she would earn her keep.

The duchess must have read her hesitant glance, because she placed a hand on her upper arm and pressed it gently. "Fear not, young Fleur. Your uncle has described your ordeal to me, and you will have my reassurance that I will help you seek revenge on that wastrel, whatever-his-name-is, oh, and your mother. How could she!" The duchess's eyes moistened.

"Thank you, Your Grace, for your sympathy. But I seek to earn my keep in your household."

The duchess smiled. "Your uncle is a close acquaintance of mine. He is also a wonderful writer who often graces my salon with his beautiful readings and witty conversation. You, dearest Fleur, have nothing to concern yourself about. You shall accompany me to court for the first time a few weeks after your arrival." The glint in her eye turned mischievous. "There is going to be a masked ball, before the more serious season of Christmas begins. The perfect occasion to bring you back."

Fleur's heart pounded in her ears. "That soon?"

"Oh yes. Marguerite and I will see to your wardrobe in the meantime. One tiny piece of advice, though." She hesitated, and Fleur held her breath. "Ditch the black gowns! I understand your reasons, but it is unbecoming of a young lady at court, and it would raise unhealthy amounts of curiosity."

With mixed feelings, Fleur concluded the lady was right. It would attract attention, and that was the last thing she wanted. Nodding, she said, "I agree, Your Grace. And I'll be forever grateful to you."

"Splendid. I'm looking forward to welcoming you to my humble home, and to bring you with me to court. We shall have to think of an introductory title for you, but there is plenty of time to ponder on that." She took a step back. "For now, dearest, I bid you farewell. But we shall meet again, very soon."

Fleur curtsied with a broad smile. "Thank you. Until then."

Later that night, as she sat with Marguerite and Uncle Marin in the lady's small, intimate drawing room, Fleur sipped her port. Was she going too far? And once she was at court, what would she do?

Suddenly, she was not so sure anymore.

"What is it, Fleur?" Marguerite came to sit beside her on the settee, sinking deep into the cushions. "You seem pensive."

"I… It's all so overwhelming."

"It might seem that way at the moment, but once you are at Marianne's, it will all work out. You will be under her protection, so your mother can't touch you."

"I would still suggest you don't venture out by yourself, Fleur." Marin leaned forward on his high-backed chair, holding his glass in both hands. "Sophie may arrange for someone to waylay you. But Marianne has excellent staff. They will ensure nobody can get too close. Or closer than you want them to come…"

"Yes, I've gathered as much, though I'm certain Mother has given up on any marriage plans for me. She's happily spending my inheritance." She took a large gulp of the strong wine. The situation was so unfair. Her mother was living a good life, from what she'd gleaned, always at court, and treating her young *amant* generously. It made Fleur's blood boil.

"You are seeking revenge, and you shall have it," Marguerite said, her hand on Fleur's. "Marianne is well-connected – much better than myself. She is a daughter of the famous Mancini family, a niece to the late cardinal. She will have ideas to help you. She is Italian!" The marquise nodded nonchalantly, her gaze meeting Fleur's.

"Ah, so she is." Fleur took a deep breath. She understood. And if that meant crossing Jacques' path in the murky alleys of Saint Denis, so be it. She would deal with him. Revenge was more important than anything, even than friendship. She pressed Marguerite's fingers gently. "I shall be fine."

"Naturally. And we are always here if you need to escape from time to time. Aren't we, Marin?" A long looked passed between them.

"Of course." Uncle Marin nodded and emptied his glass. He set it down on the small table beside his chair and rose. "Now, if you ladies would excuse me. I'm a tired old man. I wish you good night."

"Good night." Fleur smiled at him. "Sleep well."

"Thank you." He beamed. "And don't fret. I haven't forgotten about our appointment to discuss Monsieur Molière's latest scribbles."

She laughed, relieved and excited that she'd sought his company. The only relative who cared.

"Sweet dreams, dear Marin," the marquise said. "I hope they inspire you."

After the door had closed behind him, Marguerite turned to her with a serious expression. "Fleur, are you certain you want to go through with your revenge?"

"Yes, I am." She met the older woman's gaze evenly, recognising concern in her eyes. "I shall be careful, but it must be done."

"So your mother will feel your wrath."

"She shall, as will Philippe."

"And how are you planning to accomplish it?"

"Quietly and calmly. I won't rush it, if that's your worry. It takes time."

"Oh, absolutely. You must not give anyone cause for suspicion. Many secretive things are going on at court, and beyond. The services of alchemists, apothecaries and witches are in great demand. Dark powers are at work here. You must be careful."

"I lived in one of the poorest *quartiers* of Paris, Marguerite, and have come across a few of those people. I'm not planning to make enemies, but merely pursue my goal. Once I've achieved it, I'll leave for my country estate or go travelling."

"A wise decision. Now I won't ask any further. Marianne will know the risks much better than I. Please trust her, but be honest. If she thinks you are deceiving her, it could turn against you."

Fleur nodded. "I shall heed your words of advice. I'm so grateful for your understanding."

The marquise smiled. "It is my pleasure. Your mother's treatment of you was abominable. Sadly, she only follows where many have trodden before her. As for that young man – Philippe," her eyes glinted with mischief, "keep me informed about your progress, but only when we meet in person. No letters or notes."

"Oh no. I wouldn't dream of putting my thoughts in writing."

"Good girl."

They clinked glasses, and as Fleur drained the last of the port, she had the impression that taking one's vengeance was commonplace in Paris. She may have to use the services of people who were acquaintances of Abbé Guibourg. That might give her an opportunity to expose him.

Chapter Sixteen

Early December, 1676
Paris

Jacques stormed up the narrow stairwell and banged on the door. "Ninou, open!" An anger he rarely felt consumed him ever since Guillaume had sent word. Little Jeanne, Ninou's daughter, had wandered aimlessly – alone – in a nearby park, looking lost. Jacques had rushed to fetch her straight away. Now he wanted answers.

The girl on his arm rubbed her running nose with a dirty sleeve. Wet strands of hair stuck to pale cheeks. The rain had soaked her threadbare coat. She clung to him, shivering.

Footsteps sounded from inside. And a male voice. A client? He braced for an argument.

Ninou threw open the door, dressed only in a thin shift. A false smile flittered across her face. "Jacques, what a surprise! And you've brought Jeanne. I've been wondering where she was." He twisted out of reach when she extended her arms to take the child from him.

He could smell cheap wine on his friend's breath. From within the lodgings, he heard shuffling.

"Tell whoever is with you to go!" Jacques barked.

"I…" Ninou touched her neck, but she could not hide the raw bruise.

Jacques barged inside and came to stand in the open door to the small bedchamber. "You, out!"

In front of him, a man beyond his fiftieth year struggled to pull up his breeches, glaring at him. "Who are you? I wasn't finished yet."

Jacques' rage grew. "You are now. Leave!" With a gentleness he did not feel, he cradled Jeanne to his chest. It was best the man did not see her face. What was Ninou doing, receiving clients in her own home?

The man bristled, but picked up his coat and hat. Jacques stepped into the narrow corridor and let him pass. In the stairwell, the client pushed Ninou against the wall, his gaze challenging. "I've not paid yet, whore, and now you won't get an *écu*." He stood back, leering. "Next time, make sure there are no disruptions."

Jacques pulled Ninou inside and slammed the door. "What do you think you're doing? I found Jeanne in the park."

"Oh, go away, Jacques!" A stubborn glint in her green eyes, Ninou blinked back tears. "What do you know?"

Ignoring her, he stepped into the bedchamber and sat the whimpering girl on the small bunk bed on the far wall, wiping away the tears with his thumb. Gently, he kissed Jeanne's forehead. "Go to sleep, ma *chérie*. You're safe."

The girl nodded and removed her filthy clothes. He would buy her a new dress and coat in the morning.

As he turned to leave, Jeanne took his hand and whispered, "I was scared, Jacques. Thank you." In her thin shift, she slid beneath a blanket.

He drew a cover from Ninou's rumpled bed, placing it over the child and tucked her in. Immediately, Jeanne fell asleep.

Leaving a lit candle on the chest of drawers, he pulled the door to behind him. Ninou stood in the doorway to the kitchen, looking pale.

"Did you give any thought about what could have happened to your daughter out there?" He strode past her and came to a halt by the old dining table, letting out a deep, shuddering breath. When she remained silent, he repeated, "Did you?"

"When I left her, Jeanne was playing with the other children in the yard." Ninou sat on a chair, twiddling her hands in her lap.

"Don't lie to me!" He glared at the woman he'd considered a wonderful mother. Until today. "Jeanne was alone, in the park, and dusk was drawing in."

Ninou shrugged. "The children must have—"

"Stop it! Your client was due to arrive, and your daughter needed to be out of the way. That's the true reason."

She fumed. "Oh, you walk in here, all full of yourself! What do you think I'm doing? I'm earning a living, so I can feed my daughter."

"Does Claudette not pay you enough?"

Her harsh laughter sent shivers down his spine. "Claudette pays well, yes, but here, I can earn more and keep all of it."

So that was it? She sent her daughter into the streets because she'd been receiving men at home. How long had this been going on? The thought made him sick, though he could not explain why. "If you need money, I can help."

"I don't need charity, Jacques. I'm making sure that my daughter will grow up so she won't have to do what I do."

"And to do that you send her out into the streets to beg?"

"I didn't—"

"She walked around, lost, asking strangers for help! Christ, Jeanne could have been abducted or abused. Did you not consider that?"

"I'm doing this for her. Jeanne can look after herself."

"For God's sake, Ninou, she's five years old! Too young to be outside on her own."

"Other girls are—"

"And what happens to them? Do I need to remind you of your old friend Claire's daughter?" With a sense of grim satisfaction, he watched as Ninou flinched. "A stranger dragged her into the bushes and..." he struggled for the words, "she died from the injuries he'd caused. *That* could be Jeanne's fate, and I will not have it." He slammed his hand on the table. Ninou jumped. "Tell me, what is really going on?"

Ninou closed her eyes for a moment before she met his gaze. All anger seemed to have left her. "I can't pay my rent, Jacques. My landlady died last month. Not only did she keep the rent at a fair price, she also looked after Jeanne. Her greedy son promptly raised it, and now I barely have enough left to put food on our table. He's also tried to..." Ninou shuddered. "Claudette has offered to help, but I can't accept it again."

"Why not?" He sat down. Finally, she'd told him. "What did she offer?"

"Fleur's old room. But it would be too small. Jeanne would live in a whorehouse. I don't want her in such a place."

"It would only be temporary, until you found more suitable lodgings. Jeanne would be safe in Claudette's chamber during the day."

"Rents are going up all around us. As more people arrive from the countryside in search of work, landlords are taking advantage. There soon won't be anywhere people like me can afford." Tears welled up. "Do you really think I'd send my daughter into the streets if I didn't have to? I'm trying my best." Her voice broke.

Watching his friend, he noticed deep grooves beneath her eyes. Her face was gaunt, and the slim body beneath the plain shift looked more bony than feminine. An idea formed in his mind.

"Why don't you move into my lodgings? They're nothing much to speak of, but Madame Pèlerin, my landlady, is a kind woman. She might be able to care for Jeanne when you're working."

Ninou shook her head. "Oh no. It's sweet of you, but I can't accept."

Jacques sighed. Did she have to be so obstinate? "Why not?"

"It's wrong. You're a grown man with your own life. I wouldn't dream of imposing on you." She gave him a dry smile. "And wouldn't your landlady deem it unsuitable if you had a whore with a child living with you?"

"Well, I shall speak with her. She'll understand, I'm sure." He grinned. "I can always stay in the workshop. There is a bunk bed."

"All that effort for…"

He leaned forward and took Ninou's hand. "I want you and Jeanne safe. We can later search for new lodgings for

159

you, but at least you wouldn't have to work at home, and you'd be safe at Claudette's."

"Thank you. I… How can I pay you back?"

"You've no need to. You're a good friend, and this is what one does for friends."

"You're an unusual man, Jacques. Others would have suggested some kind of arrangement. But you do it for nothing."

"I do it for our friendship, and for Jeanne's future."

"Jeanne's now going to live with you?" Guillaume asked, an eyebrow raised, as Jacques sat beside him on the wall by the Seine. The dark water swirled fast beneath their feet, but Jacques welcomed the breeze.

"Yes. It keeps her from roaming the streets."

"That's good. She's too young to be out alone."

"Thank you again for sending word, Guillaume. God only knows what might have happened."

The boy straightened his shoulders. "By the time you came, I'd already taken care of her."

"I'm grateful you did. You always keep an eye on the little ones. But you can't be in all places all the time."

"I try my best." The stubborn set of the boy's chin made Jacques proud – and angry. Here was a lad who was clever, caring and quick-witted, yet his mother made him beg to support her.

"You shouldn't be here, on the streets. You should learn your letters and help others."

Guillaume looked at him. "I want to, I really do. But Mum won't—"

"Your mother is a selfish woman who doesn't have your wellbeing at heart, but only her own. You must think of your own future."

"I can't leave her. She'd die without me."

Jacques shook his head. He'd known Guillaume's mother for years, ever since he first arrived in Saint Denis. "Well, she'd have to get off her backside for once. Your mother has relied on you for the past few years. She even wanted to cut

160

off your foot, remember? Maimed children get more coins from gullible passers-by." He swiftly suppressed his rising anger at uncaring mothers like Guillaume's. Feeling sorry for the boy did not help the situation. But Jacques hoped he would agree to the suggestion he had in mind. It offered a way out. "Never mind. I have a proposal for you."

"Oh. What would you want me to do?"

Jacques sighed. "It won't be easy, and it might not prove popular with the other children on the streets."

Guillaume shrugged. "I'm not interested in being popular. You know I prefer my own company."

"You're like me there." Jacques grinned. "The police want to get as many children off the streets as possible."

The boy snorted. "They can try their luck, but I doubt they'll manage."

"The Lieutenant General has tasked me with it." He raised his hands as Guillaume sent him a sharp glance. "It's not what you think. Hell, I have no idea where to begin."

"No one will follow. The parents will beat them."

Jacques nodded. "And therein lies my problem. I want you to get an education. You're clever, quick-witted, and you could do well."

"But that would mean learning with the monks." He screwed up his face into a grimace. "They do these things to young ones…"

"Not all of them. Some merely want to help. It can lead to a better life than stealing. You're not cut out to become a criminal, Guillaume."

"I am a criminal, Jacques. Begging is a crime."

"Not if you're forced into it, and you are. Don't contradict me! Plenty of other parents play your mother's game."

"I'd learn to read and write?"

"You would; and even learn a trade."

The boy's eyes glinted. "Like yours, you mean? Working with leather?"

"Or with any other material you'd want to try, but yes, like mine, for example." He smiled. "I was only a couple of years older than you when I learned how to handle leather."

"But you're making the most beautiful items."

"You peeked through my workshop window?"

"Yes, and I saw beautiful belts and saddles and..." Guillaume's voice grew in excitement. A sense of satisfaction coursed through Jacques.

"I can teach you – provided you're willing to learn your letters too. It's important for business."

The boy nodded, then his face fell. "I'd love to, but..." Twisting his hands, he stared into the river.

"Your mother?"

Guillaume nodded. "Mum needs all I take home."

"Listen to me, please. If you're working hard to learn the craft, I can pay you a small wage. Not much, but enough for you to give to your mother." He watched the emotions crossed the boy's face. Brows drawn together in doubt, at first, before, with a glimmer of hope, a smile broke through. "Though she doesn't deserve it. I'd prefer her to find employment."

"But that means she has to see men."

"I'm aware of that, but she's not the only woman in Paris in that situation. Jeanne's mum is one. What do you think?"

"You really think I can learn?"

"I do." He did not press his point further. Now, it was Guillaume's decision. The first step for him to grow up. "Now, I need your help in getting my message across to other children."

Jacques sat on a large slab of rubble in the shell of a half-collapsed house only minutes from his own lodgings. The walls of the upper storeys had crumbled, but the remains of a ceiling gave the group that had gathered there a little shelter from the winter weather. Blankets lay piled up in the corner least exposed to the elements.

Jacques joined the seven children crouched on the floor beneath the unsafe cover, as he sat, cross-legged, beside them. Finally, they'd agreed to speak with him. Guillaume had done well to convince them.

Dampness covered their exposed heads and limbs. The

small faces that stared at him were gaunt, their bodies – huddled together against the cold – thin, and their clothes grimy and threadbare.

Their eyes darted from him to the open entrance. The longer they stayed here, the less coin they'd collect. He'd seen them all before, scurrying around the narrow lanes day and night, begging or picking pockets.

"Thank you for coming here. I'm very grateful," he began. "You are free to leave, so don't think I'm forcing you to anything."

"I don't know you," a young boy of perhaps eight years said. His left hand was missing three fingers; the wound looked too cleanly cut to have been an accident. A parent with a sharp knife…

"But I do, and if I say you can trust Jacques, you should." Guillaume's voice was firm, convincing. "Listen to what he has to say." He clearly wanted his friends to have a chance of a better life.

"I came to warn you," Jacques said. "Soon, the police are planning to make sure that no children are begging on the streets of Paris." This caused much laughter, most of it wry, and he grinned and held up a hand. "They've tried this before, I remember, and the result did not help children or families."

"No, it's only so the *seigneurs* don't have to look upon us as they pass." a girl of twelve said. Her teeth were black, and several were missing. "Although some men enjoy taking more than a glance, and no one, least of all the police, worry about that." She glared at him.

"I worry. Trust me, I have come across that type."

"Those dogs should be thrown into gaol, but never are." Her mouth formed a thin line, and she picked a louse off her sleeve with a swift movement and crushed it.

Jacques wondered if she'd suffered an attack. His heart went out to her. "I usually report them, so if anyone troubles you, tell me."

She nodded, somewhat mollified.

"What we – I – want for you all is to get an education; a

163

chance to escape this life. You pass old beggars every day. The lure of the coin is there, but if you fall ill – like 'old' Robert from rue du Temple who is merely forty – your life may be short."

"My parents rely on me," a boy of around ten said. "Papa's a cripple, and I have four younger brothers and sisters." The sadness in his eyes moved Jacques.

"Did your father do this to you?" He pointed at the cut-off foot where only a stump, wrapped in filthy rags, remained. A makeshift crutch lay on the floor.

The boy remained silent, and the others averted their eyes. Jacques sensed their disquiet. If they spoke up or failed to bring home enough money, their elders would beat them. Another of the obstacles he faced.

"I see," he said, not pressing the boy further. "Your parents are your biggest hindrance. We both know it. But to prepare for a better future, we must think ahead."

The girl who'd spoken earlier snorted, then wiped her nose with the back of her hand. "Easier said than done, sir. Mine would kill me if I didn't go back. They'd find me, and…" Her large eyes filled with fear, and an acceptance of reality. Others mumbled in agreement.

"Mine too. Paris isn't big enough for me to disappear." This boy was small, probably around six years of age. When he spoke, his voice wobbled. "I've tried." He stared at his bare feet caked in mud.

Jacques sighed. He exchanged a glance with Guillaume who nodded imperceptibly. They had to tread gently. "I want you to attend classes where you can learn to read and write, to discuss religion, and to gain a practical skill." With the education from several charity schools across the city, they could save children from a lifetime spent begging, or whoring. "We would send you to attend school either in a monastery or convent, or visit classes in charity schools every day. But you continue to live at home."

"But how will our parents survive?" The six-year-old asked.

"They will have to look after themselves for the duration

of your learning, but," he paused until all eyes were on him, "once they know that you are learning a skill to earn a better wage, they might agree. It's how you present it to them, that is important."

"Just like we convinced mine," Guillaume said. "I'm going to Saint-Eustache from next Monday, where they teach letters and cal…" He sent Jacques a sideways glance.

"Calculations and subtractions."

"Yes, that," he grinned, "and a bit of religion too."

"Guillaume will work with me. He'll be a leather-worker soon, earning honest money to help feed his mother." It had been a fierce discussion between Madame Tellier and Jacques, but he'd convinced her that her son's education would benefit them both, and eventually she'd given in. "I can speak with your parents too if you'd like."

"My father would beat me black and blue if I asked," a young girl, not much older than Jeanne, said. A purple bruise rose beneath her left eye, as if she needed proof. "He doesn't think much of learning."

"Then we need to find a more permanent solution for you. Let me help you." He peered at the small rabble of desolate children. "All of you."

He moved a few paces away, giving them privacy to talk.

After several minutes of hushed exchanges, the girl with the black teeth and the boy with the younger siblings rose and left without another word. Jacques was sad to see them go, but felt encouraged when the others stayed.

"So, what do you want us to do?" the little girl with the bruise asked.

He admired the children's bravery. It was a start.

Chapter Seventeen

Mid-December, 1676
Château de Versailles

Marianne, Duchess de Bouillon, leaned forward and gently pressed Fleur's hand. "How are you feeling, now you are back here?"

The carriage was queuing up for their turn to disembark. They'd arrived the previous afternoon, installing themselves into a three-storey house Marianne rented in the village of Versailles. The time it had taken to travel to the palace had been much shorter than their wait so far. As the minutes ticked by, Fleur's nerves became more fraught.

"To be honest, I feel sick in my stomach."

"Don't worry too much, dear. Everything will be fine. You'll see." Marianne pulled back the curtain and looked out. At that moment, the carriage moved forward a few steps. "Ooh, we're getting closer." She grinned. "Only count eight or nine others before us."

Fleur appreciated the woman's attempt at cheering her up. She picked an imaginary fluff off her elaborate gown – the first of several presents from the duchess. Fleur had insisted she would compensate her, but Marianne waved off any such concerns.

"What's a gown or two more or less?" the lady had said, before she instructed the dressmaker with the exact specifications she wanted. Now, Fleur was in her debt, something she was not completely comfortable with, especially as she could not earn a living as long as she stayed at Marianne's.

And that had been on Fleur's mind these past few nights, as the masked ball at Versailles had drawn closer. Once she had taken revenge on Philippe, what would she do? Return to the family estate, her inheritance? Or first…

Mother must pay too.

She brushed off her morose thoughts and followed Marianne's glance. Ascending the steps were dozens of ladies and lords of the court. From a distance, Fleur admired their versatility. The masks were uniquely elaborate works of art, glittering in the light from hundreds of candles. Each wig was more elaborate than the other. The display of clothing took her breath away: daring, low-cut gowns decorated with bows, freshwater pearls, feathers or bobbin lace; the men's shirts with their colourful slashed sleeves and jackets showing fine gold thread and precious stones. Most wore exquisite, heeled shoes – following the king's fashion. But she knew once up close, faces drowned beneath powder and *rouge*, to hide imperfections. It was a vicious circle. Women used powder to make themselves more attractive, but something in it blemished your skin. One needed more and more layers.

"What a display!" she whispered.

They moved again. Soon, it would be their turn to dazzle those behind them watching.

Marianne laughed. "That's what Versailles is about – the glitter and shine. Not what's hiding behind the bright exterior." She sent her a curious glance that Fleur could not decipher. "Agreeing to accompany me shows that you are willing to look behind the masks, so to speak. Tonight, your first lesson in observation will begin."

"Ah," Fleur said, not sure what Marianne was referring to. "But how will I know what to look for?"

"I shall tell you." The carriage moved again, then came to a halt at the bottom of the steps. "We have arrived. Are you ready?" The duchess huddled deeper into her fur-trimmed cloak. Then she held her mask up.

Fleur nodded, then pulled her own mask over her eyes, taking care not to upset the elaborate wig she wore, and secured it at the nape of the neck. Hopefully, this would hold it in place all night. Not that she had any intention of taking it off – the risk that someone recognised her was too great. "I am ready."

A footman opened the door and helped Marianne from the carriage. Then it was Fleur's turn, and she carefully descended the two steps.

The frosty evening air hit them, and she shivered. "Come, quickly," Marianne said, then led the way. Fleur followed a couple of steps behind to allow the duchess enough space. She tried not to grimace at the heavy perfume that wafted Marianne's wake. A melange of lavender, sandalwood and camphor, heady and sweet at once. Fleur had opted for a light lavender tonic on her skin after her bath, and she was grateful for the comparatively light scent.

Her heartbeat echoed in her ears as she followed the duchess into the palace where they left their cloaks with a waiting maid. Soon, they drifted from one room to another, and Fleur watched as everyone greeted Marianne with great reverence.

Fleur smiled as she caught sight of herself in a wall-to-ceiling mirror. The mask concealed her eyes well. Her lips were rouged. She wore Uncle Marin's pearl earrings and a necklace made of amber drops Marianne had lent her. Mother would never recognise her.

Not that she'd be looking for me here.

Unlike outside, the air indoors was stifling as people pushed past each other. Fleur felt her skin flush.

Marianne took two glasses of white wine from a tray and passed one to her. "This is delicious. From the Rhine, I hear. Try it!"

Fleur sipped the cool liquid, savouring the taste. "Mmh. Pungent."

"Come." Laughing, the duchess waved her onwards. They passed into yet another room where she turned towards her and leaned in close. "I know just the place we want to be tonight."

Fleur could see the mischief in Marianne's eyes. She admired her confidence, wishing her own would grow. But then, Marianne came from a famous family, and as a niece of

168

the late Cardinal Mazarin, she'd married well. In every respect, her new friend was so different from the environment in which Fleur had moved so recently.

But tonight was not the time to think of Claudette, Jacques and the others. She must concentrate on her goal.

They came to a halt in the ballroom. "The king and queen have not arrived yet. Let us head across to that large window." She pointed to a velvet-covered settee where a woman sat by herself. "We can see everyone from there."

Marianne wove her way through the crowds, and Fleur followed. The duchess stopped right in front of the woman, tapping the fan on her wrist. "Good day, mademoiselle. You're in my seat."

The other woman stared at her, then rose. "My apologies, Madame la duchesse." Without a glance back, she disappeared into the crowd.

Marianne looked at Fleur with a broad smile and sat. "Here, come!" She patted the embroidered seat beside her, and Fleur lowered herself into the confined space.

"What was that?" She faced Marianne. "What did that lady do to you?"

The duchess laughed. "Oh, but everyone knows this is my seat. I always await the king's pleasure here."

"The king's what?" Fleur stared at her.

A self-satisfied smile appeared on Marianne's face. It reminded Fleur of a cat – one who was about to pounce on an unsuspecting mouse. "His pleasure. Here, you shall see His *Majesty* closely."

Fleur's mouth went dry. This was not what she'd expected. She'd planned to remain anonymous. "But what if Mother hears about it?"

"Fret not, dear Fleur. You are now Rose. Close enough, but Sophie would never know it was you…"

Rose. Fleur liked it. Then the meaning of Marianne's words sank in.

"Introduce me to…?"

"Yes. The king. Look!" She stood and pulled Fleur up as a fanfare echoed through the room. "Here they come. Isn't His

Majesty divine?"

Fleur swallowed hard. She watched as King Louis and Queen Marie Thérèse wandered through the courtiers lining up on either side of a path created for them.

Marianne stepped forward, taking Fleur by the wrist, and pulling her with her. Other courtiers made way for them at the front. Again, the duchess's influence impressed Fleur. Doors opened when you were well-connected.

Her pulse quickened as the royal couple approached. They smiled politely, exchanging words with the courtiers as they progressed. Then the king spotted Marianne, and his face lit up. He guided the queen their way.

Marianne dropped a deep curtsey, and Fleur followed suit.

"Madame, what a pleasant surprise to see you returned, and looking so well."

Fleur thought she'd heard a hint of sadness in his voice. She remembered the rumours that said he'd once wanted to wed a young Marianne Mancini, but it had come to nothing.

"Thank you, Your Majesty. I have been out of town." The duchess straightened.

"Ah, good, good. But we are glad you have returned to us, dearest Marianne." He paused, then stepped closer to Fleur. "Please rise, young mademoiselle."

Fleur was still staring at his embroidered shoes adorned with little golden bows. Hurriedly, she rose and met his gaze. Was she expected to respond? He had not posed a question.

"Who is this enchanting creature, Marianne? And where has she been hiding?"

"Your Majesty, this is Mademoiselle Rose, a guest at my humble home. She is from the west."

"Well, that does not necessarily count against her."

He beamed, and Fleur thought she'd faint. The air seemed to have become thin. His eyes shone darkly through the holes in his elaborate mask decorated with precious stones, gold leaf and the most delicate feathers. Heat shot into her cheeks, fortunately hidden by the *rouge*.

She returned his smile, unsure if she was allowed to speak. She dared it. "Thank you, Your Majesty. You are very kind."

King Louis chuckled, then ran his thumb over her cheek. A shiver ran down her spine.

If Mother only knew…

"And what a pleasant voice she has. Welcome to Versailles, Mademoiselle Rose. We shall hopefully see more of your delightful company in the coming months."

"Oh, we will visit regularly," Marianne said, the corners of her mouth turned up. She sent Fleur a knowing glance.

"Good. We shall look forward to seeing you dance."

Fleur bit back a gasp and merely nodded.

"Marianne. Mademoiselle Rose." The king inclined his head, then moved on. Behind his back, the queen stared, her mouth pinched in a thin line, and Fleur lowered her gaze a little.

Behind the royal couple, Monsieur the King's Brother walked past Marianne, barely acknowledging her. His wife, Liselotte of the Palatinate, walked beside him, sending Fleur a warm smile and wishing her a lovely evening. Madame de Sévigné had called Liselotte a 'country bumpkin', though Fleur appreciated the woman's friendly demeanour. It was so different from the majority of courtiers with their false smiles and empty promises. Fleur thanked her and curtseyed.

A trail of members of the royal entourage followed, led by a woman Fleur recognised from previous visits, but did not recognise. The lady briefly stared at Fleur, then walked past with her head held high, her full mouth forming a thin line beneath a mask decorated with gold leaf. A low-cut gown more extravagant than the queen's almost simple dress hugged her curvaceous figure. Attached to her puffed sleeves was an array of bows and lace, with precious stones and gold thread weaved into her corset. Her skirts trailed behind her in silken layers. The lady's pale hair was piled up high, draped into narrow curls, and held together with strings of pearls.

Once the procession had made their way into the next room, Fleur let out her breath. Marianne pulled her gently back to the settee.

Only after they were alone, did Marianne lean over to her with a self-satisfied smile. "It went better than expected."

She waved over a footman and exchanged their empty wine glasses with filled ones.

Fleur waited until he'd left. "Why?" The cool liquid went down well. She felt like emptying the whole glass but forced herself to take small sips. She must not get too drunk.

"I'm very pleased Louis noticed you. My protection is solid, but once you have the king's favour, nothing can touch you."

Fleur blinked. "What do you mean?"

Marianne sighed. "Child, you are looking for revenge. It's your choice how you wish to play this out. If you are serious about it, I know where to go and what to do. It's simple, really, although we must not rush it." She met her gaze. "Revenge must be savoured. You understand?"

"Of course." Fleur had already realised that if she really wanted Philippe and Mother to suffer, she had to take serious measures. But only now that Marianne had put her thoughts into words did the enormity of her plan sink in.

Did she want to stoop to Sister Benedicte's level? No! Her revenge would not kill innocent children. It would only hit those who deserved it.

For a while, they sat in companionable silence, watching men and women file past, then they walked through to the ballroom. There, they made their way to a corner close to the king and queen. As they settled with fresh glasses of chilled wine – it was going to her head, but there was nothing else to drink – the dark-haired lady from earlier leaned across to King Louis, whispering something in his ear. He smiled half-heartedly, then waved her away.

"Who is she?" Fleur asked Marianne, then gazed to the royal couple.

"Who? The sour-faced woman? That's Madame de Montespan, the king's mistress of many years and mother to a brood of his children," Marianne whispered. "Beware of her! She has spent time in the company of certain unsavoury characters you might know of." She sent her a knowing glance.

Fleur gasped. "Unsavoury? As in Abbé Gui—?"

"Shh!" Marianne urged, hiding her mouth behind her open fan. "Undoubtedly."

Fleur could envisage Marianne's raised eyebrows behind her mask. "Ah." She swallowed hard. The king's mistress attended black masses? "But what for? She has everything."

"And therein lies her problem." The duchess lowered her voice further. "The king giveth, the king taketh away…"

"I see. She's worried?"

"Yes, and even though he's had their three children legitimised, he has moved his attentions to younger ladies, and she fears for his attention."

"But she looked as if she was carrying a child."

Marianne smiled sweetly, her eyes glinting with mischief. "Not surprisingly, we can expect another royal bastard. But don't be fooled! The marquise is as scheming as they come."

Fleur giggled. This was coming from a lady with a reputation for intrigue.

"Ahem." Marianne gave a false cough, then nudged her in the ribs. "I know what you're thinking."

Fleur's cheeks flushed, but the duchess was smirking, clearly revelling in her reputation.

"Ah, let me introduce you to a good friend," she said, her eyebrows raised. "You may not have seen him in my house yet – because he always leaves before sunrise." She reached out a hand as a young man approached.

A mask covered in plain black velvet obscured half his face. The cut of his jacket and shirt were of excellent quality, but he appeared understated compared to the colourful attire of most courtiers. He bowed and kissed Marianne's hand. Then he looked at Fleur. "Is this your visitor, Marianne?"

The duchess nodded, linking her arm through his. "Isn't she pretty?" To Fleur, she said, "This is my nephew, Louis Joseph, the Duke de Vendôme."

Fleur curtsied. "Your Grace."

"*Enchanté*, mademoiselle!" He inclined his head. "Marianne has told me much about you. Are you enjoying your evening?"

"She is." Marianne said, beaming at him, before Fleur

173

could open her mouth. "The king has spoken to her."

"So I saw from the opposite side of the room," he said. "Be careful, young lady. There are many here who'd take advantage of your beauty." Fleur's smile vanished, and he apologised. "I'm sorry. I didn't mean to tread on your toes."

"'Tis nothing, Your Grace. Just a dark blot in my past."

"I'm relieved to hear it's in your past. Does that mean you're not here looking for an eligible husband?"

"God forbid!" Fleur shook her head, and he laughed.

She liked him. He seemed to understand.

"Joseph has just returned from the Netherlands. He's campaigning there on behalf of the king."

"You are in the army?"

"I am, yes. But now I have a few weeks' leave, and what better to do than watch courtiers tear each other apart." He grinned, then sent the duchess a long glance.

Ooh! Fleur turned away slightly, fanning herself, her gaze sweeping the room. The rumours Madame de Sévigné had hinted at were true. Aunt and nephew had a love affair. At Versailles, nothing surprised Fleur anymore.

She watched as courtiers on the periphery glared at others closer to the king. The ring of false laughter reached her. Everything here was like in a play. People acted the way they thought the king expected of them.

Was she not doing the same?

Fleur sighed. She still had so much to learn.

Then her gaze fell on a young woman in a quieter corner, far from the royal couple. Short and evidently pregnant, she sat slumped in a chair. Mouse-brown hair was styled in a ridiculous ball of curls which did not suit her round face, and a poorly fitting mask did not hide big blotches on her cheeks where the *rouge* had smudged. The red-painted mouth drawn in a thin line, she watched a man near her. The girl looked utterly miserable.

Curious, Fleur studied the man, and her blood froze. The familiar swagger, the soft chin, and wavy hair. Even though she could not see his eyes, there was no doubt. Philippe.

It appeared Henrietta was not the happy wife she'd

174

envisaged to be. He stood with his back to Henrietta, chatting to a slender girl no older than fifteen. Her hand rested on his wrist, and she giggled at something he'd said.

Poor Henrietta.

Fleur shook herself. She should not feel pity for the woman who'd laughed at her misfortune. A content smile spread across her lips.

"What amuses you, dear?" The duchess leaned over, following her gaze.

"See the sad excuse of a lady over there, in the corner on the right?"

"Who? Ah, the frumpy one?"

"Yes. That's Henrietta de Brun."

"Brun? Not *the* Henrietta?"

Fleur nodded.

"So the man she's throwing daggers at with her eyes is Philippe de Mortain?"

"He is."

"Well, well." Marianne emptied her glass, and, without a word, Vendôme went in search of another. "So now I know our victim number one. Assuming you still want your—"

"I do."

"Then let's begin with our preparations soon."

Fleur met Marianne's gaze straight on.

"Yes, please."

176

PART FOUR

A Twist of Fate

Chapter Eighteen

March, 1677
Paris

"Oh, damn it, I can never do it." Tears welled up in Ninou's eyes.

"Of course you can." Jacques sighed. "It's hard to remember all this," he pointed at the books and handwritten notes littering the large table in his sitting room, "but it's in your head, you'll be the perfect schoolmistress."

"But I'm not as bright as those—"

"Don't!" He held up his hand. Ninou's issue was not one of learning or remembering the information, but one of confidence. "I know you're struggling but give it time. Our new school's benefactor has great plans, and those involve employing women as teachers."

"But they will never accept me."

"Yes, they shall. You've met a number of schoolmistresses over recent months, and the Ursulines are quite content with your ability to learn and teach."

"Then why do I feel inadequate? This," she waved a sheet covered in mathematical symbols, "is just beyond me."

"Just learn it by heart. You don't need to understand it, but simply have some basic knowledge of it. Your strength lies in the languages – and in religion, I'm told."

Ninou blushed. It had surprised Jacques that her favourite subject was one that was so different from the trade she'd practiced for so long. But then, he realised he knew very little about her. The Mother Superior at the convent of the Ursulines had commended Ninou's enthusiasm to discover all about the word of Christ and of the Apostles.

"They are kind to me, the nuns; as they are to the

179

children."

"That's why I sent you and Jeanne to them. And did they not praise your ability to absorb everything they've thrown at you?"

She nodded slowly. "Yes, they did. Apart from this." She slapped the sheet on the table.

"These formulae are not for everyone. They say you either have a gift for letters and literature, or for numbers. You're clearly in the former group."

Ninou sighed.

But Jacques was not finished. "You said yourself – you will have a respectable role."

She sent him a sheepish glance. "But I feel sorry for Claudette."

"Why? She'll have no problem finding a replacement. And no, I didn't mean it like that," he added quickly when she stared at him. "Your new life will be very different."

"I owe Claudette a lot."

"And she is happy for you to move on. Look," he leaned forward and took her hand, "see it as a chance for another young girl to find a safe haven from where to work her trade. You'll just make way for her."

Ninou nodded. "What you say is true, Jacques, but it still makes me feel sad."

He patted her hand, then straightened. "At certain times in our lives, new opportunities crop up, like seeing those children we took off the streets gain an education. Many of us are sad at one point or other, for the life that we led in the past – however unhappy we may have been. But change is good – for you, and for the children. You'll see for yourself how much you're going to benefit."

"Yes, master." Ninou's eyes lit up, then pulled the sheet with the equations back towards her. A strand of her long blonde hair fell over her shoulder when she leaned forward.

A new private school had been set up in the town house of a widowed countess who'd retired to the country. With the help of two of the Ursuline nuns, Ninou would be in charge of a small group of fifteen children. Ninou had studied hard these past few months, ever since the idea had formed in his head that she was well-suited to teach children. Intelligent and caring by nature, she had everything she needed, except an education. Now, they were working on that. The new private school – and Ninou – would be a success.

Jacques was proud of her. He watched as she traced each line with her fingers, silently mouthing numbers and signs. His thoughts drifted.

Whilst Ninou and Jeanne had been living in his lodgings, he'd converted the back of his workshop into a space containing a comfortable bed, a table and two chairs. The hearth provided enough warmth. But with Guillaume joining him every afternoon, Jacques had not had the time to turn it into a proper home yet.

Not that there was anyone to share it with… His mind wandered to Fleur, and he realised he'd not thought about her for weeks. The last he heard was that she'd returned to court with the Duchess de Bouillon. One of his informants had told him she'd attracted the eye of King Louis himself, and Jacques was ready to rescue her from disaster. But he accepted that life had taken her away from him. Fleur was no longer his concern.

A knock on the door drew him from his reverie, and, exchanging a glance with Ninou, he rose. "Are you expecting anyone?"

She shook her head.

He opened the door to a man he knew was one of La Reynie's spies.

"A message from the Lieutenant General for you, Jacques." The man handed him a sealed note, then turned and hurried down the stairs.

Jacques closed the door again, tapping the letter against his lips. He'd not heard from La Reynie lately, and only occasionally wrote to him about the schools and the children who attended. More and more disappeared from the streets into classrooms. The result pleased his superior. There had even been a drop in stolen purses. It had been the proof Jacques needed to continue his quest.

Intrigued, he entered the sitting room and strolled to the window. He ripped open the seal and unfolded the missive.

"And so it begins anew," he muttered.

"What?" Ninou asked, staring at him.

"Ah, nothing." He smiled.

"I see." She grinned. "Police work."

Jacques nodded. He looked out of the window as rain spluttered against the pane. A draft of cold air came through the gaps.

Then he read the message again. In La Reynie's typical fashion, it was simple but direct.

'We have arrested one Magdelaine de La Grange, a fortune teller. She has appealed to Louvois, indicating that she knows of persons of high standing involved in occult matters. It would appear the poisoners have continued their actions undisturbed. We are about to arrest several others.

I want you to join me in the interrogations.'

A shiver ran down his spine, and Jacques wondered if it came from the draft, or the sense of doom La Reynie's note had given him.

"Is everything all right?" Ninou stood beside him, her hand on his arm. He'd not heard her approach.

"Yes, it is." He sighed. "Please make sure Jeanne is never alone, Ninou. There are people out there who would harm a child for the sake of personal ambition."

She nodded. "She is with the Ursulines all day. They are looking after her well."

He took her hand. "I'm serious. She must not walk alone outside. We can't save every child in Paris, but at least we can try."

"Thank you."

Embarrassed, he stepped back and walked to the fire, dipping the missive into the flames. Within moments, it was burnt to dust.

"I have to out."

"In this weather?"

182

"Yes, I must check how Guillaume is faring. He's working on a harness for a client. Afterwards, I need to see La Reynie."

"Ah. Be safe, Jacques." Ninou returned to the table, pulling a candle closer to the bundle of papers in front of her. Her head dipped, and he saw her concentration as she worked through the numbers. The blonde strand of hair fell over her face again. Absent-mindedly, she brushed it behind her ear.

Jacques swallowed. There was something…appealing about it that he could not explain. 'Twas best he did not dwell on it.

"I shall." He pulled his cloak around him and fastened it. Then he grabbed his hat. "I'll see you tomorrow."

***

Fleur sat in the darkened room and studied the interior from beneath lowered lids.

It had taken Marianne several months for this first step. During that time, they had watched Philippe's habits at court, his time of arrival, who he conversed or danced with – usually an array of young, unwed girls – and what he drank. Fleur had frequently seen him disappear from the terrace in the direction of the small copse where he'd seduced her. At once, she knew what he was doing. Marriage had not changed him. What a cur!

Philippe was also rather partial to wine. Under Marianne's instructions, Fleur had charmed a handsome footman who would provide Marianne and her first with the coolest refreshments, before attending to other courtiers. The young man had become besotted with Fleur, but she kept him at a distance. Never again would she allow anyone to compromise her.

Marianne had explained the importance of using the help of the staff. If one were to pour a little something into Philippe's wine, one had to ensure he took the correct glass from the tray offered.

Fleur had learned fast that wishing to foist your revenge

on someone required a significant amount of finesse, planning – and time.

So they sat and watched. Not once had he looked her way, and she always ensured her fan was in place so he would not recognise her. But she was now moving in circles way above his station, whilst he maintained his place in the lower ranks of nobility.

Not that she recognised herself these days – her face painted, eyebrows lined with kohl, a powdered wig in a simple yet effective style that did not cause too much attention. Her gowns were of excellent quality, outshining those of Philippe's wife, Hapless Henrietta, as Fleur now called her. The woman had not attended court in recent weeks, and rumour had it that she'd given birth to a girl, and, in his disappointment, Philippe had banished her to their country estate. Well, it was hers, really, but now his, of course. Poor Hapless Henrietta!

But the time had finally come when Fleur would put the next step in motion. For that reason, Marianne had taken her to rue Beauregard, to the salon of Catherine Monvoisin, known in certain circles as La Voisin. A woman well-known to many courtiers, Fleur had heard, a fortune-teller and provider of potions. And poisons.

Now, as she sat in the salon, its walls covered in expensive black drapes, the furniture opulent, but all a little on the dark side, she wondered for a moment if she was doing the right thing. This was what she wanted, was it not?

"Madame la duchesse," a woman's voice reached her, and Fleur stared at the figure that emerged from an adjacent room. Whatever she had expected, this was not it. La Voisin was an imposing, curvaceous female dressed in a figure-hugging crimson velvet gown that stood out in stark contrast to the decoration of the salon.

"Madame Monvoisin," Marianne rose, as did Fleur, and the woman inclined her head briefly.

"Please take a seat again." La Voisin gestured at the settee.

Fleur lowered herself again into the thickly cushioned comfort. A soothing environment, were it not for the lack of

184

any personal items. No books or figurines, no sign of the woman's daily life. In fact, the black drapes made it resemble an unlit cave.

La Voisin sat on a single armchair next to their settee and folded her hands in her lap. In her forties, she gave the impression of a woman of business. But despite the smile, Fleur noticed cold, dark-brown eyes apprising her.

"What can I do for you, madame?"

Marianne cleared her throat. "We have a rather…delicate matter to attend to, madame. My friend here, whose name I'd rather not share, is looking for something to, umm, rid herself of someone."

"A rival?" La Voisin's eyes never left Fleur's face.

"No, nothing like that. A man," Marianne clarified.

"A former lover?"

Fleur took a sharp breath, and La Voisin laughed out loud. Goosebumps rose on her skin. This woman was as cold as the slate on a grave.

"I see."

"I believe you can assist us." Marianne's voice sounded confident. How often had she sought the woman's help?

Best not to dwell on that now.

La Voisin smiled thinly. "I can. But first, I will need to see the girl's hands."

"Why?" Fleur folded her hands in her lap. What did this mean?

"To find out the best way to achieve that what you wish for, my dear. Please join me over there." She walked to a small round table covered with a black silk cloth.

Fleur exchanged a glance with Marianne, who nodded. "It's fine. Nothing will befall you."

La Voisin's mouth twitched as Fleur followed her and sat in a chair opposite. Up close, the chill in her eyes became more obvious.

As if she were dead inside.

La Voisin reached forward and took her wrists, then she studied her hands, first on the back, tracing each finger. Then she turned Fleur's hands over, her thumb following the lines in Fleur's palm.

"Interesting," she whispered. "Very interesting."

Fleur stared at her. "Really? What is?" She looked at her palm, but it looked normal to her.

La Voisin regarded her with half-closed lids. "You've been through much."

If you only knew…

"Like many people in Paris," Fleur said.

A spark of admiration appeared in the woman's eyes, and she straightened. "Absolutely. You are not the first, nor shall you be the last. Hmm." Her index finger traced a broken line. "A man – young, virile – promised marriage."

Fleur held her breath. This could also be true for half of Paris.

"But there's more." La Voisin looked Fleur up and down, her gaze coming to rest on Fleur's stomach.

Fleur blinked.

"He left you with child."

"How do you—?" Fleur wanted to pull her hands away, but intrigued, she kept them in La Voisin's firm grip.

"That's why people come to me. I know everything!" A challenging glance met hers, and Fleur averted her eyes. The confidence the woman exuded was far above her station.

Just how did she know what happened?

"Now you're seeking revenge for your loss of innocence. Men of good standing would no longer wish to wed you."

"I don't want to marry," Fleur said.

"That's fair. Look after yourself." La Voisin brought Fleur's left hand closer to her face, staring at something. Her finger followed a line that reached towards Fleur's wrist. "See this?"

Fleur nodded.

"This brings you power. Much power." Cold eyes appraised her again, and Fleur felt like a piece of meat on a butcher's table. "Someone of high importance protects you." La Voisin glanced at Marianne, who'd remained on the settee. "Someone even higher than you, Your Grace."

"Who do you mean?"

"Ah, it's not that detailed, but let me tell you – this person has much influence. My guess would be someone close to the king."

Fleur gasped, and repeated, "Close to the king…?"

A sly smile appeared on La Voisin's lips, then she whispered, "Perhaps even the king himself."

"He has spoken to her, several times, in recent months," Marianne said.

"Good. That means that whatever happens, whatever you do, you shall be safe. This line here implies a long life."

"Wait! Safe from what?" Fleur was looking from one woman to the other.

"Persecution!" La Voisin smiled. She folded up Fleur's palm and placed her hand on the table. Then she leaned back.

Fleur's mind was in turmoil. "Why would I be—?" Then it dawned on her.

She would poison Philippe and get her revenge on Mother. She would turn into a criminal.

Marianne stared at her. "'Tis not without risks, this."

"I know." Her voice croaked, and she cleared her throat. It was what she wanted, what she'd been working towards this past year. Nothing would stop her now, least of all a darned conscience.

Fleur met La Voisin's gaze. "I believe you have something for me?"

The older woman grinned. "If you would like to wait a moment, I shall return." She disappeared through the door she'd entered, and Fleur heard steps sounding on the wooden floor beyond the door.

Fleur closed her eyes, remembering Philippe's sweet words, his touch, the joining of their bodies. She'd been happy. Then a baby's cry sounded from outside, and her mind returned to the birth of her son – a boy she'd not even cast eyes on. A child that likely had fallen victim to a dark trade.

Briefly Fleur wondered if La Voisin was also involved in the black masses, but then she shrugged off the thought. Would simple fortune-tellers take part in something so ghastly?

Marianne had risen and placed a hand on Fleur's shoulder. "Are you certain you wish to follow this through?"

She patted Marianne's hand. "Yes, I am."

The waiting is over.

Chapter Nineteen

Late May, 1677
Château de Versailles

Fleur's nerves were fraught as she rose from the curtsey, smiling at King Louis. "Your Majesty."

"Walk with me, young lady." He held out his arm, and Fleur placed her hand on it.

"As you wish."

She sent a quick sideways glance at Marianne, who smiled pointedly. Then she walked past rows and rows of courtiers. Fleur's heart pounded in her ears, and she hoped the king did not feel her shaking.

"I'm delighted to see you so often recently, here at Versailles, Mademoiselle Rose." He looked at her encouragingly.

"Who would not wish to be here, Your Majesty?"

Lines creased his sharp eyes, but despite being almost forty years of age, he exuded power and raw masculinity. She found his company mesmerising.

He laughed. "Oh, I can think of a few. But let's not dwell on them. My good friend, the brilliant Marianne, has taken you under her wing, and I'm glad she has. You will have learnt much about court, about politics, and the games everyone plays here, I'm certain."

Fleur smiled. "Yes, Madame la duchesse has enlightened me on so many subjects, I feel like I've discovered a different earth."

"I take this as a compliment." The corners of his mouth quivered.

"That it is, Your Majesty." As they walked from one *salle* to another, Fleur became aware of the stares from the courtiers, among them many faces she recognised. Some seemed surprised, but others showed envy and even jealousy. Fleur was in a position many women desperately wanted to be. She was not sure if she should delight in her small victory or worry.

"Will you grant me a dance, tonight?"

Her breath hitched. "Of course. It will be my pleasure."

Would Philippe see her? Or Mother? Then she remembered that Sophie had not been to court in weeks. Had something befallen her?

Finally, they reached the dais where the queen waited, watching them with her mouth pursed.

The king turned to face Fleur. "Stay near. I shall call you when I'm ready." He inclined his head and slowly released her hand.

"Yes, Your Majesty. I will wait right here." She curtseyed deep.

After a final glance, he turned and joined his wife. Fleur felt a flicker of sympathy for the queen. It could not be easy, being married to a king such as Louis, with his dominant character, the many mistresses, and an ever-growing number of children.

"Here," Marianne handed her crystal glass of wine, "drink! You need it."

"Thank you." Thoughts were hurtling through her head. She leaned close to the duchess. "He wishes to dance with me."

"That's wonderful. It means we can now set out plan in motion."

"Our plan? But how?"

"Leave it with me, dear Fleur. Relish your dance!" With a knowing smile, Marianne vanished into the crowd.

Soon, Fleur lost trace of her. Suddenly, she felt alone and vulnerable. The people around her were strangers. And whilst she had spoken to dozens of courtiers since her return to Versailles, she'd not become close to anyone. They were all too shallow.

In stark contrast, the witty exchanges at Marguerite's soirées always made up for the banality of courtiers. Uncle Marin was not the only writer attending, though the only one in residence, and there was always an array of visiting artists and musicians. Fleur preferred the evenings in rue Beauregard to the nights at Versailles, but she'd attend court until she succeeded in her revenge.

Sipping the wine, she watched as the crowd of courtiers parted in front of her, just as the musicians began to play.

Then he arrived. King Louis gave a deep bow in front of her, and she curtseyed low. Someone took her glass, and she placed her hand in his. Never had she anticipated that she would be this close, and even less so to be chosen to open the evening's dancing with him. But any initial concerns evaporated into the air as they walked, in time to the music, to the centre of the *salle*. The Sun King knew how to put the women at his side at ease.

In the early days of her stay at Marianne's, the duchess had enlisted the help of an acquaintance, a music instructor, and Fleur had practiced all the dances of the court with him. Much to her own surprise, Fleur found she gained great pleasure from it.

The king was an excellent dancer. His grace and flowing movements enchanted everyone, and although he no longer performed in plays, his enjoyment still showed.

King Louis' gaze never left hers. Blood rushed through her veins, and a strange sense of power took hold of her. This was not at all what she'd expected when she returned to court as Marianne's *accompagnante*, but if it aided her plan, then she would cope with it. She'd coped with a lot worse.

Fleur brushed aside all intrusive thoughts and, returning the king's smile, focused on the steps.

As they neared each other, he whispered, "I know your real name."

Fleur stared at him for a moment, uncertain of how to react. His smile did not falter. He did not seem angry at all.

"Marianne explained your, er, situation." He whirled around, and she followed his lead. "After today, your lady mother can no longer threaten you. You have nothing to fear

191

from her."

Fleur breathed a sigh of relief. The duchess had used Sophie's plans to reveal her identity, but it did not appear she had shared Fleur's plan of revenge on Philippe de Mortain.

She blinked. "Thank you, Your Majesty. I am in your debt."

Whatever that may entail…

He must have read her mind as he grinned. "Fear not, dear *Rose*! Whilst I'm very tempted to get to know you a little better, I'm sadly too busy at the moment. But who knows, perhaps one day, we might dance again. I would enjoy that."

Relief flooded through her, and gratitude to his mistresses for keeping him entertained enough. As she stepped towards him again, she whispered, "We may, yes. In the meantime, Your Majesty, please accept my gratitude."

He nodded. "I shall. By the way, I know your lady mother is in this room, in a far corner."

Fleur held her breath, then released it when he pressed her hand. "Where? Has she seen me?"

"She most assuredly has." He winked. "As you probably know, I enjoy a good intrigue. You see, when I we walked earlier, I made certain that we passed your mother. She is by the little water fountain over there, if you care to look."

During another movement, Fleur's gaze fell upon Sophie, who was glaring at her. She swivelled around, avoiding direct eye contact. The shock on Mother's face had been enough to make Fleur giddy with joy inside.

"She doesn't look content, Your Majesty," she observed drily.

The king laughed out loud, and several dancing couples turned to look. "Question is, are you, at seeing her so… furious?"

Fleur smirked. "Yes."

"Then our work is done. But don't forget to thank Marianne. 'Tis all my dear friend's doing."

"I shall, Your Majesty."

They fell into companionable silence, focusing instead on music and movement. Dancing with the king felt like she was floating on clouds. Fleur's breathing steadied, and she knew she had one concern less.

Then, as she turned, her gaze met the thunderous blue stare of Philippe de Mortain. He stood, mouth gaping open, near the door to the anteroom. Was he jealous? A surge of satisfaction swept through her.

After the next step, she looked back at him. He emptied his glass of wine and waved over a footman – the one she'd been charming on Marianne's instructions – who handed him another. Philippe took the glass and swallowed the contents whole.

Ooh, he must be jealous. Fleur rejoiced inwardly.

The footman removed the glass and moved away swiftly, without offering another. Moments later, Philippe clutched his stomach, and his face turned into a grimace. He glared at her, then, pushing aside everyone in his path, rushed out the doors to the terrace.

The dance came to the end, and Fleur met the king's gaze again. A glint of speculation shone in his eyes. Had he witnessed Philippe's strange behaviour? No, he would not know him at all, and Philippe had not been in the king's line of vision.

"Is everything in order, Fleur?" King Louis whispered as he bowed.

"Yes, Your Majesty, thank you." She dropped into a deep curtsey, a smile playing on her lips.

It is now.

***

Paris

Jacques walked through the middle floor of the three-storey house – their charity school, with Ninou in charge. A sense of pride surged through him.

Even Claudette had been forthcoming with advice on how to run an establishment – albeit of a very different kind – and Ninou had gradually gained in confidence. Initially, two nuns from the convent of the Ursulines would assist her in daily classes, which would comprise girls from middle class and poorer families.

It had taken much of his negotiations skills to convince the nuns that education of girls outside a convent was acceptable. Eventually, they had seen reason when he explained that many particularly poor parents would not wish for their children to stay in a convent all week.

So this house had become a compromise. Classes would be in the mornings, leaving the children enough time to help their parents for the rest of the day.

"How can I thank you, Jacques?" Ninou covered her nose and mouth with her hand. "This is a dream come true."

"No need to thank me, but our benefactor. And no, I don't know his or her name. But the lawyers have confirmed everything is legal and in order, and in place for the next ten years, costs included. From Monday, your school will be open."

Ninou beamed. "My school." Tears shimmered in her eyes.

"Our school." Jeanne had joined them, having been upstairs to inspect the four bedrooms. Mother and daughter would share a chamber, and they would use a sitting room downstairs for their personal space. Three other bedrooms were available for girls who lived too far away to return home after classes had ended each day. A small kitchen lean-to was at the back of the building where a cook would prepare breakfast and dinner.

"Yes, Jeanne. Make sure to help your mother when needed," Jacques said.

The girl rolled her eyes, and he laughed, pleased for them.

He grinned, then grabbed his hat from a desk where he'd thrown it onto when he entered the classroom – one of two on this floor. "I'll let you settle in. La Reynie will wonder where I am." He held out a bunch of keys to Ninou. "Good luck!"

"You will visit us, sometimes, won't you?" Her voice trembled as she took them off him.

"Yes, I shall, though not as often as in recent months, now that all your belongings are here." *And more children are off the streets...*

Jacques knew that Ninou had developed feelings for him – which he put down to him having helped her escape from her old life and given her a future. Did he reciprocate? He was uncertain. In his line of work, he had no time for a serious relationship, nor did he have the means to support a family. No, 'twas best everything stayed the way it was– a close friendship.

"You know where to find me should you need anything."

As he walked towards the Châtelet, he pulled his hat lower, braving the spring gales. Drizzle covered his skin in moments. Part of him felt relieved at being able to focus on actual cases from now on, no longer chasing children. The school would thrive, he was certain.

His mind returned to the revelations Magdelaine de La Grange had made. After weeks of interrogation, they had taken her to the Conciergerie, yet there remained plenty of doubts to her story. The details she shared of a plan to poison a high political figure – such as the king – had been vague. But even so, her ramblings could not be dismissed out of hand, and La Reynie had tasked Jacques with shadowing several of her associates.

For the past few weeks, he'd been tracing the steps of various well-known alchemists and fortune-tellers, but so far he'd found nothing untoward.

La Reynie, usually a man not taken to emotions, had confessed that he had a feeling that there was a network of poisoners active in Paris. Individuals or even entire families died suddenly without explanation over the space of mere months. When Jacques made further enquiries, though, mouths stayed shut. It was the pox, or a fever, they claimed.

The lack of evidence frustrated him.

Jacques walked along the corridor to La Reynie's office when he saw Desgrez close the door behind him. "Ah, just the man I was looking for."

"Me? Why? Has there been a development?"

"Possibly. The Lieutenant General wants us to ride to Versailles. He's given me enough funds so we can stay at an inn overnight."

"What…now?"

Desgrez nodded, scraping back his floppy, greasy fringe from his eyes. "Yes. They found a young man in a copse in the palace gardens, dead. Monsieur de La Reynie thinks this may be linked to our investigations. Did you wish to speak to him about something in particular?"

"No. I was merely stopping by to see if he had news to share."

"Ah, good. None other than this suspicious death. Come with me! Horses are already being made ready for us as we speak."

As Jacques followed Desgrez out into the yard, his mind was whirling. "Why are we getting involved? Surely, Versailles is outside our jurisdiction?"

"It is." Desgrez stopped, waiting for a stable boy who was leading two horses towards them. Desgrez lowered his voice. "The young man in question relieved himself as he died. Eyewitnesses claim that he'd clutched his stomach moments earlier as he fled the palace and into the gardens. Yet up to that point in time, he'd not shown any signs of feeling unwell."

"Ah." Poison. Jacques did not need to say the word out loud. The look his colleague sent him confirmed his suspicion. He took the reins of a grey gelding from the boy. "Thank you."

"Let's go."

Soon after, they left the outskirts of Paris behind and headed west. They did not waste time to collect any belongings, preferring to arrive before it turned dark. Most of the morning had passed already, but with the wind in their back, they would make swift progress and arrive in Versailles in time for the evening's entertainment.

Desgrez remained silent for most of their journey, which suited Jacques well. Conflicting thoughts tumbled through his head. So far they'd assumed the poisoners were active in Paris, amongst the middle and lower classes where superstitions and faith in the effect of potions prevailed. Greed was another reason, especially behind poisonings, but it had not occurred to him that courtiers could be amongst the suspects.

Those people might have even more to lose – or gain.

He was also beginning to wonder if Fleur had been at the palace at that time. Accompanying a popular duchess, herself a *confidante* of the king, would likely see Fleur attending events regularly. Jacques would never have guessed that the girl's uncle, the writer, had such influential benefactors who'd be happy to extend their generosity to his niece.

But why would they do that? Fleur had no skills to earn her living, and he doubted that she'd be helping with the sewing.

Gritting his teeth, he remembered the last contact they'd had. It was in the last winter that he'd received a note from Fleur, an invitation to an evening of Marin de La Fontaine's latest musings at the Marquise de La Sablière's fashionable salon. But Jacques had felt uncomfortable with the prospect of mingling with aristocratic ladies and lords, and he had little time for literature. He preferred to be active and create items with his hands whenever time permitted. Not for him, endless evenings enclosed indoors, mulling over words that bore no meaning to him. Therefore, he'd declined – and not heard from her since.

And to think he'd even considered asking for her hand, even though he knew he did not earn enough to support her. Jacques had thought they were close; that she trusted him. At Claudette's, she'd been part of their extended family – a family of friends he had chosen. But that was not enough to plan a future for Fleur and him.

Of course Fleur was of a different world – one into which he'd been born and where he'd grown up in, but which was no longer his. Now, he recognised the false smiles and unkept promises of the upper classes for what they were: mere proof of the entitlement and self-importance the gentry felt. It was a world Jacques had no desire to return to, with or without Fleur.

Following the move to rue de Sainte-Foy, Jaques had relished his leather work, often creating new pieces well into the night. Where he grew up, in the manor that had been in Montagnac family hands for generations, he'd not been permitted to do anything manual. Lessons always involved theory, never practice. His late mother's dearest wish had been that he joined the Church – an idea he abhorred, even more so since he discovered the clandestine involvement of priests and nuns in the murder of infants.

The only trait he shared with his mother was to ensure children came off the streets and found worthy employment. At least in this respect, she'd be pleased. It made him proud to see them learn valuable skills.

But with a heavy heart, he remembered that he rarely heard Fleur speak about her own son. Jacques hoped she'd recover one day, and for her to attend *soirées* and readings, it was surely a sign that she moved on.

Not having caught Abbé Guibourg in the act of child abduction had grated on Jacques ever since La Reynie had set him the task of getting children off the streets. The few times he'd followed the priest had been a waste of time. As if someone had warned Guibourg. After a few weeks of sleepless nights, Jacques had given up.

Now, he might see Fleur again. The thought should have elated him, but he felt almost indifferent. What had changed?

As he and Desgrez neared the palace, they slowed their horses from a run to a trot. They had headed there first, before seeking lodgings for the night in the village. The sun stood low in the sky, and the wind had calmed. It was the perfect late afternoon, yet a sense of foreboding gripped Jacques as he stared at the palace with its new wings.

"It's massive!" His jaw dropped. How could a hunting lodge turn into such a large building so swiftly?

Desgrez grinned. "Yes, that it is. Have you been here before?"

Jacques nodded. "Years ago, when I first came to Paris. It has changed much."

"It makes you wonder where the money for all this comes

from…" His colleague mused. "With the continuous wars and never-ending building works, I'm surprised the king has not run out of funds."

"Well, he had to accept terms once or twice on grounds of cost." Jacques laughed.

But as the walls of Versailles grew closer, his mood turned morose. If poison had caused the young man's death, it was likely he'd have to spend more time here.

His gut wrenching, Jacques fervently hoped that the suspects did not include Fleur.

Chapter Twenty

Château de Versailles

"It is so peaceful here," Fleur mused, looking at Marianne. "Yet I sense so many undercurrents waiting to swallow you whole."

"You're quite the poet yourself, Fleur." The duchess smiled. "Perhaps you should write too."

Fleur sat with Marianne on cushioned chairs near a fountain in the palace gardens. The spring sunshine warmed her skin. Soon, it would be too hot to venture out of doors in the afternoon. She lowered the book of poetry from which she'd been reading earlier into her lap and slotted a sheet of paper in to mark the page.

The last poem she'd recited was rather dark, foreboding, and it suited her mood. Now, memories returned. Ever since the previous night, on hearing of Philippe's dramatic demise, she'd not been able to eat a morsel. It did not help that the duchess refused to talk about the turn of events.

Did I really want him dead?

Fleur knew that she'd communicated that wish clearly, yet in the light of day guilt had crept in. But Marianne was right. They must not appear to be affected by his death.

A lady leading an entourage of six chattering women wandered over and stopped beside Marianne's chair. Madame de Montespan, the king's mistress of many years and mother of half a dozen – now legitimised – children.

There was something about the woman that made Fleur's skin crawl. She was definitely one who created plenty of undercurrents at Versailles. Outwardly, La Montespan displayed poise and grace, but beneath the surface, Fleur saw an overbearing sense of entitlement.

You don't want her as an enemy…

The woman brushed back a few strands that had escaped the dark-blonde hair piled up high and decorated with pearls. The pale-yellow gown embellished with lace, bows and precious stones encased a round figure that almost burst out of the seams. Of course, the marquise had only months earlier given birth to yet another daughter.

The marquise leaned closer to Marianne's ear, and Fleur averted her gaze from the lady's bosom that tried to escape its confinement. She was grateful that her fan covered the smirk she could not suppress.

"Have you heard what happened last night?" La Montespan's eyes sparkled with excitement Fleur deemed misplaced, and she sobered.

"About that poor young man? Yes, we have. A tragic situation, isn't it?" Marianne glanced solemnly at the woman.

Fleur tried hard not to fan herself too furiously to hide her shaking hand. They should not have come here today. Soon, everyone would know.

"Word has it he was…" glancing over her shoulder, the marquise lowered her voice as she hovered, "poisoned. Isn't that…incredible?"

"Quite so, dearest Athénaïs," Marianne replied. "What a frightful way to depart this life!"

La Montespan clearly saw Marianne's response as an invitation to join them. At her signal, a lady in her entourage rushed to pick up a vacant chair nearby and placed it beside the duchess. Only a nervous twitch in the corner of Marianne's mouth showed Fleur that she was not content with this. But it would be unforgivable to take their leave the moment the king's mistress joined them.

"I'd wager it was a spurned lover. He was a pretty boy, they say." She raised a delicately plucked eyebrow. "Although I'm told he leaves a young wife and an infant."

"He does, apparently." Marianne gave a sad smile.

"What's the poor girl going to do? A babe, and no husband?" The marquise tutted, clutching the pearls at her neck.

Fleur wanted to roll her eyes at the drama. To her, La Montespan's behaviour was a performance. She was expecting a reaction. But from Fleur and Marianne, she received none.

"Oh, but she's one of the Bruns," Marianne said, her voice passive. "Her family will look after her until they can marry her off to another man once six months of mourning have passed." The duchess leaned back in her chair.

The marquise sighed. "Sometimes I wish I knew every person who attends court. And I mean that." She giggled. "That way we knew for certain what has befallen that beautiful young man. But you know how it is, Marianne…"

"I do. One cannot be in all places at all times, Athénaïs. We would not have enough time to spend with everybody. Isn't that right, Fleur?"

Blinking, Fleur nodded, aware of the marquise's eyes on her. The woman was taking her measure.

"Oh yes." Fleur lowered her gaze to stare at the book lying forgotten in her lap.

"What have you been reading? Anything of note?"

"Nothing new. Merely a collection of poetry by Marin de La Fontaine, the uncle of my *accompagnante*," Marianne said.

"Your uncle? How intriguing." La Montespan smirked. "Is he still in residence at Marguerite de La Sablière's house? That particular habit appears to run in the family." A glint appeared in her eyes. "Well, as long as you don't think you would have the remotest chance to become His Majesty's next favourite…"

If looks could kill… Then Fleur remembered her dance with the king the night before.

Is the famous Madame de Montespan jealous?

She returned the gaze with a smile. "A favourite? Me? You jest, Madame la marquise."

In the corner of her eye she saw Marianne's mouth twitch again, and she knew she'd responded correctly. Clearly, the horrible woman had meant her comment as a threat. Had she threatened other mistresses in the same manner?

How far would she go?

A chill ran down Fleur's spine as La Montespan held her gaze, then rose. Turning to the duchess, she said, "I must dash, dear Marianne. Be well and keep an eye on your little companion. As we saw last night, you never know what might happen…"

With a whoosh of her skirts, the king's favourite continued her stroll, and the giggle of her women at something she said as she walked away reached them.

"Don't pay any attention to her, Fleur. She is terrified of losing her position."

"I can imagine. Those other ladies the king visits must give her constant headaches."

Marianne laughed out loud. "Just look at the woman. She has been putting on so much weight that she is turning into a caricature of herself."

Fleur felt a flicker of sympathy for the king's favourite. It cannot be easy to be pregnant almost year on year whilst trying everything in your power to hold his interest.

What would I do if he asked me? She'd have no choice. *You cannot deny a king.*

She prayed it would not come to that.

As her gaze followed the marquise and her entourage, she noticed they'd stopped by the path that led to the copse where Philippe had seduced her – and where he'd died. The irony was not lost on her. What was he thinking when he fled there? Had he realised it was her revenge?

Two men emerged from the path and strode towards Madame de Montespan, who swiftly engaged them in conversation. Then she pointedly looked over to where Fleur and Marianne sat.

Fleur shielded her eyes from the glare of the sun and squinted. If only she knew what was being said. She gasped when the men walked in her direction. Then, to her horror, she recognised him.

"Jacques!" she whispered.

"What? Where?" Marianne followed her gaze. "Do you think La Reynie sent him to investigate?"

Fleur stared at the duchess. "Yes. That would make sense." She bit her lip. "It means they are suspecting poison."

Marianne patted Fleur's hand that clutched the book. "That means nothing, Fleur."

"But he knows of Philippe."

"He has no proof. You, my dear, were dancing with His Majesty himself when that silly young man ran outside. No one can associate you with it."

"What if Jacques hears about the footman?"

A smile played on Marianne's lips. "The good man should by now be halfway to Lombardy, with a nice little parting gift from me."

"He's what?" Fleur's eyes widened. Now, she was even more in the duchess's debt. A sense of unease gripped her. "But how can I ever thank you?"

"There is no need. I'm serious." Marianne leaned back in her seat as Jacques and the other man approached. "I enjoy helping friends in trouble."

Fleur's mind was still in turmoil, but the duchess's words sank in and her breathing calmed. No one would see the link. Her visit to La Voisin had been months ago, and they had been careful to hide their faces. And with the young footman out of the picture...

She smiled when Jacques stopped in front of their seats and bowed. "Madame la duchesse. Mademoiselle de La Fontaine."

"Hello Jacques. It's good to see you," Fleur said. Absent-mindedly, she put her hand over her heart, feeling it race. It had been too long since they last met. He looked well, and content. She brushed aside an unwanted sense of jealousy and closed her fan, not wishing to hide her face from him.

"Good afternoon," Marianne said, beaming at him. "So, you are the man who helped dear Fleur escape from her tormentors? How wonderful to meet you finally."

"The pleasure is all mine, Your Grace. Unfortunately, we're not here for our amusement. This is Monsieur Desgrez from the Police in Paris."

The other man, a few years older and bulkier than Jacques,

bowed. "Your Grace. Mademoiselle de La Fontaine. You must have heard of last night's…unfortunate incident?"

Marianne nodded, then covered her throat with her hand. "Yes. So tragic. To pass away at the height of your youth."

Jacques' gaze did not leave Fleur's face. "You know who he was, of course. Don't you?"

"Yes. Poor Philippe." She returned his look evenly. "What happened?"

"We're still trying to form a picture. From what Monsieur Desgrez and I have seen, there are no outward signs on his body that may hint at a violent attack."

"You've seen him?" Fleur gasped.

Desgrez nodded. "Yes, just after we arrived. His mortal remains are kept in a cellar in the palace. Tomorrow the morning, they will move him to the Hôpital de la Charité for a closer inspection of his guts."

Fleur swallowed under Jacques' scrutiny. "What does that mean?"

"He will be cut open and his organs removed. If they show any signs of an anomaly, someone likely poisoned him."

"What? Here at Versailles?" Marianne glanced around as if a suspect was hovering nearby. "What about the king? If it was the food…"

"No need to concern yourself, Your Grace. It can't have been the food or the wine as many courtiers have partaken of the same," Jacques said.

"But we will still speak to the chefs and serving staff, as a matter of routine." Desgrez' jaw was set. "We can't rule out anything yet."

As Fleur nodded her understanding, relief flooded through her that the footman was far away.

***

"Did you notice anything unusual last night?" Jacques asked, looking from the Duchess de Bouillon to Fleur.

Both shook their heads. Then the duchess patted Fleur's arm, smiling indulgently. "Well, apart from the fact that this

205

young lady here danced with the king. So she might not remember anything else at all."

"Is it true?" What did he expect, now that she spent her time in the company of courtiers, back at Versailles where she belonged? He had not wanted to believe Madame de Montespan when she'd told them moments earlier. "How did that happen?"

Looking at Fleur, he had to admit she'd done well for herself. No longer the simple dresses from the time at Claudette's; the exquisite gown she wore now was of a much higher quality. Strands of her blonde hair fell in soft curls over her exposed shoulders. She was like a vision. Out of his reach…

Yet he could not find the answer to a niggling doubt in his mind: Why would the Duchess de Bouillon support a young, penniless girl whose mother was spending her inheritance?

From his work with the charity schools, Jacques knew that benefactors came in many guises, but they usually expected to see positive results. What did Fleur have to give the duchess in exchange?

"He asked me." Fleur blushed, averting her gaze. It jolted him back to the present. "It was only the one dance."

"That's a great honour, but how did he know of you? I mean, not that you don't deserve to be noticed by His Majesty, but…" His thoughts were running wild. Whatever next? Would Fleur become King Louis' mistress?

"Jacques," Fleur leaned forward and took his hand between hers, repeating, "it was merely a dance."

"But one at an interesting time, from what we've gathered from the Marquise de Montespan," Desgrez said, his tone suggestive.

Fleur dropped Jacques' hand, and he crossed his arms, feeling the bond they'd shared for so long dissolve. "As the king distracted you, you saw nothing unusual, Fleur? Madame la duchesse?" He kept his tone calm.

"No, it would have been rude to focus my attention away from His Majesty," Fleur said sharply, then glanced at the duchess.

"I for one was chatting to my sister, Olympe, when Fleur was dancing with the king. We were admiring how well they moved together. But I was later told that, by strange coincidence, it was at that moment the young man took ill and left the *salle*. Is it true?" The older lady looked alarmed.

"That's what we believe, Your Grace," Jacques said. "There was a bit of a commotion, apparently."

The duchess shrugged. "Oh. I'm afraid I can't help you…"

Jacques frowned. "Never mind," he said through gritted teeth. "Several courtiers noticed Monsieur de Mortain rush outside, clutching his stomach."

"So it was the food!" The woman's eyes blazed, and she placed a hand on her stomach.

"Perhaps," Desgrez mused, then turned to him. "Jacques, I think that's all the questions we have for now. It's time we headed to the kitchens."

"Yes, of course, François. Madame la duchesse. Fleur." He gave a slight bow. "I wish you a pleasant afternoon, despite the…unfortunate…events."

Fleur blinked as he straightened, and his expression softened.

"Goodbye, Jacques," she said, then she opened and closed her mouth as if she'd wanted to add something.

"I shall pay you a visit soon if I may," he suggested.

She smiled, nodding. "That would be lovely. I will send you an invitation to our next soirée."

"I shall attend, thank you." He would have to overcome his reluctance and go. If only to see her again. But was that really what he wanted?

As Jacques walked with Desgrez to the back of the palace, where the kitchen buildings were located, he tried to make sense of what they'd learnt so far.

"One. They found the body in a small clearing surrounded by trees, but within easy reach from the terrace where several courtiers had seen him." He counted with his fingers. "Two. Although people thought he was unwell, no one took the trouble to follow him. Why?"

"It's truly telling behaviour," Desgrez interjected.

"It is. They're not a caring bunch, these courtiers. Which leads us to point three – his dead body was found hours later by a couple seeking, er, privacy."

Desgrez grinned. "That spot seems to have been popular with people retiring from the crowds."

"Yes, that's my impression as well." A thought struck him. Was that the place where Mortain had seduced Fleur? "I should have asked Fleur if she was familiar with the location."

"Check with her when you accept her invite, Jacques."

He laughed. "I'll do that, though listening to hours of literary waffle might send me to sleep before I get the chance." He sobered, continuing his count. "Four, the poor man had shat himself before he died—"

"Or during?"

"A good point. It is possible. In any event, that would imply he'd consumed something that didn't agree with him."

"And more than merely the wine, I'd wager."

Jacques nodded. "It'll be interesting to see what they discover when they cut him open. Five, if it is indeed poison, who wanted him dead?"

"What was he like? From what you've told us, he was a wastrel."

"Yes, he was. He took advantage of her, and no doubt of many other girls at court or elsewhere. But we have no way of discovering who. Their families would've hushed it up."

"But he was married."

"That was after Fleur's...misadventure. She came across him fumbling with his fiancée in a...clearing." He stopped.

"Like the one where he fled to?"

Could it be? If yes, Fleur was a firm suspect. "Possibly. It will be worth finding out. Then there's point six." He stared at the tall windows and the embellished façade of the palace.

"Which is?"

Jacques' eyes met his colleague's. "Where did they get the poison?"

They continued to walk.

"That brings us back to our lovely bunch of fortune-tellers, false priests, and other persons peddling dubious wares."

"It does. When we're back in Paris, I shall watch Abbé Guibourg again. He seemed to have become more circumspect in his activities."

"That makes sense. And the nuns with whom he conducted his 'business'?"

"I'm certain they're still helping young ladies in need, for coin and an infant to sell." It galled him that he had not been able to gather the evidence he needed to present to La Reynie. These people were getting away with murder, and there was nothing he could do to stop them.

They were not dumb, these charlatans. They'd concealed their activities, so the Lieutenant General and all his spies across Paris could not find proof.

"We're here." Desgrez mounted the few steps to the entrance of the main kitchen. "Let's see if we can add to your list."

Jacques followed him inside, where a major-domo was already waiting for them. He led the way into a tiny office and closed the door behind them.

"Monsieur, thank you for agreeing to meet us," Desgrez said, taking a chair indicated.

Jacques leaned against the wall, more comfortable to watch whilst standing up.

The steward threw his hands in the air, an expression of annoyance on his flabby features. "I don't know why you're here. Our food and wine is above reproach."

"That's for us to decide. As you know, the Lieutenant General sent us. Therefore, we appreciate your cooperation."

"Of course, of course." The man wiped a speck of dust from the desk behind which he sat. Then he shifted a bundle of loose papers and ledgers to his left, piling them up. Finally, he leaned forward on his elbows and folded his hands. "What would you like to know?"

"Did you know the dead man, Philippe de Mortain?"

The major-domo shook his head. "No. I don't really know any of the courtiers, except for the royal family and a number of dukes and duchesses."

"So you've never seen him?" Desgrez asked.

"No."

"What did you serve at the time of his death, which occurred around eight of the clock?"

"Only wine, monsieur. His Majesty usually dines after the evening's entertainment, a tradition witnessed by many courtiers. They eat afterwards."

"We heard the king was dancing when witnesses say Philippe de Mortain fell ill."

"That's what I was told, too, because His Majesty asked us to delay his dinner due to this gruesome discovery."

"You were here?" Desgrez shifted in the chair.

"I'm always going back and forth in the evenings, so I could have been here, or not. My role is to convey the king's culinary wishes to the cooks, and to ensure he is satisfied with the quality of the food."

"I see." Desgrez' voice was dry.

Jacques suppressed a grin. Neither of them had time for the fanciful workings of the court. Their world was different.

"Therefore, I'm afraid I can't help you any further." The major-domo rose, but Jacques gestured to him to sit down again.

"The wine that you offer every night, what's the procedure?"

"We take vats from the cellars to various *salles*. The larger *ones* have tables where we set out dozens of filled glasses for people to pick up. In addition, footmen walk around, carrying trays which are regularly replenished."

Jacques exchanged a glance with Desgrez. "Do you have a list of names of all the footmen who worked last night?"

"I don't." The major-domo's cheeks grew red. "I saw this morning that last night's account was missing."

"When did you notice that?" Desgrez asked sharply.

"After the royal family had broken their fast."

"Who has a key to this office?"

The man's colour deepened. "No one. It's always unlocked. I've nothing to hide."

"Even with your valuable accounts here?"

"Oh, I lock the ledgers of expenditure into the sideboard over there every night."

"But not the staff lists?"

"No. They're usually on that shelf over there."

"That means anyone could've just walked in during the night and taken yesterday's sheet."

He nodded, his gaze lowered to stare at his fingernails.

"Now we can safely assume that someone plotted Mortain's death." Desgrez' expression was grim.

"Yes," Jacques agreed. "And whoever planned it had help amongst the staff."

"That means we have to revisit everyone he had a link to, including his wife – and Mademoiselle de La Fontaine."

"It appears so. His wife is in her country estate. I'm saying 'her' as it came with her dower. Fleur told me," he added when Desgrez sent him a questioning glance. "If you want to pursue the wife, I'll see if Fleur has more to say."

"Are you sure it shouldn't be the other way round?"

Jacques stopped.

Would I let Fleur get away with murder?

Chapter Twenty-One

June 29th, 1677
Rue Neuve-des-Petits-Champs, Paris

"Good evening, Monsieur de Montagnac. Please enter." The marquise welcomed Jacques warmly as he stepped over the threshold into the salon, and he inclined his head.

"Thank you for the invitation, Madame la marquise."

The room was as opulent as he'd imagined it, with large dark green drapes covering the tall windows. Portraits of what he assumed to be family members of Marguerite de La Sablière decorated the walls covered in costly tapestries.

"Ah, Jacques!" Fleur rushed up to him. "You've come."

"Fleur, it's lovely to see you again, and so soon after our last encounter." He took her hands in this, but still, he could not shake off the feeling that the bond they'd shared for so long was gone. He shrugged off his dark thoughts at the sight of her smile.

"Wonderful to see you too. Here," she took a glass of white wine from a table and handed it to him before she picked up one for herself, "refresh yourself. It's rather hot outside today." She opened her fan.

Her eyes were sparkling, and he hoped it was on his account, but Jacques was realistic enough not to harbour any such hopes. Looking around, he knew exactly why. Literary evenings were for those who did not work for a living. Heirs to fortunes, wives of men of station. Not people like him who got their hands dirty. She likely felt sympathy for him.

Fleur took his arm and led him across the room to a man old enough to be her father. Jacques could see a vague resemblance in the shape of Fleur's face and chin, but she did not share her uncle's long nose or thin mouth.

"Uncle Marin, this is Jacques de Montagnac – the man who saved my life."

Jacques felt uncomfortable at the reminder, but the older man took his hand and shook it, regarding him warmly. "Dear Monsieur, you shall forever have my gratitude. If only I'd have known in what dire circumstances my niece had found herself."

"It was fortunate that I was close by."

"Oh, but what a nasty woman my sister-in-law is. I've always promised to create a character that is just as evil as she is."

"That would be wonderful, Uncle Marin. And she would never know, as she abhors reading."

Marin de La Fontaine tutted. "You see, young man, my late brother adored books as much as I do. He amassed an extensive library – which your mother hopefully has not destroyed, Fleur – and used to publish fables and poetry, too. And I write. Sophie never did fit into our family. Fortunately, this young lady here is like a ray of sunshine."

Jacques nodded, smiling. He recognised a strong bond of affection between uncle and niece. As he watched La Fontaine extol Fleur's virtues – reading, and her love of music and dance – he noticed that the writer's clothes were rather simple, almost austere, despite the finery of the fabrics. He wondered how much the writer relied on the purses of his benefactors. The marquise had opened up her home to him years earlier, and the Duchess de Bouillon had also funded his publications, he'd discovered.

As La Fontaine excused himself to welcome further guests, Jacques observed those already gathered. Beneath the shine, he noticed several men's coats had been mended, and the gowns of a couple of women were of lower-quality fabrics.

So not everyone who came here was rich in funds.

"What amuses you, Jacques?" Fleur nudged him, pulling him out of his reverie.

"Am I amused?" He frowned.

"Yes. You were smiling." She hit his upper arm playfully

213

with her fan. "But I was watching you." Leaning closer to him, she lowered her voice. "You are trying to discover who our audience is."

Fleur knew him too well. He gave her a lopsided grin. "I'm curious, that's all. I've never been to a *soirée*."

"I know." She pouted. "Your visit tonight is long overdue." But beneath the playful exterior, sadness lurked in her eyes. Then it was gone, and she laughed.

"Oh, I'll just have to greet Marlise." She dashed across the room, taking the free hand of a plump, elderly lady who leaned heavily onto a walking stick, and took her to the nearest seat.

Jacques welcomed the break. It gave him time to think about something that puzzled him. Was she trying to distract him from the investigations? This was not the Fleur he remembered from Claudette's. The Fleur he encountered today was too cheerful for his liking. She put on a mask. But for what purpose?

Now, watching her in the environment she inhabited, Jacques wondered not for the first time if she was keeping something from him.

She was still angry at Guibourg – and, Jacques was certain, upset that he had not found proof to arrest the priest for the abduction of her child. And although she'd stopped asking him about Guibourg, instinct told him she had not truly moved on. Unfortunately, the priest was still not showing any obvious signs of dubious activities.

Jacques hated to disappoint Fleur. Perhaps that was why her current behaviour puzzled him. He sipped the wine. It was of excellent quality, bursting with freshness in his mouth.

Then, the marquise clapped her hands and bid everyone take a seat. He walked over to the other side of the room where five rows of chairs had been set up in a small, intimate semi-circle, and veered towards the back.

"No, Jacques. Please join me here." Fleur pointed at two seats at the front. "This is so exciting."

Reluctantly, he followed her, and they sat near the centre. Her cheeks held a heightened colour, or was that merely the *rouge* she applied? Contrasting with the whiteness of the face powder, her eyes glowed. Had she drunk too much wine? He looked at the glass in her hand. It was full. This was not the selfless, quiet girl who'd always put others first. Something in Fleur had changed, and he found it disconcerting.

"Uncle Marin is so nervous," she whispered. "He's about to reveal a new poem tonight. And we're the first to hear it."

Jacques smiled at her enthusiasm. "That's wonderful. I must admit I've never read your uncle's works."

"Then you must promise me to return soon again. It's all so…enlightening."

He nodded. "I'm certain it is." He racked his brain for something else to say, but there was nothing. They'd grown apart.

Perhaps we've never been close.

The thought filled him with sadness.

The marquise clapped her hands, and everyone took their seats. Jacques looked around.

"Is the Duchess de Bouillon not here tonight?" he asked Fleur.

She giggled. "No. Her nephew is visiting for a few days, which always means she's, er, preoccupied."

The rumours about the duchess having taken her nephew as her *amant* were true. He grinned. "Ah. I see. And where is her husband?"

"In the country, as always. He doesn't interfere in her life. Now you know why I'm staying at dear Marguerite's for a little while." Her smile wavered.

They pushed her from one to the other. Again, he wondered what interest the highborn ladies had in supporting Fleur. Unlike at Claudette's – where she had at least been sewing for her living – here she only sat around, greeted guests and made polite conversations. Was that what an *accompagnante* did? To keep you company and chat to you all day? Or was it only because she was the niece of a famous – if often destitute – writer, allowed to stay as a favour to him?

"Then you'll have time to spend with your uncle." He

215

tried to cheer her up.

"Yes, that's true."

As Marin de La Fontaine faced his audience, a hush descended on the room and several candelabra were extinguished, except around him.

Jacques leaned back, watching Fleur, and grew concerned. She was pale tonight, although it could be the powder she used. But he sensed that not all was well. Barely taking in the Marin de La Fontaine's words, Jacques' mind wandered again.

Perhaps Fleur knew something about Mortain's death after all, and it was eating away at her.

Later that night, he sought Claudette's company. He needed to talk. In her sitting room, small and simple in comparison with the marquise's salon, they sipped at glasses of red wine. He'd shared with her his conversation with Fleur, and his thoughts. Now, he was looking at the woman who had over a lifetime's experience with girls in need of help.

"You've lost her, Jacques," Claudette said. "I'm sorry." She picked up the carafe and refilled his glass.

"Thank you." He took another deep draught. "I don't think I ever 'had' her, as you put it."

"You're in love with her." A sad smile on her lips, she held up a hand when he opened his mouth. "No, don't deny it. I saw it in your eyes whenever you visited her." She sighed. "And I could've sworn she liked you too."

As the sudden heat in his cheeks receded, he nodded. Claudette was right. "That's what I dared to think, but looking back, it must've been gratitude, or something. I got her out of that nunnery." He paused, remembering, then met Claudette's calm gaze. "But I never found a trace of her boy."

"That's no reason to stop liking someone. She never accused you of ignoring his plight. Fact was, she knew that you staked out many nights by the church of Saint Marcel and outside the convent to catch them in the act. It's not your fault they covered their tracks and laid low. And then you had the order to gather the children off the streets, and I'm sure she approved of that."

"I don't know." He raked a hand through his hair. "I told her about Ninou and her new position at the school, and she barely acknowledged it. Yet, those two were good friends, I thought. Her mind is on other things these days. Poetry, music, chattering mindlessly."

Claudette frowned. "It's true, it doesn't sound like the Fleur we knew here, but the world at court is so different from ours. My contacts tell me Marin de La Fontaine's funds are constantly low, and both the marquise and the duchess keep supporting him. They seem to extend this courtesy to his niece. But when he has served his purpose – entertaining is costly, and even with their riches, their resources will not always be as available. What will then happen to Fleur?"

"I've concluded they will cast her out, eventually. Now, that might not happen for several years, so what purpose could she serve in the meantime?"

"Could they matchmake and suggest she marry someone to their advantage?"

"That's one possibility. But I fear worse." He emptied his glass and put it on the table.

Claudette leaned forward. "What?"

"I can't explain it, but I have a feeling that she's somehow involved in the murder of Philippe de Mortain, with the help of the Duchess de Bouillon."

"The rogue who left her pregnant?" Claudette folded her hands in front of her face, tapping her nose with her index finger. "She became a little obsessed, I think, near the end of her stay here. Bitter, almost. So it wouldn't surprise me. But you said she was dancing with the king when the bastard fell ill."

Claudette could not hide her contempt for Mortain. She had a low opinion of men who left young women with child.

"That's true, and confirmed by many witnesses, as are the whereabouts of the Duchess de Bouillon. But she didn't need to be the one administering the poison. We know one footman has disappeared without a trace."

"And you think he's dead?"

Jacques shrugged. "Possibly. Or they've rid themselves of him too."

***

Fleur paced the bedchamber. She'd changed into her nightgown, but sleep eluded her. Perhaps it had been the wine she'd consumed – following Jacques' departure moments after Uncle Marin had finished his recital, she'd gulped down three glasses.

He knows.

She'd seen it in his eyes. He was watching her all evening. What was she going to do?

Even Marguerite, usually kind and talkative, had not exchanged too many words with her tonight, although it had been kind of her to offer Fleur a room when Marianne had asked her.

Sitting on the edge of the bed, Fleur finally admitted to herself that she had nowhere of her own to go. For the past year, she'd brushed aside that thought, but now, her mind dulled by the wine, it returned.

Uncle Marin was always sweet and helpful, but he was not one to challenge Sophie on behalf of Fleur. And what would she inherit? Her mother was alive, spending it all on the young man who accompanied her at court. Fleur feared there would not be much left for her.

For now, staying in her new friends' company kept her safe. Both ladies were acquainted with the king, and that was one link her mother would heed, without doubt.

But what happened next? Philippe was dead – not by her hand, but she might as well have wielded a knife and stabbed it into his cold heart. With Marianne's help, she bought the poison at La Voisin. She toyed with the footman until he was willing to do their bidding. How much the duchess had paid him, Fleur had no idea.

She adored Marianne's vivacious nature. The woman cared not about conventions. She played no part in her

218

children's upbringing other than a brief daily visit before their bedtime. And although Marianne was only nine years older than Fleur, she seemed much more worldly.

"Something I'm seriously lacking," Fleur mumbled. Her gaze fell on to the mirror on the toilette table across the room.

Tired eyes looked back at her. Her long, dark hair hung limp over her shoulder. Spots had appeared on her skin from the regular use of powders and *rouge*. Before going to court, she'd never needed to cover her face in paint. Now, it sapped all the life from her skin.

What's happening to me?

Tears pricked her eyes. She slid beneath the cover. Blowing out the candle, she sighed as darkness descended on the room. A sliver of moonlight shone through a gap in the curtain which fluttered in the breeze. Breathing in deeply the fresh air, she fell into an exhausted sleep.

Chapter Twenty-Two

June 30th, 1677
Paris

Jacques left the house of Catherine Monvoisin, commonly known as La Voisin, on rue Beauregard with the distinct sense of needing to wash his hands.

The Lieutenant General had instructed him to speak with the woman after he'd received an anonymous note accusing her of selling poisons.

But when he'd entered the salon of La Voisin, goosebumps covered his skin. She'd been helpful – yes, she created the odd potion to help lovelorn young men or women along – but what stayed with him now were the things she'd not mentioned.

Usually not one given to superstitions, Jacques had found the room so oppressive, he had the sense darker things happened in La Voisin's life. A midwife dabbling in potions sounded harmless. La Voisin did not come across as such.

Her haughty attitude and the way she dismissed the accusations had not secured his confidence. Despite her smiles and reassurances, her eyes had stayed unmoving, as if made of marble.

Dead.

His instinct told him there was more to the woman. He strode down the *rues* until he arrived at the Châtelet. Desgrez was descending the stairs as he entered.

"How did it go?"

"You might want to hear this. Come with me," Jacques pointed up.

Moments later, both men entered La Reynie's office. Jacques accepted a chair but Desgrez stood, leaning against a tall shelf filled with books about laws and bundles of paper piled up high.

"I gather your visit was fruitful?" The head of the Paris police looked from one man to the other. "Or you wouldn't have brought Desgrez back in with you."

Jacques nodded. "I think so. The midwife you asked me to see – one Catherine Monvoisin of rue Beauregard – she's hiding something."

"So the suggestion of La Voisin selling poisons is correct?"

"It's likely, although she would not admit it. She was adamant that on the few occasions she suggested potions, she'd sent her clients to an old apothecary. But that was apparently years ago, and the man in question is no longer alive."

"How convenient!" Desgrez snorted.

"It is," La Reynie said. "But there's more, I take it?"

"Yes. I think she hides something worse than mere potions."

"Why? What's she done?"

"I can't explain it. Her whole demeanour is bizarre. She is all smiles, with much waving of hands, but her eyes never change. The last time I saw such a hard look in someone's eyes was at my encounter with Abbé Guibourg. La Voisin has that same look about her."

"That doesn't make her a poisoner, Jacques."

"No, not that alone. But the room itself…it squeezes the life out of you."

Desgrez scoffed. "That's quite dramatic. Don't you agree?"

Jacques glared at him. "You pay her a visit. Then you'll see what I mean."

"But you found no proof of any wrongdoing?" La Reynie regarded him with half-closed lids. He leaned back in his chair and held his folded hands against his pursed lips.

"Unfortunately, not. But she might be worth watching."

"Half of Paris is worth watching, Jacques. These people are careful, they do nothing under our gaze. We have to catch them in the act."

"What about those we have arrested?" Jacques asked. "Do they never give away their sources?"

La Reynie shook his head. "Not so far. But I'm certain there's more to this. I agree with you, Jacques. We need to renew our effort."

"Yes, sir, we do. I can keep an eye on her and the priest. One of them will make a mistake, I am sure of it."

"Do that. It's not too far from your quarters, too, but be careful! These people won't hesitate to get rid of anyone in their way."

Jacques knew what La Reynie meant. "I will be, thanks."

"Speaking of getting rid of someone, any progress on that case at Versailles?" La Reynie's gaze went from Jacques to Desgrez.

"It must be a lady bearing a grudge," Desgrez said. "The man had a reputation as a seducer, and about a dozen young *demoiselles* from respectable houses had to hide in convents until they gave birth to his offspring."

The memory of Fleur's face when she stared as Guibourg rode away with her son sprang to Jacques' mind. Was she capable of revenge?

"Perhaps she merely meant to scare him, but the poison proved too strong," he suggested.

"Impossible. The damage to his stomach and liver was so severe, it must've ripped them apart whilst he was still alive," La Reynie said. "Whoever did it knew what they were doing."

"You think it's a group of people, sir?" Desgrez asked?

"Of course. If it was a woman, she must have had the help of a footman, at least. Witnesses who saw him before he ran outside saw him stand there alone, drinking two glasses of wine in quick succession. We do have a useful description of the footman. But where has he gone?"

"He must have left straight after serving Mortain the wine."

"A good point. That means he clearly knew what he was doing."

"So either someone paid the man off or…" Jacques paused.

"Or he was killed," Desgrez finished for him.

La Reynie's expression was grim. "His Majesty wants to stay informed throughout our investigation, therefore, I'm due to visit Versailles tomorrow morning. Yet I've nothing to tell him." He balled his hand into a fist. "We must solve this murder."

"We shall." Jacques rose.

"I have a sense that if we succeed, we'll be able to flush out the person who'd provided the poison – and probably catch a whole school of other fish in the net."

As he left the Châtelet, Jacques' mind was whirling. He wanted to be certain Fleur had nothing to do with Mortain's murder. But how could he find out? Her behaviour towards him had changed. Was it only because she was now moving in upper circles of society? Or did she have something more sinister to hide? Acknowledging that she had suffered the loss of a child, and of the life she'd known, he'd given her the benefit of a doubt. But would those losses really lead to murder?

People get killed for less. Fleur would not be the first to think of revenge.

Gritting his teeth, he walked out of the passageway and turned away from the river when he heard his name.

"Jacques! Wait!"

Turning, he saw Guillaume push away from the wall that separated the street from the river. The boy raced towards him.

"Shouldn't you be in the workshop?" He'd given the boy clear instructions that morning. They had several urgent orders to fulfil.

"Yes, but a messenger came with an urgent letter for you. As I wasn't sure where you were, I took the liberty of relieving the man of it before he waited in vain. Here." He held out a folded note.

Jacques took it and turned it over. It was secured with a

seal he did not recognise. "And how did you find me? I trust you locked up?" he asked as he ripped it open.

"Of course." Guillaume grinned and touched his nose with his forefinger. "I might no longer spend my days on the streets, but I still have my sources."

Jacques laughed. "You're growing up too fast, lad. Now back to the workshop! And thank you." He waved the note in the air as Guillaume hurried away.

Then he read it.

"Damn!" His heart sank. These were not the tidings he needed. He re-read the words the Marquise de Sablière had written clearly in haste, given the unsteady hand:

'Monsieur de Montagnac,
I beseech you for your help, as you are the only one I can turn to. You have been Fleur's good friend in need, and I would ask a favour from you.
Fleur has disappeared.
After our late soirée last night (which I sincerely hope you enjoyed), she retired to bed as normal, but her room was empty this morning. She has vanished! Yet, her valise and all her dresses are still there.
Please come to my home at your earliest convenience. I fear dear Fleur's life is in danger.
I await your arrival.
Yours,
Marguerite de La Sablière'

Jacques folded the note and shoved it into his coat pocket. The breeze from the Seine suddenly gave him the chills. He buttoned up and weaved his way through the bustling streets towards the quieter *quartier* where the marquise lived. He could have hired a chaise, but he needed time to think.

With Philippe de Mortain dead, only one person might have an interest in abducting Fleur. Sophie de La Fontaine. But he did not have the woman's address. He racked his brain for snippets of information he'd gleaned from Fleur over time, he concluded that there must be a town house. But she'd never revealed where it was. He'd have to send his informants out to do some digging.

When he eventually reached the marquise's home, he walked up the steps. The door opened before he'd knocked. Clearly, the lady had been awaiting his arrival. Jacques was led into the salon where the night before Marin de La Fontaine had recited his works.

Today, only two large settees stood in the centre of the room. Marguerite de La Sablière rose and rushed towards him. The Duchess de Bouillon remained seated, dabbing her eyes with a handkerchief.

The marquise took his hands in hers. "I'm so relieved you came, Monsieur de Montagnac. I'm going out of my mind with worry."

"Please calm yourself, Madame la marquise. Take a seat again." He led her back to her settee, and she dropped herself into it as if unable to remain on her feet. He extracted his hands and bowed to the duchess. "It's good that you are here too. It saves time. May I?" He pointed to the seat opposite, and the marquise nodded.

"Would you care for refreshments?"

"No, thank you. You're very kind, but I'd prefer to hear what happened, then I can begin my investigation as soon as possible."

"Of course. I understand." The marquise fanned herself.

Marianne de Bouillon patted her friend's arm. "All will be well, Marguerite. I have full faith in Monsieur de Montagnac."

A sense of unease prickled at the nape of his neck. As much as he wanted to find Fleur, in time and alive, the lady's optimism seemed premature.

"Thank you, madame. I imagine you are up to date with the details?" To him, the duchess seemed the calmer of the two.

"Yes. Marguerite has told me all. If I had not asked her to move here for a few days, she'd still be safe at mine."

"Don't blame yourself, dearest! No one could have foreseen this."

The duchess nodded, then met Jacques' gaze again. "We will do anything to help find her. If you need financial support, please say so."

He shook his head, stunned by her unusual suggestion. "No, thank you. That won't be necessary. My sources are all over the city. But now, Madame la marquise, please tell me what happened. Then I'd like to see Fleur's room."

Marguerite de La Sablière sighed. "Fleur retired last night as normal. We always chat a little while over a glass of something, to help us calm after such a noisy soirée."

Jacques nodded. His head needed clearing after the event, so this did not surprise him.

"Nothing untoward happened during the night. I've asked the servants, and even they noticed nothing unusual. This morning, Fleur's maid arrived to wake her, only to find the bed empty."

"Had it been slept in?"

"Yes. That's what puzzled us. Fleur must have fallen asleep."

"And you said all her clothes are accounted for?"

"That's right. Fleur would certainly not leave the house in her shift!" The marquise's eyes widened. "Therefore, I suspect someone has taken her by force."

"I see." He shifted on the seat. "Did you see any signs of forced entry?"

Her hands flew to her mouth, and she stared at him. "Oh, my god."

The duchess placed her hand on her friend's shoulder. "What is it?"

"Why did I not think of it at the time?"

Jacques' pulse quickened. "What did you not think of?"

"The doors." The marquise groaned. "Fleur's chamber opens to a small balcony which you can access from the garden. The doors were wide open this morning."

He nodded. "That might explain the fact you found no signs of forced entry. But how would anyone get onto your property?"

She paled, and her hand flew to her throat. "There is a

narrow path at the back. High walls surround the garden, but there is an old gate leading to it."

"Thank you. I will need to see this gate too. But first," he stood, "can you please show me her room?"

"Of course. Please follow me. Marianne…?"

"I'll come with you, Marguerite. I want to see this for myself."

Jacques let the ladies go ahead as they climbed the stairs to the first floor. It surprised him that Marguerite de La Sablière did not delegate this task to a maid, but then, she was clearly concerned for Fleur's wellbeing.

"Here we are, monsieur." She held the door to Fleur's chamber open, and he entered.

Sparsely furnished, it was clearly a guest room. The bed, with two small side tables, stood against the wall to his right, and a chest of drawers beside the door. Along the wall opposite, a large, ornately decorated wardrobe took up most of the room. Small chairs sat in the corners. On one of them, he saw Fleur's stays and a shift slung carelessly over the back.

"I apologise, monsieur, but I thought you'd want to see everything as it was this morning." The marquise's cheeks reddened.

"Fret not, madame. You did the right thing."

He walked into the centre, coming to a halt at the foot end of the bed. The covers lay thrown back, as if someone had been in haste. A small rug beside the bed lay ruffled up. Perhaps Fleur had fought the intruder? As he looked around for other signs of a scuffle, he found none.

He scanned the room once more, then his gaze fell on the shut glass-panelled double doors to the garden. "These were open this morning?"

"Ah, of course. I forgot. The maid closed them as it was getting cold in the chamber." She stared at him. "I hope that wasn't a mistake."

"Not at all." He walked over and checked the lock. The key was in place on the inside.

Both ladies joined him. "It looks untouched," the duchess remarked.

"It is." Jacques turned the key in the lock and opened the door. "Ah."

A wooden balcony extended to the side, with steps leading down into the garden. Like many town houses, the space at the back was small. A high wall surrounded it on all sides, shielding it from the neighbours and the lane beyond. He leaned over the wooden railing. Below, a terrace spanned the width of the building. The garden was pretty. A path wound its way between flower beds, many only just beginning to bloom. At the far end stood four trees.

Jacques turned to check the lock, but, again, there was no sign of a break-in. He looked at the ladies beside him. Both were quiet, lost in thought, as they stared at the greenery.

"I'm going downstairs to check the grass and the gate at the back. If you prefer to stay here…"

He'd have preferred it, but both shook their heads. "We'll come with you," the duchess declared.

"Follow me, but please don't veer off the path. I'm trying to retrace Fleur's steps – or those of her abductor."

"Of course," the marquise agreed, her voice shaky.

He came to a halt at the edge of the lawn. No fresh footprints were visible on the grass. Loose stones covered the path. It was impossible to spot any tracks here. As he followed the trail, he noticed some deeper holes, as if someone had walked there, carrying a heavy load.

When he reached the gate, he halted. Right in front of it, the stones were disturbed, as if several people had gathered.

"When was the last time someone entered this way?"

"Oh, when the gardener came last, a few weeks back. He is due another visit, to be honest. No one in my household uses that gate."

"Not even your servants?"

"No. There is a small door at the bottom of the steps, below the main entrance at the front. They only ever use that." She huffed. "I won't tolerate muddy shoes."

"I see." He stifled a smile. "So our intruders might have caused this mess."

The duchess leaned forward. "Yes. That makes sense. But

how did they come in?" She looked from Jacques to her friend.

"Only my housekeeper has a key." The marquise's tone was sharp.

"Calm yourself, Marguerite. We're not accusing your staff."

Jacques left the women to their discussion and approached the gate. It was not fully latched. He grabbed the handle and pulled the gate open.

"It's unlocked." Marguerite de La Sablière sounded surprised.

Checking the outside of the door, he sighed. "And this is why." He opened it wide. The metal was twisted, the wood around the lock splintered.

Someone had forced their way into the garden. He scanned the narrow alley behind. Weeds had grown on the path, but right outside, they were trampled. Imprints from wheels were embedded in the half-dried mud.

A cart had taken Fleur away.

His heart sank.

Chapter Twenty-Three

Fleur woke and tried to stretch her limbs, but her arms or legs.

She wet her dry lips, blinking. This was not Marguerite's guest chamber. She stared at the low ceiling in the dim light. Was she in an attic?

"Where…?" she murmured. Her throat burned, and she swallowed a few times, but could not rid herself of the bitter taste in her mouth. Was this an after-effect of all the wine she'd drunk last night, or something else?

She stared at her hands, encased in broad shackles which were tied with rope to iron rings in the wall behind her. "What on earth?" she croaked, trying to pull her wrists free, but only ended up chafing her skin.

At the bottom end of the narrow, plain bunk bed, she saw her ankles tied up in the same manner to the feet of the bunk.

The room was empty apart from the bed, a table with two chairs and a chest set against the far wall. Above her to the right, a sliver of daylight came through a small window covered with what looked like a rag.

Panic surged. Her last memory was of her falling asleep at Marguerite's house. How much time had passed? And where was she?

Fleur forced herself to calm her breathing. It was of no use if she passed out with fear. She would rather be awake to deal with whatever must face.

Should she scream for help? A glance at the eaves told her it would be in vain. She was upstairs, and the only people likely to hear her were her abductors.

The thought chilled her to the core.

Had Mother finally found her?

Then she remembered. She'd opened the door to the

garden to air the chamber, but must have fallen asleep.

Everything became clear. Whoever had taken her must have watched her movements. She'd only recently returned to stay with Marguerite.

But how did they take her without her waking? And why had no one heard anything?

Perhaps they had, and someone was already searching for her.

"Jacques…" she whispered, and her heart filled with hope. Marguerite might have asked for his help. But where would he start searching?

And who had snatched her?

Philippe was dead. His wife rarely came to Paris, and Fleur doubted the girl was too sad about his demise.

It could only be Mother. But would she be callous enough to have her abducted in the middle of the night? She'd been busy spending Fleur's inheritance. By running away, Fleur had saved her the price of a dowry.

As far as Fleur could think, she had no other enemies.

Heavy footsteps sounded outside the door. When a key grated in the lock, Fleur closed her eyes and kept her breathing low. It was best not to let her abductor guess know she'd awoken.

Someone entered, the tread telling her it was a man. Not seeing what was happening gave her a sense of vulnerability, and she found it hard not to blink. Then a second person entered with lighter steps. A woman?

Mother?

"She's still out," a male voice said. Fleur racked her brain, but it did not sound familiar. "I must've used too much of the soporific."

Ah. That explains my lack of memory.

"You fool!" The woman spoke, her voice imperious. It was not Mother. "We cannot risk her screaming when she wakes."

He laughed, the sound sending shivers down Fleur's spine. Cruel. Uncaring. "Don't worry, my lady. There's no one around, apart from me. As you have seen, the houses on

231

either side are empty."

Fleur's heart sank. She was now seriously fighting the urge to peek. Her stomach rumbled, and she sucked in her breath.

"Is she waking?" The lady's steps retreated.

Who is she? The voice sounds vaguely familiar.

The man prodded Fleur's shoulder, but she remained unresponsive. "No, not yet. I'll return later with some bread. She'll be up soon enough."

A calloused finger trailed from her shoulder down the rim of her shift towards her breasts. Fleur's heart beat faster, yet she did not stir.

"Don't! I don't want her spoiled. I mean this to serve as a warning only."

Something clicked in Fleur's memory, and she hoped the woman would speak again.

"Shame. She's a pretty flower I'd love to pluck."

"I'm not sure La Voisin would like to hear you say that, Lesage. The girl is not to be harmed, merely kept out of sight for a while." A sigh followed. "For now, see that she's fed, and don't let her out of this room. She must not escape. Am I clear?"

"Perfectly, Madame la marqu—"

"No titles!" she hissed. "If she has the faintest idea of who I am, or causes trouble, you know what to do. It would be a shame, but needs must. We cannot risk compromising my position."

"Of course," he said in a tone Fleur found surprisingly submissive. "I shall keep you up to date with any developments."

"Good. And Lesage, once more," the woman paused, "do not take advantage of her!"

"Such a waste…" A whisper reached Fleur's ears, and she suppressed a shudder.

As two sets of footsteps receded, Fleur peered through half-closed lashes. A tall, slim man followed by a stout lady dressed in a simple black gown. A veil of the same colour covered the woman's face, but something in the way she carried herself triggered a memory. Then the door fell shut.

Fleur let out a long breath. Where had she seen her before? He was going to call her 'Madame la marquise'? Perhaps she was a lady at court. That would match the way she spoke. But who would want her out of the way 'for a while'? And out of the way of what?

Frustrated, Fleur kicked at the shackles that tied up her feet, but all it did was graze her skin, burning into her flesh. She yelped and held still again.

"Think, Fleur!"

As she could not free herself without help, she revisited her times at court in her mind, starting with her first day – when she met Philippe.

No one associated her with his death, she was certain. Perhaps Jacques had wondered about it, but he had no proof. Philippe's family lived in the north, and his wife was likely relieved he was dead. Fleur remembered the young woman's face. How naïve they had both been!

She gave a dry laugh. Everything had gone wrong from that day onwards. Tears pricked her eyes when she thought of her months held in the convent, at the mercy of the sisters. Anger tore through her that none of the nuns had faced justice. It was not Jacques' fault that he could not find any evidence. Even witnessing Guibourg riding off with her son had not been proof enough. They had never found the boy. Or any others.

"My boy is dead, and no one cares." Her voice was hoarse, and she let the tears roll. For the past year, she'd forced herself not to think of him, or of the brutal way he likely lost his young life. Her own life had continued, and even whilst plotting her revenge on Philippe, she'd kept her brief glimpse of the little body being carried away confined to a distant memory. For her own sake, she'd refused to think about him.

Now, alone in a filthy attic room, the thoughts tumbled through her head. Of course he'd be dead by now, used in the most despicable way.

"It's all Mother's fault."

Slowly, the tears dried, and her breathing calmed. Instead,

a plan formed in her head. If she got away once, could she do it again?

La Voisin. The woman she'd visited with Marianne to get the poison. The lady in black had mentioned her name. It seemed the man who guarded her was close to the witch.

Lesage, the woman had called him. Marianne had mentioned an associate's of La Voisin called Lesage – her *amant*.

But he'd touched her skin until the strange woman had forbidden him to. Did he want her? What if she encouraged him? Perhaps it would help her escape.

A smile formed on Fleur's lips.

"I will avenge your death, *mon cœur*..."

***

Paris

Jacques knocked on the thick oak door of the town house owned by Sophie de La Fontaine. It was not an imposing building like the Duchesse de Bouillon's, or even like the slightly smaller home of the Marquise de La Sablière. Instead, it had a sense of normality to it. Comfortable, but not wealthy.

A maid opened, eyeing him up and down. "Yes?"

Jacques smiled. "I'd like to speak with Madame de La Fontaine. I'm with the police."

"The police? Do come in."

The stout woman stood back, and Jacques walked past her into a narrow corridor that branched off into two rooms on either side, and a door at the back, likely leading to the kitchen. A staircase led to the upper floors.

"Please." The maid let him into a sitting room. "Take a seat. I will inform Madame de La Fontaine." The door closed behind her, and Jacques looked around.

His first glance confirmed his expectation. The furniture was dated. He lowered himself into a chair that creaked. Several small threads of the embroidered armrests were hanging loose. The pale green cover of the settee had faded in places, and the rug beneath his feet was well trodden.

The La Fontaines were not rich, and it appeared Fleur's mother detested her lack of status. Her daughter's appearance at court should have secured a wealthy husband. Instead, it had been the beginning of a nightmare.

The door swung open. He rose. A woman in her forties entered, her back straight, her chin pushed forward. Sophie de La Fontaine had a reputation for arrogance, and even without having spoken to her before, he could tell by her whole demeanour.

"Madame de La Fontaine," he said, inclining his head.

"Monsieur." She walked past him, then sat on the settee and gestured to him to do the same. "You are from the police? What seems to be the problem?"

Jacques perched on the edge of the seat, leaning forward, his hands folded. "My name is Jacques de Montagnac, and the Lieutenant General sends me. I wish to speak with you about your daughter."

"Blanchefleur? What has she done now?" She sighed, drawing her mouth into a thin line. "If she needs money, I have none to give."

Surprised, Jacques stared at her. Could it be that she was truly ignorant about Fleur's whereabouts? Or was she merely an accomplished liar?

He cleared his throat. "She is missing."

Madame de La Fontaine laughed; a dry sound devoid of humour. "Has she? Perhaps she found herself another unsuitable *amant*. Or she's with child again." She eyed him, taking in his appearance. "You are acquainted with my daughter."

Jacques was prepared. He'd expected to reveal their connection.

"I was the one who helped her escape from the convent."

"Ah. I see." She leaned back, placing her hands flat on the plush seat either side of her. "And now you have lost her again?"

"She was with one of her friends, the Marquise de La

Sablière, when she appears to have been…taken."

"She was what? Ah." Sophie de La Fontaine smirked. "And you think I have something to do with it? Let me tell you what I think of my ungrateful daughter, then you can decide what to believe." She looked around the room, as if to prepare what she wanted to say, then met his gaze. "I have seen Blanchefleur at court, in the company of certain… ladies. She now attends soirées that promote her uncle – that overrated and heavily indebted writer. Is it true that Marin introduced her to Madame de La Sablière?"

Jacques nodded, his mouth in a thin line. "Yes. She was asking for his help – as she did not want to marry the man you chose for her."

She smirked. "Of course she didn't. But he would've been perfect; even prepared to overlook her…indiscretion. It's difficult, finding a suitable husband for a daughter who'd just given birth."

"He sounded more like an old lecher than a man giving an unfortunate girl a chance."

"And?" She sighed. "You are a man of the world. In your line of work, you would have come across men like him, I have no doubt. For Blanchefleur, it would have meant financial stability for the rest of her life."

"And for you?" Anger rose within him. How could a mother be so heartless? He brushed the memory of his own mother to the back of his mind.

"I admit it – I love spending money, and our estate does not bring in nearly enough. It costs too much to maintain; something dear Blanchefleur never concerned her pretty head with. Oh no. She left it all to me."

"Why did you not re-marry after your husband's death?"

"Why should I? I did my duty. Émilien and I had not been close. This time, it was my daughter's turn, but of course the little *mademoiselle* had other ideas."

"I'm certain she was not the only girl seduced by Mortain."

"Of course not. The man was a rogue, but it was all so obvious." She picked at a loose thread on the cover of the

236

Chapter Twenty-Four

Fleur woke after the first good night's sleep in days, this time without the shackles. She stretched and rose to pull the grimy curtain aside. Rain was drumming against the thin window pane.

She dipped her hands in a bowl of cold water and rubbed her face. Guessing that it was not too long until Lesage would arrive with breakfast, she returned to the bed. Today would be the day.

Leaning back against the wall, she smiled. It had been four days since her abduction, and she'd slowly chipped away at his mistrust. Last night, he'd arrived late, and Fleur pretended to be asleep. He sat on the bed, running a finger along the rim of her shift. But he had gone no further. Something – or someone – stopped him.

Over recent days, they'd talked. Slowly, conversations turned personal. Bashfully, Fleur told him about her time at court. In turn, Lesage revealed minor details of his life, though nothing that could be regarded as suspicious. Yesterday, he spoke for the first time about his associates – the fortune tellers, midwives and creators of potions. The man was almost boasting of his connections.

Oh, how Jacques would have loved to listen in!

Firmly brushing the thought of him far from her mind, Fleur now realised she'd never get close enough to Sister Benedicte or Abbé Guibourg.

Criminals stuck together. Lesage had not once mentioned the woman in black, who had not returned since that initial visit, nor had he revealed any names of other acquaintances.

Eventually, Jacques would trap them all, but he would have to do it without her help.

Today, she would tell Lesage she was seeking revenge. It had become clear that causing pain excited him, and Fleur was sure he would be a willing partner in her plot. He seemed to enjoy the sense of power.

Whatever fate held in store for her after she'd rid herself of Mother, Fleur's conscience was clear, and her son's death avenged.

Footsteps sounded on the stairs, and she shuffled into position. The door cracked open, and Lesage poked his face through the gap, checking where she was.

Fleur smiled. "Good morning." She stretched her leg out a little more from beneath her shift.

Lesage entered slowly, the corners of his mouth quirking, and kicked the door shut. Then he set down the tray he carried on the table. It held a bowl of something steaming, a chunk of bread, freshly baked by the scent of it, and an apple.

"I've brought you broth, Fleur, as it's cold and miserable outside. You should eat whilst it's hot." His gaze roamed the room, then fastened on her eyes. "Or are you not hungry?"

She made no move, waiting for him to come over.

For a long moment, he stood by the bed, then sat on the edge, his fingers picking on a thread in the blanket. "I know what you're trying to do, girl." He sent her a calculating look. "But it won't work."

Dismayed, Fleur took a sharp breath. "Why not? You want it."

A dry laugh escaped him, and he ran his forefinger around her chin, then grabbed it firmly, forcing her to look at him.

"I might want you, but there is a woman who'd feed my balls to the ravens if I gave in to my lust."

She jerked her head away, freeing herself from his grasp. "The one in black, who came with you the first day?"

"Ah, you weren't asleep? I thought not. How much did you see?"

"Only that she was dressed in black. A veil covered her face."

"But you didn't recognise her." It was a statement, not a question.

Fleur shook her head. "No, though the voice sounded familiar. Why are you holding me here?"

"To keep you out of someone's sight."

"The king's?"

He said nothing.

She folded her legs beneath her and sent him a challenging look. "So that's what it is. Someone was worried about my dance with His Majesty." Realisation hit her as she remembered the sway of the woman's hips – in the grounds of Versailles. "Oh, it's Madame de Montespan, isn't it? Of course." She clapped her hands, remembering the arrogant voice of the king's favourite. "She was furious about it."

Lesage nodded, watching her with something akin to awe. "You're intelligent, Fleur. You could go far at court."

"I'm not interested in court, nor in becoming the mistress of the king, or any other *seigneur*."

"No?"

"No. So La Montespan can stop worrying about me."

He cocked his head. "I'm intrigued. Many women would…kill…to share a dance with Louis. Or his bed."

"Not I." A chance opened up. "That's not what I would kill for."

"Oh." A slow smile crept across his unshaved chin, making him look almost handsome. The glint in his grey eyes was unmistakable. "What would young Fleur kill for, then?"

She met his gaze evenly. "Revenge."

Lesage grinned. Then he stood and brought over the tray. He set it on the bed beside her. "Eat. And tell me everything. But no lies!"

Her stomach rumbled as the scent of the broth tickled her senses. It smelled of beef. A costly treat. The king's mistress clearly did not want her starved. And now, she no longer had a reason they might release her.

She drank deeply from the bowl, then wiped her mouth with the back of her hand. Picking chunks off the bread, Fleur dipped it into the remnants of liquid and devoured them. All the while, Lesage kept watching her. La Voisin must have a powerful hold over him, or he'd have taken advantage. Or perhaps he was in love with the woman.

No. A man like him did not know the meaning.

After Fleur had eaten the last morsel, he put the tray on the floor, then sat back, making himself more comfortable.

Fleur sighed. She could not tell him about Guibourg or the nuns. It was likely Lesage had crossed the priest's path; perhaps he'd even taken part in those black masses. She suppressed a shudder.

"I wish to punish my mother."

"What has she done?"

"She's responsible for the death of my son."

His eyes widened. "She murdered your child? How evil of her!"

Fleur nodded. This was going better than expected. "She did."

"What happened to him?"

"Does it matter? Isn't the fact that she's guilty enough?"

He took her hand, his thumb stroking her skin. Fleur found it disconcerting. Here was a man who dabbled in abductions – possibly even of infants – and poisons, and he appeared to comfort her, all because of her vengeance. She sent him a shy smile while she wiped away the tears with her free hand.

"Have you considered…how…you would wish to enact your revenge?" he asked calmly.

"Preferably, with something quick and silent." Poison. The word hung unspoken in the air. "I don't want a bloodbath."

"I see." He understood. "And you have the means to pay?"

He's nothing if not greedy.

"I do." She was convinced Marianne would help again. After all, she'd taken her to La Voisin. Or perhaps it was simply enough to drop her name. "I have a friend who is a regular client of a woman of your…close…acquaintance."

"You've called on my associate?" His eyes narrowed. "When?"

Fleur had to tread carefully before revealing too much. She must not rouse his suspicion. "Oh, earlier this year. I accompanied my good friend, the Duchess de Bouillon."

"I see. And that visit, it related to your quest for revenge?"

"Yes. There was another person involved."

The grin on his face made him look like a wolf. "That person, I presume, is no more?"

"No. Something he drank did not agree with him."

"Ha! Very good." He rose, a gleam in his eye. "I shall speak to my associate, but I'll return soon." Suddenly, he kissed her on the mouth, brief but fierce. "And that, my dear Fleur, is the primary reason you never betray your partners. You may have need of them one day."

Lesage collected the tray, then left without another glance. The key turned in the lock, and his steps soon receded.

Fleur let out a deep breath. Relieved and apprehensive at once.

She was so close.

***

Five days later

Frustrated, Jacques walked through the gateway out of the Châtelet, heading for the river. When he reached the waterfront, he leaned on the wall and breathed in deeply the stench from the Seine. It was the freshest air he could get. Clouds hung low, and it had not stopped raining for days. The damp clung to his clothes, his hair, his skin.

Pulling his hat over his face, he bent his head and turned in the direction of the gate of Saint Denis, trying to make sense of it all.

La Reynie had suggested that Fleur was in hiding. In his superior's eyes, her guilt had become clear at the moment of her disappearance. In fact, she was now the prime suspect in Philippe de Mortain's death, and La Reynie was keen to question her – if need be with the help of the water torture.

Jacques swallowed hard. Could the sweet girl he rescued from the convent – the girl he'd spent many evenings chatting to, who was darning stockings, gowns, and shifts all

245

day at Claudette's without a word of complaint – be a cold-blooded murderess?

Despite his reassurances that someone had abducted her, for he was still certain of it, the Lieutenant General blocked all his arguments. Now, it was up to him to uncover the truth.

But Jacques was still unsure what the truth was. Had Fleur fooled him?

As he hurried towards the workshop, he wondered if his intuition had deserted him. Perhaps he'd focused too much on the tragic situation, and her beguiling looks, to realise what went on inside the girl's head. Her sad eyes captured him. But had they been a front behind which she plotted revenge all along?

"Damn!" Jacques hated being taken for a fool. He stopped at a corner and swore again. Taking turns left and right, he'd lost his way, thinking of Fleur.

He decided he needed clarity and entered a lane that ran towards the Porte Saint-Denis. Then he stopped short. About fifty yards ahead, a man and a woman left a house that had seen better days. Its front looked shabby, and the wooden beams brittle. But it was not the building that caught Jacques' attention. He darted beneath an overhanging entrance before risking another glance. Fortunately, the couple were not heading his way, but he still recognised the way she moved.

Fleur.

When he saw the woman's profile as she said something to the man, he sent a small prayer heavenwards. He'd got lost for a reason. La Reynie had been right about Fleur. She walked freely beside the man, therefore she could not have been taken by force. Her companion pointed to the north, and they continued at a sedate pace. Clearly, wherever they were going, they were in no hurry.

What a stroke of luck! Now to discover what Fleur was up to. Keeping a safe distance, he was always ready to hide behind a cart or in a doorway if needed, but neither of them looked over their shoulder.

As if they were an ordinary couple on a stroll.

That in itself could be deemed unusual in this bustling part of Paris, but no one took notice. On his side of the street, merchants walked towards him, gesticulating wildly, discussing whatever trade they were involved in. He swerved around them. Further up, a cart carried wood to a house, and Jacques had to side-step.

Riders, urgent and insisting on their right of way, veered between carts and donkeys. Ahead, Fleur and the stranger swiftly crossed rue de Cléry, continuing further north.

So they were not heading towards the Porte Saint-Denis, but where, then? The new roads to the north held a variety of people, mostly with some funds, but not rich. Writers and poets lived beside butchers and alchemists. Fleur's uncle still resided at the Marquise de la Sablière's house, so she would not seek him here. Marin de La Fontaine's associates were of a higher society.

Content that the path was clear, he scurried to the other side, keen not to lose sight of Fleur and the man. They walked without talking now. Her back was straight, and her stride held determination. A purpose.

What was she up to? This was not the impression of a woman abducted in the middle of the night, against her will. It was very much that of a woman who knew what she wanted – and who was about to get it.

His breath hitched. She'd deceived him; him, Claudette, and all the other girls. Even Marin de La Fontaine would have no inkling about his niece's true intentions.

As he passed the corner to the little rue Saint-Roch, a movement distracted him. Two boys tried to scurry away, but, having recognised them from Ninou's school, he was faster. With a curse, he held them by their threadbare shirts and glared at them.

"What are you doing out here? Don't you have lessons to attend to?"

They squirmed, and he let them go.

"Our *Maman* is sick, sir. She needs medicine." Paul, the elder of the brothers, stared at his feet.

His little brother's eyes welled up. "She can't move."

Jacques sighed. It was always the same – children ended

247

up in the streets when their parents were ill or inebriated.

"I have an idea, boys. You're out today, so you might as well continue, but I'll speak with Mademoiselle Bourré and ask her to visit your mother. Perhaps there's something we can do to help. Does that sound fair?"

"Thank you," Paul said, nodding, then took his brother's hand. "Come."

For a moment, Jacques stood and watched the boys, their shoulders hunched, their heads unprotected against the drizzle.

'You can't save every child in Paris.' Ninou's words came back to him.

"I can but try," he muttered, then he remembered Fleur. There was no sign of them up and down the chemin des Poissoniers. "Damn!" In large strides, he walked up to the next corner on the right, but they had disappeared. Several lanes veered off from rue Beauregard. Fleur and the stranger could be anywhere. As he ran up the street, one entrance caught his eye, and he halted. He'd been here before, visiting a midwife suspected to be involved in witchcraft – and poisons. A woman he'd found unnerving. Madame de Monvoisin.

Was Fleur visiting La Voisin?

His blood froze. What could she possibly want there?

Poison.

Keen not to be spotted, Jacques pulled his hat lower over his face and walked away swiftly. Back at the corner, he waited, out of sight. As the drizzle deepened, so his mood darkened.

Fleur had deceived him. La Reynie had been right. A slow-burning anger spread through him. When she reappeared, he would confront her. No, he shook his head. It was better to see where she was going.

When darkness fell, the man finally emerged from La Voisin's house. But Fleur was not with him.

The man walked away in a determined stride, and Jacques was in two minds. Should he follow him or wait for Fleur?

Oh, how he wished one of the children were around, so he could send a message to the Châtelet for help. On his own, he might make a wrong choice.

A life could depend on it.

After taking a deep breath, he decided to wait. She would have to emerge before night fell.

Two hours later, his body chilled from the rain and wind, he had to admit he was wrong. Had she seen him?

A thought hit him, and he retraced his steps. Walking into a courtyard behind the house on the corner, he saw a maze of yards and gardens at the back of the connected buildings on rue Beauregard.

"God's teeth!" Rage tore through him and his fist hit the wall.

Fleur had escaped.

Chapter Twenty-Five

Paris

"Of course, I'll speak to the boys' mother, Jacques." Ninou wrote a few lines into her small notebook, then she put the writing utensils aside. "Thank you for telling me. I was worried about them."

Jacques had stopped off at Ninou's lodgings above the school rooms. Jeanne was already asleep in the bedroom, but the kitchen was warm and inviting. From the hearth, enticing scents emerged from a closed brass pot set on hot bricks beside the fire.

A cup of warm ale in hand, he sat opposite her at the sturdy dining table that also served as a desk by the look of the piles of books and papers gathered in one corner. He grimaced. "Paul looked very guilty, and little Nicolas was crying. I think they both felt bad about not attending their lessons. They were wet through, too."

She nodded. "I'll visit their home at daybreak to see what we can do." Rising, she placed a hand on his arm. "You look tired, and soaked. Let me get you a bowl of broth."

"No need, Ninou. I—"

"That wasn't a question, Jacques. You can be glad it's June, not November. Now take off your shirt and give it to me. I'll hang it beside your coat to dry. Oh, and your boots."

He paused a moment, then removed his wet clothes. Conscious of her watching him, he remembered Claudette's words. *'The girl's been in love with you for years...'*

He'd always been careful not to encourage her, as if some instinct had stopped him. Strangely, he realised he did not mind her looking anymore. Memories of their conversations before Fleur's arrival sprang to mind; true, the light tone

250

Ninou and he used to share had changed with Fleur's arrival. Jacques had become more reserved.

But Fleur no longer had a hold over him, her betrayal clear for all to see. Why had he not seen it earlier?

"Here you are." Ninou placed a bowl and a wooden spoon on the table, pulling him from his musings. "When was the last time you ate?" She whisked away his sodden garments and deposited them by the hearth, then she sat down and took a sip at her ale.

His hand stilled on its way to pick up the spoon. "I can't remember. Yesterday at some point."

"You look gaunt, Jacques. Is something bothering you?"

He snorted. "A few things, yes. But I don't want to burden you with my failures." He shoved a spoonful of broth into his mouth. Immediately, the taste of vegetables and herbs assaulted his senses, and he took another, savouring the moment despite his dark thoughts. "This is good." He smiled as her eyes met his.

"Don't change the subject!" Ninou put on her tutor's voice. "What troubles you?"

"Let me finish this first, then I'll tell you." Truth was, what would he say? And where to start?

He ate in silence whilst Ninou flicked through her notebook again. Scribbled paragraphs covered pages after pages. "What are you writing in there?"

She looked up. "I keep a diary about the children's progress. Some need more help with learning; others need a stronger hand to keep their attention on the tasks. This way," she tapped her index finger on an open page, "I can see how each is faring."

"You've really grown into your new role." Pride for her achievement surged through him. And relief that she no longer needed to see men.

"I enjoy working with them. Most are keen to learn and quick to adapt to their new routine. For all of them it's a way out of their hopeless lives."

Jacques nodded. La Reynie's push to help boys and girls off the streets was working.

It had been a big step into the unknown for Ninou, especially having to hide her previous occupation. But the children benefitted from her enthusiasm. Although he'd been very protective of Ninou ever since they first met, her fierce independence had always kept him at a distance. Jacques suspected her attitude had not changed. If you found yourself abandoned, with a child, you had to help yourself. Ninou's only way to save them both from starvation had been prostitution.

It could have been Fleur's fate, too.

After his last spoonful, Ninou took the bowl and put it aside. Clearly, she would not let him get away this time.

He sighed. "You know when Fleur left Claudette's to stay with a lady?"

"The Marquise de La Sablière," Ninou nodded, "where her uncle is in residence."

"Yes. But it seems that she moved on to darker circles than the literary world."

Ninou furrowed her brows. "What do you mean, darker circles?"

He met her gaze. "Poisoners."

She gasped, then let out a long breath. "Go on…"

"The Lieutenant General considers her the prime suspect in Philippe de Mortain's murder. He doesn't believe she was abducted, even though the evidence speaks for it."

"Why not?"

"For La Reynie, it was too much of a coincidence. Fleur danced with the king at the same moment witnesses saw Mortain running into the gardens, doubled over. I still defended her yesterday, but…" He raked a hand through his hair.

"But?" Ninou prompted.

"I was ready to prove La Reynie wrong when she emerged from a house, together with a man I didn't recognise. They talked as if they'd known each other well."

"And you followed them?"

"Yes, until I spotted Paul and Nicolas and spoke to them. When I looked again for Fleur, she'd disappeared."

Ninou cocked her head. "Do you think she saw you?"

Jacques closed his eyes briefly, then felt her hand covering his. "I believe so. She and the man had vanished – on rue Beauregard. So I waited. They had to appear eventually."

She pressed his hand. "And did they?"

"The man, yes. He walked away in the opposite direction. Fleur didn't. I checked the house he'd left and remembered visiting a midwife there with Desgrez."

"Ha! Of course, a midwife!" She nodded slowly. "They know so many things, those women."

"And this one in particular. They call her La Voisin. She presents a respectable front, dabbling a bit in fortune-telling aside of her skills. But when we entered her house, it sent shivers down my spine, as did the woman."

"I've heard of La Voisin. She's well known in our circles for getting rid of unwanted babes, but not in the safest manner. Many whores go to her, though. The woman has quite a reputation."

He regarded her, wondering.

"No, in answer to your unspoken question, I've never been to see her. I wanted my daughter, despite the bastard her father was. It was not Jeanne's fault."

"Good." Relief flooded through him. "What else do they say about her?"

She grimaced. "Nothing that you could use in your investigations, Jacques. Everyone fears her. She has ways of making people…disappear."

"But you have no proof." He did not have to ask.

Ninou shook her head. "La Voisin is very careful. She works with several associates, one of which is believed to be the priest you used to follow."

"Guibourg?"

"Yes. Another is her *amant*, a man called Lesage. He is as nasty as they come."

A thought struck him. "What did he look like, this Lesage?"

"I've never seen him, but he's older than her."

"Tall, thin?"

"I'm sorry. I don't know. Maybe if you watch her home, you could spot him when he visits."

He might have to do that. After a lull in activities, it appeared the poisoners were more daring again.

"Anyway, you were saying Fleur did not emerge from La Voisin's house?"

"No. I waited until it had grown dark, but all was still. Then I retraced my steps, around the corner back into the chemin des Poissoniers, and discovered that the houses had gardens to the back. More like small yards, really, and all interconnected by a path. Fleur must have left that way to avoid me." He felt so stupid. Deceived.

"It's not your fault." As if Ninou read his mind, she pressed his hand. "Your concern for the boys made you lose sight of her. Yes, perhaps she'd seen you. Or perhaps she – or La Voisin – thought it was safer for her to leave through the garden."

He sighed and sent her a half-smile. "I know it's not rational, but I can't help blaming myself. She visited La Voisin for a reason."

"To get her hands on a potion or poison?"

"Yes. But Mortain is dead, and his wife is staying in the country. She has no interest in court. There is no way Fleur could get close to Guibourg or enter the convent without Sister Benedicte's knowledge. Those were my first thoughts. She wouldn't harm her new friends, the Marquise de La Sablière or the Duchess de Bouillon, either, so why did she visit the woman?" He shrugged his shoulders. "You spoke to her often. Did she mention anyone else in her life?"

Ninou let go of his hand, then closed the notebook that had been lying open before her, and put it onto a pile of books at the end of the table. Then she stared out of the rain-streaked window. "Fleur obviously seeks revenge. That was my impression all along. She seemed to carry this…this feeling of injustice in her heart, and nothing I said would ever make her change her mind."

"She never spoke about this with me." He realised how much Fleur had withheld from him, all the while he thought she'd trusted him. His sense of betrayal deepened.

"No. She always regarded you as a friend, whatever you may think now." Ninou looked down at her hands. "Please don't blame yourself. She is a lost soul, beyond reach of reason." She blinked back tears that welled up. Swiftly, she wiped them away. "And with Guibourg and the nuns untouchable, and Philippe gone, there's only one other person Fleur will hold responsible for the loss of her son."

When Ninou locked eyes with him, he knew. The blood drained from his face. "Madame de La Fontaine." He rose. "I must go to her."

Ninou nodded. "But you don't know when Fleur will strike – or if."

"Well, after her visit to La Voisin, I'm certain she will." Jacques pulled the now dry shirt over his head and grabbed his boots. Sitting down again, he slid the wet leather over his feet. "The sooner I warn her mother, the more on guard she will be."

"Are you thinking of setting a trap for Fleur?" Ninou rose and took his coat from the hook near the hearth, then handed it to him.

"I hope so." He wriggled into the warm garment. "Can you do something for me?"

"Of course. What?"

"Can you get word to La Reynie at the Châtelet to meet me at the house of Sophie de La Fontaine in an hour?"

"I will search for Guillaume straight away." She grabbed her shawl from the back of a chair.

He took his hat, then stared at her for a moment, before he pulled her close and kissed her forehead. "Thank you."

***

The rain had stopped by the time Fleur reached her family home. She stood, staring at the façade, feeling empty.

With a sad smile, she remembered she always preferred their country home. Memories of rolling hills, of tilled fields, and forests teaming with deer. It had been a happy childhood.

255

She'd enjoyed the freedom to go for long walks, exploring the surroundings with her friends. It was the first place where Fleur had learnt about the healing potential of plants – and the dangers.

Back then, she'd found it intriguing. Now, she realised how valuable that knowledge would have been had she retained it. Fleur detested having to rely on the likes of La Voisin – and everything the woman stood for.

Once Mother was dead, Jacques would hear about the woman's real dealings – but only after Fleur had left Paris. Where she would go to, she did not know, but she would take a few items with her, heirlooms from Father, and some other valuables. These would secure the journey, and perhaps a position in a noble household abroad.

Italy sounded interesting. Sunny and warm. Perhaps Marianne would give her a recommendation. Or perhaps not, given that Fleur had provided La Voisin with a sealed letter to the duchess, asking for payment on her behalf. The poisoner looked at Fleur for a long moment. Then, with a slow smile, the midwife agreed.

One devious mind acknowledging another.

No! Fleur pushed the thought away. *I am not like La Voisin!* No, she was merely…desperate.

Despite the late hour, a light still shone through the curtains of the sitting room. Mother was still awake. Good.

Her hood pulled down, Fleur craned her neck and took a deep breath, then laid a hand on her stomach. "This is for you, *mon cher*!" She slid her hand into her pouch and wrapped it around the small vial. It was reassuring. Right.

Slowly, she took the steps to the front entrance and tried the handle. Relief flooded through her. It was unlocked.

Mother is getting careless.

Fleur entered the dimly lit corridor, leaving the door ajar. In three steps, she reached the living room and glanced through the half-open door. Mother was sitting in a chair by the hearth, staring into the flames of a dying fire, as if deep in thought. A full glass of red wine stood on a small side table next to a half-empty carafe. Had her *amant* left her, or was she unwell? It was not like Mother to be so morose.

Not that Fleur cared either way. Whatever troubled the woman, she deserved it.

Nudging the door open, she entered. Sophie still did not move.

"Good evening, Mother."

Sophie startled and rose from the chair. "Blanchefleur? What are you doing here, at this late hour?"

Now, facing Mother, Fleur paused. It had been so much easier with Philippe. She'd been on the far side of the *salle de dance*, distracted by the king's attention.

"The door was unlocked. Are you expecting someone?"

Sophie straightened. "That is none of your business."

Fleur snorted. "So your fancy young man did not turn up, as expected, did he?"

"If you are here to mock me, I'm not in the mood." Sophie picked up the glass and took several sips, before setting it down again. "I thought someone abducted you, though you seem to be here of your own free will."

"How—?"

Sophie laughed, the sound harsh in the silent house. "How I knew? Your friend, that man who works for the police…he came to me with a wild story about you having been taken from La Sablière's." She paused, looking Fleur up and down. "Hm. So that was a ruse?"

"No." Fleur hated having to defend herself. "I was indeed abducted."

"But you miraculously escaped." Sophie's cynical voice grated in Fleur's ears.

Mother just could not be nice to her. Not once.

Anger surged in Fleur, and she swallowed it back. Digging her fingernails into the flesh of her hands in her coat pockets, she wished she'd come prepared with a plan. Then her gaze fell on the carafe, and an idea formed in her mind. Mother had to leave the room.

Fleur took a step forward. "I won't bother you for long, but was merely looking for something Father left me."

Sophie rolled her eyes. "Then get it and begone; back to

your duchesses and marquises who only use you for their own little games. But don't worry, Blanchefleur, they will soon tire of you. Then you will come running back home." She turned away. "But don't think you are welcome here."

Seething inside, Fleur glared. But she needed to know. "Why do you hate me so much, Mother?"

"Are you serious?" Sophie prodded the logs in the hearth. "Marrying your father was a grave mistake, but my parents gave me no choice. I had my sights on a wealthy vicomte who had asked for my hand, but your grandfather deemed us unworthy to move in the same circles as nobility. He declined Geoffrey's offer."

"Ah, that's why you wanted to do the same to me?"

"It's how things are done, Blanchefleur. Why should you have a voice in who to wed if my parents ignored mine? You should never have been born, or at least, you could have been a boy. A legitimate heir."

"I am a legitimate heiress. And Father loved me." Fleur's voice trembled.

The flames were hissing as Sophie kept attacking the wood. "You are a girl. And as we have seen at Versailles, one with no sense of propriety."

Fleur bit her lip. "Perhaps you should have prepared me better for what to expect."

"Oh, now it is my fault Mortain got you with child? Take whatever it is you have come for, then leave. I can't bear to even look at you." She put the poker into its stand and stared into the flames.

"I want the small clock Father had bequeathed to me."

"The clock?" Sophie whirled around. "What do you want with that?"

"I've always liked it, and it's mine."

"Everything in this house is mine, Blanchefleur."

"It's mine, and I want it."

Sophie sighed loudly. "For all I care, fetch it. It's in my bedchamber. You know where."

"I don't want to enter your rooms, Mother. It's too personal."

"It never bothered you in the past. Why the sudden concern? A maid can get it, then." She passed Fleur on her way to the door.

Blood pounding in her ears, Fleur grabbed her mother's arm. "They're all asleep. Can't you…collect it for me? Please?" She gazed at Mother with a shy smile, hoping to appear demure.

Sophie sighed. "This once, only. You think about other items to take with you because, after tonight, you are no longer welcome here." Then she left.

Moments later, Fleur heard Sophie's footsteps on the stairs. She strode to the small table and pulled the dark green vial from her pouch. Carefully, she prised it open and sprinkled some of the coarse powder it contained into the glass. The rest, she dropped into the carafe and swirled it around, hoping the poison would dissolve quickly. Fleur put it back in its place and dropped the vial into her pouch the moment one of the wooden steps creaked, announcing Sophie's return.

Scurrying to the window, Fleur smiled. She pushed aside the curtain and looked out into the darkness. The street seemed deserted. A sigh of relief escaped her. No one would see her leave. All she had to do was take Mother's jewellery, the silver coins she knew were sewn into Mother's bed linens, and a few of her own clothes.

Tomorrow I shall be—

"There you are." Sophie stood in the doorway, holding out the clock.

At the sight, tears stung Fleur's eyes. Father had loved it dearly, and she was glad it would be with her forever.

"Thank you." She took it, cradling it in her hand. The turquoise paint on the front had faded, but it was still a beautiful piece of craftsmanship.

"You're welcome. I never liked it anyway." Sophie passed her and came to a halt beside the small table. "Anything else?"

"Oh," Fleur put the clock and her pouch on the settee, pretending to remember. "I want to take my pale blue gown and its matching scarf. You don't mind if I fetch it?"

"Of course I don't." Sophie turned towards the fire, absent-mindedly picking up the glass.

Fleur's heart pounded in her ears, and she forced herself to smile at Sophie. "Thank you." As Fleur walked to the door, Mother took a sip. It would need more than one sip to have the full effect, La Voisin had said. "Do you think your *amant* will come tonight?"

Sophie snorted. "No, he won't." And gulped down the wine.

Hiding her shaking hands in the folds of her cloak, Fleur stepped outside the room and drew the door closed. She took the solitary candle that stood on a sideboard in the corridor and climbed the stairs. When she neared the top step, there was a thump. She smirked. It was done. Now, time was of the essence.

Determined to see her plan through, Fleur entered her old room and looked around. She put the candle on the dressing table and rummaged through the wardrobe, pulling out four respectable gowns. They were nothing fancy – she did not wish to attract any attention – but they would see her through. The hoops she left behind. Climbing on a chair, she pulled the travel bag from the top of the wardrobe and folded the gowns into it, together with her few necklaces and rings.

In Mother's room, Fleur found the jewellery and slid it between the dresses. Then she ripped apart Sophie's bedding and pulled out the silver coins, careful not to make a sound.

Eventually, she closed the case and left the room without a last glance.

In the sitting room, Sophie lay on the floor, her mouth wide open, her hands clutching her middle. The wine glass had fallen onto the carpet. It muffled the sound. A small pool of red liquid stained the cream fabric.

Fleur wrinkled her nose and placed the bag on the settee to pack up the clock when a gurgling sound made her spin around. Sophie was pointing a finger at her, trying to speak, but no words emerged. Then a groan escaped her, and she curled into a ball, her breath rasping. The smell of faeces grew stronger, as bouts of diarrhoea racked Sophie.

Oh, how the mighty have fallen.

Fleur took a step back and watched, fascinated, as the wheezing grew fainter, and eventually stopped. Mother's eyes, unblinking now, stared at the ceiling. Fleur dared not breathe. The only sound left was the ticking of the clock.

Tick tock...tick tock...tick tock...

Mesmerised, Fleur stood, unmoving.

Tick tock...tick tock...tick tock...

After what seemed like hours – but could only have been mere minutes – the sound sent shivers down her spine, and she stirred. It was time to go. She breathed a sigh of relief.

A sound from the doorway made her turn around. Her blood froze.

"Jacques!"

Epilogue

September 27th, 1677
Place de Grève, Paris

Autumn had arrived with storms, destroying much of the harvest, as in preceding years. People from all over France came flooding into the city. Many had lost their livelihoods – and family members – to the ensuing famine.

The streets were littered with detritus, and the never-ending rain had brought with it disease and pestilence.

Huddled in his coat, Jacques stood in the doorway of a house. Beside him, Ninou looked around, frowning. Like him, she was wrapped in her cloak, her hood drawn deep over her face. Her cheeks were damp, and for a moment, he wondered if it was due to the rain, or if she was crying for Fleur.

Truth be told, he felt like crying too. No, it was more than that. He wanted to scream at God for allowing such an injustice. But God had long ago deserted Fleur.

"There she comes." He pointed at a cart pulled by a donkey that made its way through the crowd.

Ninou nodded. This was a moment he'd dreaded. Jacques wrapped an arm around her and pulled her close. She leaned her head against his shoulder.

A hush fell over the square. The hairs on his neck prickled. Soon, the wonder of seeing a doomed criminal would give way to insults and jeers.

But as he waited, silence remained.

The cart reached the scaffold, and the hush changed to murmurs.

"What's going on?" Ninou whispered.

"I don't know." Like her, Jacques kept his voice low. The

mood of the people differed from any other execution he'd witnessed. In their faces, he read pity; concern even.

Ninou raised her head. "They feel sorry for her."

"Yes, you're right."

As Fleur, shoulders slumped, the soaked execution dress hanging limply from her thin frame, took the first step, she stumbled, and several women at the front went to help her. She smiled in thanks, a shy smile that Jacques had not seen in many months.

"Everyone knows how she was duped," Ninou said.

"That's no reason to let her get away with murder, though." He sighed.

Speaking to Ninou every night had helped him face his guilt. He'd saved Fleur from her mother, yet he could not save her from the deep pain of her son's murder.

Not unexpectedly, Ninou understood Fleur's reasons.

"*If I caught someone harming my child, I would no longer be responsible for my actions.*"

"What?" Ninou stared at him.

Jacques had not realised he's spoken out loud. "I just thought of what you said to me the other day."

"Ah, yes."

They watched as Fleur spoke briefly to the executioner. With La Reynie's tacit approval, Jacques had given her coin to pay for a swift death by the sword. At least, she would not be burnt alive.

"I just wish she'd told us she had the poison from La Voisin. I don't know why she was covering for the woman who may even have been responsible for her child's death."

"She's not covering for her, but for the Duchess de Bouillon. Remember?" Ninou sent him a brief glance. "It was that lady who took her there in the first place. If Fleur had mentioned La Voisin, she would have revealed the link between the midwife and the duchess."

Jacques nodded. "You're right, of course, though neither woman deserved Fleur's loyalty. I just wish she'd given me more than just a request to see Guibourg brought to justice. And I don't even know where to start again there..." He huffed, and Ninou placed her hand on his chest.

"You'll find a way, Jacques." She kissed him lightly on the lips. "I know you will. You're determined."

A cry went up from the front, and they fell silent. Sadness coursed through him as he watched Fleur kneel before the block. She glanced around Place de Grève, as if looking for them. For a moment, he wanted to raise his hand, to wave at her, to show her they were there for her. But Fleur's eyes were dead, as if she did not really see anyone. Eventually, she knelt.

Ninou hid her face in the folds of his coat, and he pulled her close. A shudder went through her the moment the sword hit Fleur's neck.

Jacques closed his eyes and took a deep breath, waiting for the crowd to roar. But the silence continued. He blinked, then stared around him.

"Ninou, look!"

She extracted herself with a sniff, then turned. Her eyes widened, and she crossed herself. "They're praying."

All across Place de Grève, men and women stood, hands folded. Some even went down to their knees. The sound of wailing reached them as the women at the front raised their hands to the sky.

Fleur's head and body were gathered on a stretcher and placed on the pyre raised beside it.

Still no one jeered.

A small glimmer of hope ran through Jacques. "They feel her sadness."

"Women lose babes all the time. It's part of our life, our fate."

"But the judge never made the details of the abduction of her son public." He stared as a lit torch touched the pyre. Soon, the flames would swallow up Fleur's earthly remains, and nothing but dust would be left of the beautiful but tragic girl he'd rescued from the convent. That fateful day seemed a lifetime ago.

"Word gets round. You know how it works." Ninou linked her arm through his. "Please take me home." She looked away from the growing fire.

"Of course. Come."

They walked away from the praying crowds, away from Place de Grève, with its sharp scent of burning flesh.

Once, he'd thought his future lay with the girl he'd rescued, whose babe he'd tried to find, and failed. Now, he knew nothing he did could have saved her from herself.

His arm weaved around Ninou's waist. She leaned into him as they slowly wandered back to the schoolhouse. Where a sense of adventure had surrounded Fleur, Ninou – now confidently in charge of the children in their *quartier* – represented stability.

Watching her from the corner of his eye, he hoped that she also meant something else.

Trust.

Follow Jacques de Montagnac's continuing quest to bring the poisoners to justice in **The Alchemist's Daughter**, released in 2021.

When Jean Moreau, popular apothecary and alchemist in Saint Denis, falls ill, his widowed daughter, Anne, becomes concerned for his health. On his death, Anne comes to a dreadful realisation: Louise, her mother, must have poisoned him. Then Anne remembers her own husband's unexplained demise, and her suspicions are raised.

But why would Louise poison Jean? And what influence do Louise's new acquaintances, the fortune-tellers La Voisin and Marguerite Joly, have over her?

As poison goes missing from their stock, Anne begins to follow Louise to rue Beauregard...

Meanwhile, Jacques de Montagnac is on the trail of La Voisin, and by sheer coincidence does he uncover a link to certain ladies at court – women with direct access to King Louis XIV!

Glossary

Abbé:	priest, abbott
Accompagnante:	companion
Château:	castle, palace
Confidante:	a person of trust
Débauché:	debauchee
Décolleté:	cleavage
Écu:	currency
Enchanté/e:	pleased to meet you; lit. enchanted
Ensemble:	together; a group of musicians
Fleur:	flower
Ma chère:	my dear (a female)
Ma chèrie:	my darling (a female)
Ma petite:	my little one
Maman:	mother
Mon cher:	my dear (a male)
Mon cœur:	my heart
Quartier:	quarter, area in a town
Rouge:	red; blusher
Rue:	street
Salle:	a large room
Salon:	reception room

Author's Note

During the years *The Shadows of Versailles* takes place, the brand-new palace of Versailles had still not been completed, but it was already far more extensive than the former hunting lodge. But in the late 1670s, even whilst the building works continued to progress, Louis XIV already used Versailles for entertainment, even though he did not officially move his court to the new château until 1682.

The *Affair of the Poisons* was a momentous event during the reign of Louis XIV. It not only brought to light a vast network of alchemists, midwives and fortune-tellers operating in Paris, who dabbled in more than a few harmless herbal potions. Interrogations soon revealed that a number of nobles were also caught up in it. An official enquiry was set up with the creation of the *Chambre Ardente* – the Burning Chamber – to investigate, and to conduct trials, often away from public scrutiny.

The case of the Marquise de Brinvilliers kick-started the suspicions. She was a lady from a well-regarded family who had poisoned her influential father, a former Lieutenant Civil in charge of law and order, and her two brothers for their inheritance. Rumours insisted there was more to the relationship with her father, so when he incarcerated her lover, Jean Baptiste Godin de Sainte-Croix, she started to consider revenge. Incidentally, Sainte-Croix met an Italian accused of poisonings during incarceration, and is said to have learned much from his fellow inmate.

Everything came to light when Sainte-Croix met an untimely – but natural – end. Unbeknown to Brinvilliers, he had kept notes and letters relating to her intentions to poison her father and brothers, and her unusual curiosity in getting her hands on these aroused suspicion. She was sentenced to death by beheading by sword, as befitted a member of the gentry.

Over subsequent years, a number of fortune-tellers accused of dealing in poisons were arrested, and soon, the first accusations of high-profile clients trickled in, amongst them: the Duke de Luxembourg, a distinguished Marshal of France and one of Louis XIV's most distinguished generals; Marianne (or Marie Anne), Duchess de Bouillon, a former favourite and close to the king; her sister, Olympe, Countess de Soissons – in charge of Queen Marie-Thérèse's household – who was exiled for life, and who was said to have threatened the king's safety.

I chose the Duchess de Bouillon as Fleur's re-entry contact to Versailles as she was influential, but not as intriguing as her sister, Olympe. Marianne's relationship with her nephew, the Duke de Vendôme, appeared true, and when she was accused of wishing to poison her husband, she appeared in court with her lover and her husband. Both men swore they did not believe the rumours, and she was acquitted. Yet a whiff of suspicion remained, and she was effectively banned from court, her good relationship with King Louis destroyed.

The Marquise de La Sablière was well-known for her support of the literary circles. Widowed young, she let the writer Jean de La Fontaine reside at her home in Paris, and her literary evenings were renowned. I based Fleur's uncle, Marin de La Fontaine, on the famous writer.

The letters the Marquise de Sévigné sent to her daughter provide much insight into the intrigues and machinations at Versailles. With her acerbic wit, she avoided being accused of spreading rumours, but the 'victims' of her tales did not always see the funny side.

Finally, the investigations turned too close for comfort for Louis when the lady most involved in the Affair of the Poisons turned out to be his long-term mistress, Françoise 'Athénaïs', Marquise de Montespan, was accused of having taken part in black masses to keep the king's attention. She was also said to have acquired potions to rub into the king's garments – and poison to rid herself of potential rivals!

In light of those developments, the *Chambre Ardente* was closed in 1682, mainly to keep the revelations from the public. The king promptly distanced himself from Montespan.

Many men and women were executed following the trials – by hanging, decapitating or burning – but the majority of the over four hundred people involved was locked up for life by *lettre de cachet*. They were imprisoned in remote fortresses and not allowed visitors.

They were treated as if they had never existed.

Translation of *Salve Regina*:

Latin:

"Salve, Regina, mater misericordiæ. Vita, dulcedo et spes nostra, salve.
Ad te clamamus, exsules filii Hevæ.
Ad te suspiramus, gementes et flentes in hac lacrimarum valle.
Eia ergo, Advocata nostra, illos tuos misericordes oculos ad nos converte.
Et Jesum, benedictum fructum ventris tui, nobis post hoc exilium ostende.
O clemens, o pia, o dulcis Virgo Maria! Amen."

English:

"O, holy Queen, Mother of Mercy, Hail our life, our sweetness and our hope.
To thee do we cry, Poor banished children of Eve;
To thee do we send up our sighs, Mourning and weeping in

this vale of tears.
Turn then, most gracious advocate, Thine eyes of mercy toward us;
And after this our exile, Show unto us the blessed fruit of thy womb, Jesus.
O clement, O loving,O sweet Virgin Mary. Amen."

Acknowledgments

I want to thank my husband, Laurence, for his continued patience. He happily lets me share my life with a number of 'men' from different eras! He also creates the most amazing covers.

A big 'thank you' goes to my fellow authors at Ocelot Press. The 'Ocelots' are a very supportive clowder of writers of historical fiction, and contemporary fiction with historical hints. Please check out their novels.

My special thanks goes to my three critique partners, all writers of historical fiction, whose eagle eyes have spotted my inconsistencies and (especially!) those pesky duplications. Already, they are well-acquainted with my love of 'then', 'know' and personal pronouns. Their strong sense of writing in a historical setting has also been extremely helpful in creating the right atmosphere. Any remaining errors are entirely my own.

Thank you for reading this Ocelot Press book.

If you enjoyed it, we would greatly
appreciate it if you could take a moment
to write a short review.

You might also like to try books by fellow
Ocelot Press authors. We cover a small range of
genres, with a focus on historical fiction (including
mystery and paranormal), romance and fantasy.

Ocelot Press

Find Ocelot Press at:
Website: **www.ocelotpress.wordpress.com**
Facebook: **www.facebook.com/OcelotPress**
Twitter: **www.twitter.com/OcelotPress**

Printed in Great Britain
by Amazon